Dancing to Broken Records

Jack Moody

BEACON
PUBLISHING GROUP

For information, or to order additional copies,
please contact:

Beacon Publishing Group
P.O. Box 41573 Charleston, S.C. 29423
800.817.8480| beaconpublishinggroup.com

Publisher's catalog available by request.

ISBN-13: 978-1-949472-44-8

ISBN-10: 1-949472-44-8

Published in 2022. New York, NY 10001.

Second Edition. Printed in the USA.

To all the failures.

"Make no mistake about people who leap from burning windows. Their terror of falling from a great height is still just as great as it would be for you or me standing speculatively at the same window just checking out the view... The variable here is the other terror, the fire's flames: when the flames get close enough, falling to death becomes the slightly less terrible of two terrors. It's not desiring the fall; it's terror of the flames."

— David Foster Wallace

"I went to the worst of bars hoping to get killed but all I could do was to get drunk again."

— Charles Bukowski

Dancing To Broken Records

Table of Contents

"Moody's ability to capture the melancholy that many of us experience is unmatched. I don't want to compare him to any other writer because his work stands independently. This author has an enormous amount of talent that I believe is needed. We often shy away from the brutal moments in our lives, but Jack Moody illuminates them and shoves them in front of our eyes." — Courtenay S. Gray, Pushcart Award-nominated author of *Strawberry*

"This book is a goddamn masterpiece. I've never read something that dealt so well with the icky intersection between family trauma, mental illness, substance abuse, and toxic behavior. It neither praises nor judges. It only shows hurt people hurting each other, and asks that we see them as human." — Jacob Ian DeCoursey, author of *Vivid Greene*

A Considerable Fate

"Do you believe in fate, Tom?" Mathew asked as his bat made contact with the car window.

The alarm went off but I did my best to talk over it as I kicked out the taillights.

"That's a good question. I suppose one could argue that at the moment of the Big Bang, every moment and every piece of matter in the universe was put in its place simultaneously, y'know? Like, the universe knew from the beginning how it was gonna end, and so in a way, *we* know. It could be argued that time is an illusion and every moment there ever was already simultaneously exists at the same infinite singular moment. So I guess I do, yes."

Mathew reached in through the broken windshield and lifted the pack of cigarettes resting on the passenger seat, lit one.

"I hear you, yeah—you want one?"

He handed me a cigarette and lit it for me, then continued.

"I hear you, I do, but assuming that's true, what does that mean for us?"

I picked up a nice rock off the sidewalk and threw it at the plate glass window to a pizza shop. It shattered much easier than I thought and again an alarm went off.

"Well, that would mean that essentially we have no free will. Everything we've done and will do was already laid out for us however many billion years ago."

1

Mathew moved onto the next car and ripped off the left rear view mirror with a single well-placed swing of his Louisville Slugger, 42 oz.

"Assuming that's true, doesn't that depress you?"

I took the liberty of kicking open the hood of the first car and used the Bowie knife tucked in my jacket to cut the wire to the horn.

"Well, not really. Otherwise, It's kind of like, *too* much freedom. Y'know what I mean? If everything that ever happens to us is purely on us, and we really do have total control of our futures and ourselves, then, fuck man…that's a hell of a burden to throw on a guy who didn't ask for it in the first place. I mean, I sure as hell didn't sign up for that kind of commitment. I didn't ask to be born, y'know?"

Mathew jumped through the broken glass window of the pizza joint and started lurking through the kitchen. I followed.

"You think there's some food in here? I sure hope so, I'm famished."

I shrugged and cracked open the register.

"Pass me the lighter, yeah?"

"What're you gonna do?"

"I'm fulfilling my destiny."

We both laughed.

He tossed it to me with the Slugger leaning against his shoulder. I picked up the stacks of ones and fives and twenties and fifties, sat them on the counter, lit them all on fire.

"C'mon, let's get out of here. That alarm is driving me crazy."

"Agreed," he said. "But to answer what you were saying, I would say this: One hundred percent of the time, I would rather have too much freedom than not enough. The idea of being boxed in by some force outside of myself just bugs me out. If anyone's gonna make me wrong or right, it's gonna be fucking *me*. I don't like the idea of anyone, no matter how big or omniscient, telling me what the hell I can or can't do."

We stepped outside and wandered down the sidewalk, darkened by broken streetlights.

"But let's say that's the case," I said. "What then?"

A young couple was walking down the sidewalk towards us.

"You or me?" Mathew said, dragging the bat across the cement.

"I think it's you. Remember the last guy—with the poodle?"

"Yeah, yeah," he said. "Hang on."

Mathew produced the rusting pistol from the back of his waistband.

"*Hey! HEY! Wallets! WALLETS ON THE GROUND!*"

The couple froze with large eyes. The man stepped in front of his woman with his arms out wide. He was shaking.

"Hang on, man. Just stay cool."

"I'll be cool when you drop your *fucking* wallets on the ground," Mathew said.

"Okay… okay, man."

He motioned towards his woman to drop her purse on the ground.

"You made the right choice," I said.

Mathew handed me the bat. It was heavy in my hands but it felt right. I swung hard and connected squarely with the man's temple. He dropped to the cement and began convulsing.

"*That's* a HIT! Mickey *fucking* MANTLE over here!" Mathew screamed.

I smiled and faked a swing at the woman. She took off down the street.

"So, what were you saying? Oh right—If that was the reality, despite what I prefer to believe. Well, then anything I ever did, even if I thought I was breaking the flow of my predestined path, it wouldn't mean anything. So everything I've *ever* done has been meaningless. So by extension, my *whole life* has been meaningless. Meaning can only be real if made by man's choices that aren't predetermined."

I pondered that as I kicked the purse into the gutter.

"So either we were meant to do what we do, and really can't be blamed for these particular cards we've been dealt, or we are what the general population would call 'terrible people'."

"What's the difference?" Mathew laughed.

"Well, that's what I'm trying to figure out. …I'm thirsty," I said. "Is that a bar down the road?"

"It certainly looks like it."

He handed me the rusted pistol and I tucked it into the back of my jeans and passed the Louisville back to its rightful owner.

"Think it's happy hour? I'm short on cash."

"I'm sure it is, Thomas. Don't do anything I wouldn't do."

"And if you do, name it after me," we chimed in tandem.

The bar was nearly empty—a few regulars slouched over their drinks and a single bartender, most likely without a sawed-off resting beneath the counter. But you never know these days. There are a lot of crazy people out there. Mathew gently leaned the bat against the counter, sat down and ordered a whiskey ginger with a twist of lime. I walked up to the bar next to him and waited to make eye contact with the bartender, a green-eyed balding fellow with a long, graying beard better suited for a much older man.

"What can I get you?" he asked.

"I need the money in your cash register. All of it."

"Excuse me?"

I pulled out the rusted pistol.

"I'll need everything you've got. And a whiskey ginger for my friend here."

Mathew gestured towards me with a shrug, indicating to treat myself.

"And a whiskey neat for myself, if you're not too busy. A double."

He reached under the bar for something. It could have been a bottle to pour our drinks, but I wouldn't have known. The nine mm bullet slid loudly into the center of his skull, just above and between his two green eyes. He dropped.

"*Fuck*, MAN!" Mathew screamed. "We could've gotten free drinks out of him! You ignoramus!"

I shrugged and holstered the smoking weapon.

"Fuck it, grab the bottle of Jim Beam."

"You don't want the nice stuff?"

"No, this was a deal gone sour. He deserves a certain amount of dignity."

Mathew grabbed the bottle off the shelf and stood triumphantly, facing the small crowd of drunks.

"Free drinks for everyone!"

His enthusiasm was greeted with silence. No one moved from his or her seats, shrunken by horror and the dim light of the room.

"Well, they're just a little frightened. They'll get over it, let 'em be," I said.

We waved goodbye to the stone faces and walked back outside, trading swigs from the pilfered whiskey bottle.

"Y'know, now that I think about it, I have a bone to pick."

"Please, shoot," Mathew chirped.

"Now, you said that life is meaningless if it's beyond the control of man. Essentially, if fate exists then life is devoid of purpose. Correct?"

"Precisely—do you wanna…"

An elderly man was walking his dog about a hundred meters ahead of us, heading in our direction.

"No, no. No animals, Mathew. They deserve to catch a break, you'd agree?"

"Fair enough. What about *him*?"

"Well that's fair game, buddy. I believe you're up."

"I believe you're right."

We juggled the whiskey bottle between us, trading his bat for my Bowie knife and continued forward.

"Hold that thought, though, Tom. I'd like to hear what you have to say."

Once the man came within range, Mathew swooped down upon him.

"*Oi oi*! How's it goin', old timer?"

He tried walking past us but was blocked by my outstretched arm holding the Louisville Slugger, 42 oz., across his path at a horizontal angle.

"Lovely evening, isn't it?" Mathew smiled.

The knife plunged into the man's lower abdomen. He dropped to the ground rather softly, all things considered.

"Go free! Go free, pooch! You did it!" I undid the collar around the dog's neck and motioned for it to join the great wilderness of the city streets. It looked at me a bit puzzled before wandering off in the direction behind us.

"Look at that! Look at that, Thomas! No loyalty to this man!" Mathew pointed down at the expiring septuagenarian violently gasping and bleeding out on the sidewalk. "This man believed he had a relationship with this animal just because he fed it and allowed it to shit while chained to a leash that won't allow it to go farther than ten feet away from him. This man was wrong! What this was, Thomas, was slavery. We're not in communion with nature, don't you agree? Just look around." He threw his arms up in the air, his eyes directed towards the tops of the skyscrapers looming over us in all directions. Blood from the knife in his hand was dripping down his forearm. "Look at all this gray and black and cement and granite." He then pointed back to the man at our feet. "That blood running into the gutter is the most natural thing *in* this fucking city. This man should *be* so lucky to experience this."

I looked down at the dying man briefly, taking in the moment, and drank from the bottle dangling in my free hand. His eyes were bugged out of his head like a puppet, chest heaving up and down, desperate for air as the pools of blood filled up his lungs. He was seeing true fear and I envied him for that. For the next couple minutes before his death, he was going to be more present than he ever was in his life. I left the Louisville Slugger next to him in case some hoodlums came by and tried to take his wallet.

"So, as I was saying—"

"Oh right, right!" Mathew shouted.

It was getting darker as we made our way deeper into the city. The crescent moon was hidden somewhere behind a thick blanket of gray clouds. The air tasted of car exhaust.

"Why is life meaningless if fate exists?" I said. "Wouldn't that mean that life could be *even more* meaningful, *full* of meaning even, if the truth was that we were all unsubstitutable—pardon the word—all-important cogs that the universal machine simply couldn't continue without? What's more meaningful than that? Knowing that just by existing, you are all-important to the ability of the universe to continue existing?"

"Freedom, Thomas. Freedom. That's why. *I* want to make my bad decisions, my good ones too. No one else can make them for me. I want to be to blame for everything I do. It's too easy to play off your mistakes nowadays: *God willed me to fall so that I can rise again; it was just a lesson to be learned so that I can have new opportunities provided for me.* That's bullshit. No one takes responsibility anymore. Look."

7

He pointed to a homeless man curled up under a pile of rags resting in a side street we were passing by.

"Hand me the pistol."

I did.

"Now watch."

He raised the rusted handgun, took aim at the motionless derelict and fired. I could hear a muffled grunt behind the muzzle flash and saw the man slump over just enough to know he died.

"Now, see, I don't want that to be a necessity—an action made to fill the appropriate space in the universe so that the machine can keep turning. I want that to mean something. You understand? I want that to equal chaos. I want that to be *my* choice, something that could have been avoided. I want to make a difference by my own design. Not some fucking invisible force compelling us to do what's supposed to happen. Freedom, Tom."

The sound of police sirens erupted a few blocks down the street before I could articulate my answer.

"Hear that?" he said. "That's control. Yeah? That's order."

Mathew began walking back out into the middle of the road, dropping the pistol on the ground by the dead homeless man. He was smiling wider than I had ever seen.

"Well? Are you coming or not? Come embrace your destiny, right?"

I flinched and whipped my head around, eyeing the chain-link fence at the end of the alley behind me. I dropped the whiskey bottle to the cement, letting it shatter like a gunshot upon impact.

"*What're you doing?*" I yelled at him, both hands cupped around my mouth.

He waved over his shoulder without turning around, facing the glow of the red and blue lights.

"*You dumb motherfucker! You dumb motherfucker!*"

If he was planning on responding, it was stifled by the shrieks of the policemen, surrounding him in a half-circle with two vehicles blocking the street, their sirens howling like banshees. I stood frozen, hidden in the shadows behind the alley wall, watching—waiting for Mathew. Through their shouts and commands, I saw Mathew turn to me ever so slightly, that stupid goofy grin painted across his face, and he winked. His right hand then went to the back of his pants, came out lightning fast in the shape of a handgun; thumb pointed up and index finger pointed squarely at the armed policemen.

"BANG," he screamed.

The flashes from the responding gunfire blinded me momentarily and I stumbled back against the wall. When my vision returned, Mathew was lying flat on the street behind splotches of reds and blues and yellows swimming through my retinas. Before I had time to decide if he was dead or not, the barrels of four police-issue handguns were pointed at my head.

The hood of the police cruiser was cold against my skin as they slammed me down and handcuffed me. While the officer was pushing me into the backseat, rambling off my Miranda rights, I craned my neck up to the sky. I figured it would be the last night sky I would ever see, clouds or not. But when I looked up at the night hovering over my dirty metropolis, I saw *stars*. I saw a black sky and white, glittery stars. Everywhere. Boy, that sure was something.

Happy Birthday

Henry drives down a road with a blurry street sign, onward to the next bar. He's pretty sure that he's going in the right direction. Henry turns to the left when he notices a group of well-dressed families walking down the sidewalk. Small children wearing blue suits and pink knee-high dresses hold the hands of the adults. They're walking towards the open door of a church. He checks his watch. The big and little hands tick just behind the four. He's going to miss happy hour at the Guilty Sparrow but decides to pull into the parking lot. Henry hasn't been to church in ten years, since he went to a Catholic middle school. He isn't sure why he's about to go into the mass, but he's going to. Everyone goes to mass during Christmas season. Maybe mass is more interesting during Christmas season, and that's why everybody comes.

Henry climbs out of his vehicle, giving his legs a moment to acclimate to solid ground and the weight of his body. He checks his breath with the palm of his hand. He reeks of whiskey but maybe no one will notice. The door is heavy and wooden and Henry shuffles into the back of a line at the entrance of the church. He's late, apparently. Mass has started. The people in the line at the entrance are murmuring how there's no seats left and Henry agrees. Hundreds of heads—bald heads and hairy heads—are arranged in a sea under the yellow lights and the giant metal crucifix hanging from the ceiling over the pulpit. Henry is surprised he remembers the name for the pulpit. The pews are full and Henry will have to stand with the rest of the latecomers.

The priest is quoting something from a book of the Bible that Henry can't remember anymore. Henry scans the crowd, watching the sleeping elderly folks and the bored children. One kid is staring back at him. He's skinny, with the eyes of a wild deer, wearing a black suit that would look smart on, perhaps, a midget, but looks mournful on a child. Henry stares back at him until a droplet of snot starts to hang from the kid's nose, so he looks away. Then the priest says something and the sea of people rises.

People in the line of outcasts near Henry are staring at him. He realizes he's still wearing his beanie and takes it off, deciding that that's probably a rule about being in church but he can't remember. The priest is in white robes and leads the sea of people in a song. The people near Henry are still staring at him and he can't see very well from the back, so he decides to leave. On his way out, he hears the voice of a little girl asking her mother why that man smells like gasoline.

Henry walks back to the car and starts the ignition. It chugs for a few seconds but starts. Ten minutes later, he's sitting at another barstool. He's missed happy hour but it's still early afternoon and most people work, so only two white-haired old-timers and the bartender populate the building. The lights are dim and on the jukebox a woman sings about heartbreak and cigarettes. Henry orders a pint and stares into the bar mirror. He looks the same as he did the last time he was in front of the mirror.

The two old-timers are drunk and speaking loudly.

"You remember back when we stole that farm pig from Billy Barnum? Boy, he musta SHIT yelling at us, tryna get it back ha ha!"

"Sure I do," says the other, "his father came home and beat him senseless for that one ha ha!"

"Ha ha ha!"

"Ha ha ha!"

"But boy, that's nothin'. Remember when we went to the county pen for setting that old, abandoned house on fire?"

"Sure do. They gave us a cold floor, an itchy blanket and cockroaches to sleep with for the night!"

"Ha ha!"

"Ha ha ha!"

They drink from their pints and look down at the wood of the bar counter from under drooped eyelids.

"Say, remember when I..."

Henry looks away and finishes the pint in his hand. It unsettles his stomach and tastes like earth and grass. He orders two more shots of whiskey, drinks them, and pays the tab. In the mirror the old-timers look at Henry and Henry looks at them. They are many decades apart, but their eyes don't look much different than his.

The outside alley is spinning and Henry rests his left hand against the concrete wall while he vomits brown-yellow bile. It helps a little but not a lot. He checks his phone: 4:46. He's supposed to meet his parents in fourteen minutes. They haven't seen him in months and have repeatedly asked for him to visit while he's in between binges. He isn't quite in between binges but plans to show up anyway.

The car starts without chugging this time. The roads are smooth and the street signs are less blurry now.

Henry sits on a couch between two old people. They look like him and they are all quiet. A game show that Henry can't stand is playing on the television. There is a white haze behind the eyes of everyone. The man on the TV with the gray hair and a black suit makes a joke and the contestants all laugh. The woman stands next to a wall of letters and wears a blue dress. The old people ask Henry questions and he answers the way he imagines they would be happy to hear. Then it's quiet again and the old woman asks if Henry has been drinking. He says he has. She asks if he will keep drinking. He says he will. Then the three people that look a lot like each other are silent and continue watching the smiling man and the laughing contestants and the letters on the wall.

Once he decides that he has sat between the two old people for long enough, Henry stands up and says he's going to leave. The old man doesn't say anything and the old woman is sad and tells him to be careful. He doesn't answer and leaves.

The night is cold and the moon is almost full, so Henry drives to a liquor store and buys a bottle of whiskey so he can drink and look at the sky. The liquor store clerk doesn't ID him because she knows him and he looks much older than his age. Henry drives for a while, listening to a pop radio station because it makes him feel bad and when he feels bad, Henry feels better about drinking after seeing his parents.

He drives until he finds a nice park. It's lined with trees and there's an open field that looks full and healthy, and seems like a good place to see the moon and the stars. He parks and walks down to the very center of the field, letting the whiskey bottle dangle at his hip. The grass is wet from rain but Henry can't remember the last time it rained. He sits down anyway because he's drunk and tired and he can see the moon just fine. The whiskey goes down like water and the stars are coming out. Henry tries to name all the constellations but can only remember the Big Dipper.

Soon the whiskey in the bottle is empty and Henry feels about the same as he did before. The glow of the moon is the only light he can see. The phone in his pocket vibrates and he answers after the fourth *bzzzzz*. It's a friend of his whom he's been avoiding but doesn't know why. She tells him that she and a group of his friends are going out together to a bar downtown. Henry would like another drink but tells her that he's busy. She asks him what he's doing. He says he's caught up with the job that he doesn't have. She says okay and sounds sad, but Henry thinks that maybe he just wants to think that. He hangs up the phone and watches the moon until he falls asleep.

A policeman is prodding Henry in the stomach with a nightstick. It's very bright outside and the moon is gone. The officer tells him that he can't sleep here. Henry rises to his feet and holds in the vomit bubbling at the top of his stomach. The officer tells him there's a homeless shelter a mile down the road, and Henry tells him he's not homeless. The officer tells him to clean himself up and get the fuck out of the park before any kids arrive. Henry checks his phone: it's 10:32. He waits until the officer leaves in the patrol car, vomits on the roots of a tree with no leaves, and gets back into his car on the street next to the park.

The car chugs longer than normal and Henry has to wait ten minutes before the engine starts. He drives along a road that he doesn't remember ever being on. Men in suits holding briefcases and cups of coffee are walking along the sidewalk, going to jobs that Henry decides he would kill himself if he ever had to work. He drives until he finds a bar with half the lights on the neon sign burnt out.

The bar is dark and it takes Henry a few minutes for his eyes to adjust. There's no one there besides the bartender. The bartender eyes him uncomfortably as he sits down on a barstool that wobbles under his weight. He asks Henry if he'd like a cup of coffee or to see the menu. Henry says no, asks for a beer. The bartender brings it to him without saying anything. The foam bubbles up over the edge of the glass and pools on the counter. Henry lifts up the glass to drink, and there's a circle of beer left from where it sat. Henry thinks it's beautiful but doesn't know why. The beer tastes like oranges and spices. He looks at the bartender until he returns eye contact.

Dancing to Broken Records

"It's my birthday," Henry says, and smiles.
The bartender smiles back.
"Happy birthday, Henry."

Success

His mouth was moving rapidly but all that came out was a thin string of gibberish pouring out the front of his face like a garden hose. I was fairly certain that my eyes were focused upon his to produce the illusion that I was listening, but then became uncomfortable once I failed to realize whether I was blinking or not. My head was in an entirely different place than my body. My body may as well have not been there.

Scott was talking about his job. We were in his new house. Scott had gotten me incredibly stoned. I was not used to being stoned, to this extent or otherwise. My god, the amount of words that could come out of this man's face—it was staggering. I made a point of nodding, chuckling or releasing a shaky "yeah" every few minutes to keep up the charade that I was interested in what he was saying. It's not that he wasn't interesting me at all—I'm sure whatever he was saying was of decent entertainment or at least, valid, but the only thing I could be bothered to think about was how much of a failure I was slowly becoming.

Scott was hard working, fit, healthy and happy. He had a well-paying job as a cook in the most well regarded, high-end vegan restaurant in the city (there's nothing wrong with being vegan, but failure or not, I'm going to keep eating the seared flesh of dead animals and goddamnit Scott, you're going to have to be okay with that); a girlfriend (whom it turns out I'd fucked back in my leaner, happier days. That was a fun time when he finally reintroduced us; I had just figured she was a different Sally Yates) so attached to him that he had to ask her to move out so he could have his own personal space; a new little house on the east end with one of his best friends for a roommate; a healthy relationship with drugs and alcohol, and such an enthusiasm for life that I found it almost nauseating. I was a struggling alcoholic, overweight, painfully depressed with debilitating paranoia; no job and no girlfriend; not even a semi-recent, one-off drunken sexual encounter under my belt to help satiate my lonesomeness; dancing between living at home and crashing on couches; broke. The more I thought about the far juxtaposition between me and the beautiful soul sitting to my right, jabbering on without a care in the world, the more the pale yellow walls of his adorable little east end home began to close in around me and my drug-soaked brain.

I inhaled sharply to regain my composure and caught the tail end of one part of Scott's ramblings.

"People come from all around the world to taste our food. They wait on a list for years to be able to get in. There are only fourteen seats in the whole place, and we require total silence while the chefs are serving you. They perform everything right in front of the guests; explain where every ingredient came from and how they're preparing it. And every ingredient we use has been procured from only local farmers, all within no farther than a hundred miles of our restaurant. This is *the* most top of the line dining experience in the entire vegan world, Henry."

I nodded, said "yeah," and maintained a watchful gaze towards the open liquor cabinet across the room. He didn't seem to notice that I didn't care, or was just so wrapped up in his own life that he just wanted to talk out loud about it to someone that wasn't his own reflection in the mirror.

"Have you ever spent four hours carving the meat out of chestnuts with a knife the size of your pinky?"

"What?" I asked, shaken back to reality momentarily.

"I once spent three hours skinning mini San Marzano tomatoes."

He then showed me a few pictures on his Instagram of the tiny little meals on their tiny little plates. It was the exact kind of food that I imagine snobby, silver-haired ex-pats in turtlenecks losing their shit over while having well-informed, cordial discussions about an article that appeared in the latest edition of The New Yorker. It's twelve courses of the smallest portions you could imagine—strictly vegan, strictly fucking expensive, strictly I-did-better-in-life-than-you-did food. Even the fucking plates were hand-made and exported by an award-winning potter on the other side of the country.

I began to grow sick with myself again, and brought my attention back to the liquor cabinet, thinking about how perfectly the liquid in those tall bottles could wash away the feeling of gnawing inadequacy from the back of my throat.

"Yeah, so things are just going really well lately, man. I've just been crushing it." I could tell by the inflection in his voice that Scott was wrapping up his extended monologue. That was a nice feeling. "But anyway, what's up with you? How's the writing going?" He looked right into me with his brown eyes and a well-meaning, weak smile. I could tell he really wanted to hear something positive come out of my fat mouth. My friends—the ones who hadn't yet given up on me—were becoming desperate to see me in a better place, if only by a small margin. I figured that most of them only kept me around anymore to be comforted by the fact that this is what they could have become, but through hard work and a positive attitude, they instead became who they were oh so proud to be. I had become a walking, breathing cautionary tale.

"It's going," I said. "I'm still writing if that's what you're asking."

"Good. That's good, bud. Anything published?"

"A poem. That's all. It was just a small journal."

"Well hey, that's great! Hell, let's celebrate!"

I knew what that meant. My eyes lit up, and immediately darted to the floor to mask my excitement.

"If you insist, Scott."

"Whatdya want? I got Session, Captain Morgan, Tanqueray, Absolu—"

"Whiskey," I interrupted him.

He stopped mid-sentence and hesitated before reaching in and pulling out a half-empty bottle of Wild Turkey. "This work?"

"Definitely."

I was starting to feel a little kick in my step finally. He poured two glasses and sat back down, handed me one. "So... to—"

"To success," I interrupted him again.

"Right... to success."

Scott sipped gingerly at the brown drink while I emptied my glass. It wasn't until the alcohol entered my body that I became aware of my immediate surroundings and not just the tunnel that my vision and thoughts had been squeezed into. A Violent Femmes record was playing on vinyl. It sounded lovely. There were pieces of artwork and photography hanging across the living room walls, done by friends and friends of friends. Scott's roommate's pet snake was coiled into the corner of its terrarium, a mass of yellow scales tasting the air with a red tongue darting in and out of its mouth. My palms were glistening with sweat and my left leg was bouncing up and down uncontrollably. Scott was handsome: dark features and darker eyes, a narrow face and a growing but trimmed beard. His long hair was pulled to the back of his head in a bun. He wore a wool sweatshirt that reminded me of wet earth.

Scott finished his drink and looked back up at me earnestly, thinking of something to say to fill the silence that I alone appreciated. "You workin' right now?"

"Yeah," I lied, "been doing some landscaping with my neighbor's business. It's good work, keeps me busy." I hated myself more with each word that escaped my mouth, but I couldn't stand my friend knowing that I was doing any worse than he already did. If complete honesty were to be maintained from my end, the conversation would quickly become blisteringly depressing. Through my lie, though, Scott seemed to be pleasantly surprised, and so decided to continue with the line of questioning in hopes that it would continue to be pleasantly surprising.

"Any girls?"

"God no," I said in honesty.

My straight-faced answer proved to be humorous. A smile grew slowly across his face until his mouth was open, laughing with his teeth and his brown eyes and all. I poured another drink from the bottle of whiskey without asking, drank that down in one gulp. Scott took my silence as an opening to talk about himself once more, which was just fine with me. Conversations with others regarding my own wellbeing and personal life normally ended quickly.

"Man, it's such a different experience going into bars by myself now that me and Sally aren't really seeing each other as much. Last night, I walked into the bar down the street, and there's this bartender working there that I've seen all the time, and she's never paying me any attention—always being snarky and shit. But this time I'm not with Sally, and all of a sudden she walks up and introduces herself to me—says, 'Hi, I'm Melody, it's really nice to meet you', and starts laughing at all the things I'm saying, even though I know I'm not being funny. And then there was this sexy-ass blonde tattooed woman across from me at the bar who just starts feeding me food from her plate! I didn't even say anything, just looked at her and she starts feeding me! Like fuck, man, if only I was single."

"Yeah," I said.

"Doesn't that stuff ever happen to you? You're at bars alone all the time!"

"No. I don't look quite as approachable as you do, Scott. Mostly my hands are on my head. I don't really go to bars to be happy. I go to get drunk."

It wasn't until I spoke the words out loud that I realized how sad they were. Scott struggled to find an answer, eventually spurting out, "Well. That's cool too."

No it wasn't. We both knew that. Scott was too nice and pleasant and I was too dark and distant. We were not the same people. We would never be. So it goes.

The world will always need its golden boys to succeed and serve as evidence of the goodness and luck that exists to keep the failures from hanging by a rope, just like it needs its failures to mow their lawns and cook their food and fight their wars and serve as their deterrent examples so the golden boys can avoid their mistakes and continue to shine. It's a natural societal balance that keeps the banks open and the executioner on time and the toilets flushing and the booze pouring. It keeps the failures working in the belief that one day they too can shine. Everybody needs a good lie to survive on this planet. Don't listen to anyone say otherwise. The only shit of it is, no one gets to choose on what side of the fence they'll land. All I knew was that I wanted to climb it.

Sensing my removal from my surroundings once more, Scott poured me another drink. "Well, hey! There's always tomorrow, right?"

"Right," I said, and drank the whiskey in my glass.

It was raining outside. I've always loved the sound of the rain from inside a comfortable home. I decided it was time to go, and bid goodbye to Scott.

"Keep your head on straight," he said to me as I walked out the door into the black and blue night. He'd tried, anyway.

The rain was falling heavily like a sheet of water and obscured my vision as it drummed on the street and the houses and the hood of my car. The faint yellow glow from the streetlights illuminated each drop as they careened down to Earth. For a moment, my brain was silent. I reached into my jacket pocket, pulled out a cigarette and lit it with a trembling hand over the flame. I looked up into the great, starless expanse arching over me and let the drops land on my face and the cigarette hanging from my lips. The rain was going to fall whether I looked at it or not. The dark canopy would be overhead for always and ever. The rain was wet and perfect and it came from a stark blackness that I couldn't pull my eyes away from. I stood there in the rain until it soaked through the cigarette and extinguished the flame, and I smiled.

June

She had switched to vodka-Red Bulls once we started talking. I can't stand them, myself. She insisted I drink one with her and I did, but after six whiskeys it just tasted like a pink glass of sugar. She paid for my drinks and rather forcefully invited me to come with her. As we walked under a cold moon and rain I entertained long-held fantasies of having a sugar momma to pay for my every need and vice if this whole writing thing never panned out. I imagined a warm bed, trips to the coast, a life of luxury and leisure. I'd never have to work again.

She was a well-earning construction engineer—she designed all the fancy new condos on the waterfront that the locals loved to complain about—but what I never took into account was that any attractive 36-year-old woman who was willing to take home a 23-year-old from the bar was bound to be unhinged in a major fashion. As if chosen to warm through her cold exterior, she was named June.

It wasn't until we stumbled under the roof lights of her Porsche that I gauged the full extent of her drunkenness. Her blue eyes were glazed over like still water. Her nose was red with broken blood vessels obtained from a lifetime of alcohol abuse. Deep wrinkles spidered out like cracked glass in the corners of her eyes and beneath the rouge painted across her face. She stunk of vodka and depression and I found her beautiful. She asked me where I wanted to go.

"I don't care," I said.

She stared at me for a moment, thinking of an answer, and finally arrived at, "Watch this."

June pressed a button next to the wheel and held out her arms as if she had performed a magic trick, and the roof of the car opened up. Rain began falling over us, sliding down the leather seats. She didn't seem to notice.

"Isn't that something?"

"Sure," I said.

She babbled on, something about work. I ignored her and shook the rain out of my hair. "That's nice, but will you close the roof? I'm sure it's better in the summer."

"You don't like the rain?"

"I don't mind, I just don't think it's good for the car."

"Who cares about the car? I can buy ten more of them."

"Then leave it open. Where are we going?"

"I know where."

With an abrupt jerk, June peeled off the side of the street and burned through a red light at the intersection. She made very little attempt at watching the road, instead staring into the side of my head while I did my best to let the whiskey eat away at my anxiety. "You know you're cute? You're cute."

I nodded and laughed nervously as the dirty black Porsche ran through a stop sign into an unfamiliar side street.

"I don't do this much," she said. I could hear the slur in her voice becoming more prominent. "I'm really not like this. I work a lot. I'm a busy person."

The rain was hitting my face at an angle due to the speed of the vehicle, and the wind whistled past my ears.

"Do what?" I said.

Before she could answer, June whipped the car around a dark curve in the road, narrowly missing a ditch filled with overgrown bushes.

"You know I liked you right away?" she said. "You aren't like most guys I talk to. You look damaged. Like you drink too much. You're shorter too. But that's okay. I liked you right away."

I wasn't sure what to say.

After a few more close calls and broken traffic laws, we began to slow down in a residential neighborhood. The houses were pristine and large, with trimmed grass and white fences lining the properties.

"Are we going to your house?" I asked.

June hesitated and looked around.

"I'm not sure. I'm not sure. Hey, lemme take you to the hill where I broke my leg."

At this point I was becoming less interested in sex and more interested in getting this drunken woman out of the driver's seat.

"Why? Let's just go to your place. We can *walk* and you can show me where you broke your leg."

"No, no. I can just drive us. C'mon, Henry."

June began speeding up and passed the row of pristine houses. I mumbled something about a DUI and she snapped at me: "No, look—I appreciate that you're trying to take care of me but I have…" She paused and did the mental math while the car stalled in the middle of the street, "…thirteen years of experience on you, and I know things you don't. Okay? You're a child and I'm the adult here. It's fine."

We pulled up at the top of a long, steep hill that I recognized from a story my friend had once told me.

"Wanna see me skateboard down this hill?" Her hair was strewn across the makeup and contours of her face, straight and blonde.

"No, no I don't. Don't do that. My friend's old babysitter died riding her bike down this hill. I know you're the adult and everything, but don't do that. Let's go to your house, and then you can skateboard down whatever hill you want to while I'm not responsible for you as a witness."

"Fine. I have somewhere else to take you anyway."

June turned the car around and started heading back towards the neighborhood behind us.

"Why don't you wanna take me home?" I asked. "We don't need to have sex, y'know. We can just hang out. I'll get a ride home. I just don't want you driving."

"No, no, no. No, we can't hang out."

"Why?"

"Because I don't wanna hang out. I wanna have sex with you. I think you're cute and you think I'm crazy. And if I take you home, I'm gonna molest you and then I'm gonna start having feelings for you and I'm gonna have to see you again, and you're not gonna do that."

"What if I have feelings for you too? Did you ever think that I'm crazy too? I like you."

I wasn't sure if I was lying, but anything felt like fair game if it kept me from smashing through the windshield of a sports car.

"No you don't, you're just saying that. And I'm gonna take you home and molest you and fuck you and then you're gonna run away like everyone else."

"Okay, maybe I don't wanna fuck you," I said. "Maybe I just wanna hang out with you because I like you. Can we go home now?"

"No, no, you don't understand. I'm very persuasive. I always get my way. I'm very good at getting my way. If we go home, I'm gonna have sex with you and you'll never wanna see me again. You understand? So I can't take you home."

26

I breathed heavily through my nose and checked my front pocket for the pack of cigarettes that wasn't there. The rain was growing fierce but neither of us noticed now. I looked up for the moon but couldn't find it behind the trees standing over the blurred houses moving past us like a movie reel.

"Just trust me," she said. "You'll like this place."

I gave up and gave in to whatever future was in store for me. I got the feeling June was taking me with her whether I wanted to or not. There was nothing more to say.

It was an abandoned house. The floodlights of the Porsche lit up the untamed lawn behind the gate. We sat in the driveway and June's face was flushed red, a puerile grin filling up the inside of the car. When she smiled I saw somebody I didn't want to leave, despite her mental instability—or maybe because of it. There was this haunting, tragic sort of beauty that seeped out through the cracks in her mannerisms. The sort of beauty you experience during that brief moment of anticipation before a firework explodes. Whatever it was that screamed and trembled underneath her surface, I wanted it.

"This place has been empty for months. I've wanted to go in forever," she said.

I remained silent, thinking of some way I could convince her to park the car somewhere where it wasn't illegal for us to be.

"Let's go in," she said.

"In there?"

"Yeah, stupid." She laughed and grabbed the inside of my thigh. "Unless you're scared."

I looked out through the floodlights and eyed the ominous, shadowed house watching me from up the hill. It appeared decayed and dilapidated. "Yes, I'm scared."

"C'mon, don't be a pussy. You're a writer, right?"

I shrugged.

"Well, here's a story. Let's go explore it."

I weighed the options, trying to think how much bail would cost for when I called a friend from county at three in the morning after catching a B and E charge.

"I saw it in you," June said. "You need a little adventure."

Well, she wasn't wrong. I forced myself into the mist of my drunk, mumbled something like "fuck it," and reached my hand into her thicket of blonde hair. She shouted "finally!" and slid her tongue violently into my mouth like a snake attacking its prey. The taste of vodka and cigarettes stung the back of my throat and my cock hardened. In that moment, any trace of fear and hesitation drained out of my body. Her open lips breathed into me a vibrating high and the concept of death faded into a soft static. Overpowering warmth replaced the harsh cold of the falling rain. We parted and I was perfectly, simply numb.

"So, do you wanna go in?"

"Yes," I said.

She tossed her high-heels into the back of the car and grasped my hand, leading me towards the gap in the locked metal gate.

"Duck."

I did and found myself enveloped by the shadow of the building. A porch stood on molding high beams. We walked up the steps and stood tentatively on the aging wood until it was apparent that we weren't going to fall through.

"How do we get in?" I asked.

"There's a door somewhere. Have you ever broken into some place?"

I thought about it.

"I don't think so. It depends on what that means exactly."

We found the front door. It was closed with a padlock.

"Well, we tried."

"No," she said, "there's always another way in."

We walked around the corner and I watched the adjacent street for any signs of headlights. I could see through the broken windows repaired with 2x4s and there was nothing but an open, dark room.

"Why did you wanna go in here?"

"Haven't you ever just wanted to do something wrong?"

"Not on purpose," I said. "It just seems to happen."

June let go of my hand while she spoke, disappearing around another corner of the house. "You know what your problem is? You don't live with enough intention."

"Thank you, Doctor."

"Hey! Come here!"

I ran after her, expecting to find a loose nail pierced through her bare foot, and instead found June beaming next to an open sliding glass door.

"What'd I tell you?"

I leaned into the empty space and tried to let my eyes adjust to the pitch-blackness inside what once was probably the living room. It looked like a bomb had detonated in the house. Broken pieces of wood and debris littered the ground. Piles of glass from the shattered windows sat glittering in the dark.

"Was this always open?"

"I'm not sure. I've never gotten this close. Isn't this exciting?"

Before I could back away, June took my hand and pulled me inside the building. We were greeted by a gaping hole in the center of the floor. It could have gone down for miles for all I could tell. I imagined this place to be a perfect hideaway for someone to do heroin, and told her so. This excited June, and she whipped around to kiss me with a passion that seemed inappropriate for the situation. She released herself from me, and the glow from her eyes lit up the room. She felt bigger than life.

"You think we'll find a dead body?"

I ignored her and reached for her hand as the curiosity began to overtake me. There was a stairway that appeared to be the most logical next step. June screamed at the top of her lungs: "*Hey! If anyone's here, keep doing your drugs! Don't mind us! Really!*"

I could feel the weakness of the house's infrastructure moaning under each step. The air tasted like rotten death. I tried to say something clever or charming but nothing came out.

Upstairs was what was left of the bathroom. Black mold grew across the cracked tiles. A hole fell through the Earth where a toilet must have once stood. The windows were intact but covered with layers of Saran Wrap. The wooden floorboards felt like permeable rubber.

"I could totally buy this place," June said. She repeated this a few times. "I could turn this place around. I could totally buy this place." She spun around and smiled at me triumphantly as if we had stumbled upon a rich gold mine. "I could really do something with this place."

I stepped carefully around loose planks and ran my fingers against the wall. It felt like I was inside the soul of a dead relative. I began to feel very alone.

"I think I wanna leave," I said.

"But we haven't even checked to see if there's a basement!" June squealed, taking off back down the stairs, her voice trailing off with her. "Maybe that's where they keep the bodies. Or where the junkies are hanging out. Don't you wanna see dead junkies?"

There was no basement, and no dead body, not even a homeless drug addict. This disappointed June.

"Life is never as exciting as you think it is," she remarked.

We walked back outside and stood on the porch, watching the Elms sway with the late-winter wind. I could no longer tell if it was cold or not. I was growing sick with confusion and people and whiskey, and all I could think about was another drink to stave off the incoming jag of depression. Whatever effect June's presence had had on me was quickly losing its efficacy.

"Let's go back," I said.

"Fine. I have to pee. Where the hell did I put my shoes?"

"In the car."

"Oh, okay. Okay, I trust you."

We headed back into the yellow glare of the streetlights and entered the Porsche. June sat motionless in the driver's seat for a while, as if expecting something exciting to finally happen. "Y'know, you're not as fun as I thought you'd be."

"I get that a lot," I said.

"But I still like you."

"Lucky me."

"Where do you wanna go?"

"I don't care anymore."

"Are you hungry?"

"If it gets us out of the car."

"Okay, I know where to go."

"Of course you do."

As we drove down dimly lit streets and through empty intersections, I imagined how life could have been different if I had made fewer mistakes or was born with more intellect than what I was given. I decided that not much would be different.

The loneliness eating away inside me battled with the broken woman sitting to my left, driving far over the speed limit. A thought lodged itself in the front of my mind that I wasn't sure how to explain away: that death wouldn't feel so bad right now. Any happiness I'd ever experience would always be ephemeral. The only answer that came to me was the only thing I was ever able to come up with: that it would just have to do.

I never expected much from life. Maybe that was my problem. I tried to bring back the feeling of excitement that came from this expectation of something better, and like so many times before, I was left feeling nothing but emptiness. I looked over and forced myself to take the hand of this woman, and felt nothing but the grasp of another stranger. It was as if the person who was attracted to her had suddenly disappeared behind a vast, dark wall, and I had been thrust back into the world. I no longer knew how to act. I was grasping at the warmth of long-gone ghosts.

We pulled up to the parking lot of the bar we had just met at. June turned off the car, smiled and reached in to kiss me. I failed to reciprocate, letting her lips taste utter indifference before unlocking from mine. Her eyes grew dark. The wrinkles became more pronounced. Her age was showing.

"You don't like me, do you?"

I looked away, out the window, where a white moth was fluttering aimlessly around the streetlight above us. It glowed, translucent in the orange glimmer.

"Look at me!" she shouted. "I knew it! You don't like me! What did I do? What did I do *this time*?"

"You didn't do anything," I said, and I knew I was telling the truth. I looked back over cautiously and saw that the blue mirrors staring at me were filling with tears.

"Nothing ever works out." She choked out the words between small sobs.

I tried to think of something to say, but nothing seemed to be able to convey the complication of what was occurring within me.

"I'm fucking lonely," she said. The tears were pouring down her face and mascara stained her cheeks like running watercolors. "My brother is dead and—and… he died. My best friend is gone— can you understand that? My husband left me and took everything and I don't think I'll ever not be alone again until I die. I just want to feel okay again."

I looked back into her eyes, silent, and the guilt began hollowing out the inside of my chest. She didn't want me to speak. She didn't want me to tell her what she knew was coming. So she continued: "My ex-husband took fucking *everything*. He took everything and I'm 36 and living with a *goddamn roommate* like some fucking college student. All my friends are getting married and they have *kids*, Henry—they have families and lives and I have *nothing*. I feel like it's just too late. I'm so used to feeling alone that I don't know if I *can* be not—not... *alone* anymore. And now you're here and even *you* don't like me—a *fucking kid* doesn't even like me. And you don't even have the *balls* to tell me, you fucking asshole."

It was then that I realized why I was so attracted to her in the first place. I felt the urge to explain my need to satiate the lonely demon aching inside me, my uncontrollable desire to fill the emptiness lingering in the depths of my being like an injured stray dog; the failure of any attempt with booze or sex or passing romance to keep it from coming back. But any words I could use didn't seem to matter any longer. So I took her hand like an idiot, and to my surprise, she intertwined her fingers with mine and squeezed. And that seemed to mean more than any words ever could.

A smile appeared on her face and she wiped away the tears and tarnished makeup dressed messily under her eyes.

"I'm sorry," she said.

"It's okay," I replied. "Nothing lasts forever anyway."

"Is this the best we'll ever get?"

"I'm not sure," I said, "but it's something."

"Yeah. I guess it is."

We both laughed. I didn't know why we were laughing, but something finally felt good again. I didn't want to question that anymore.

June leaned her head against my shoulder and held onto my hand with a tight grip. I could feel the tears wetting the top of my shirt.

"I'm happy right now."

"Me too," I said.

I turned to look out the window, and the white moth was gone.

Death Wish

"Look, just don't use the fuckin' picture out in the hallway, I hate that fucking picture." Frank choked out the words between hyperventilating breaths as the big, salty tears ran down his face, staining his cheeks red. "The one with the dog that you made me dress up for and look all happy—I'm not happy and I hate that fucking dog. Use a picture from when I was a kid or something."

Frank's wife stood over him as he rocked back and forth in the corner of the living room, his arms wrapped tightly around his knees. Her curlers were in. She wore a pink bathrobe. This wasn't the first time and she had grown tired of it; he always chose the middle of the night to have these episodes. "We're not doing this, Frank. Go to bed. Just go to bed."

Frank ignored her and pretended to ignore the thin line of snot dribbling from his left nostril, clogging his nose and stuffing up his voice. "And—and don't put me in a coffin. Okay? It makes me uncomfortable. But don't leave me in the urn like a genie in a fucking bottle. I don't care where you pour it—it's all the same—but don't leave me in the urn."

"Frank, just stop. I won't listen to this."

"You better fucking listen to this, this is important. Do you not think I'm serious? I'm done. *I'm done.* I'm fucking done. Burn everything I've written—or... don't burn it. Just don't read it at the funeral. I don't want that shit to be the last words people hear from me."

"Frank, I'm going back to bed. I have work. *You* have work."

"Not anymore I don't. I quit. I'm done. Are you not listening? I'm killing myself. I'm doing it."

"Goddamnit Frank, you can't quit the world every time you get depressed. Be a fucking man."

"FUCK YOU 'BE A MAN'! I'M *ALWAYS* DEPRESSED. I'VE ALWAYS *BEEN* DEPRESSED. THIS LIFE HAS BEEN ONE GIANT FUCKING WHOPPING HUNK OF A SHIT SANDWICH AND IT HAS NEVER GOTTEN BETTER. IT WILL *NEVER* GET BETTER. AND I'M FUCKING DONE."

Frank's infantile screams echoed through their empty home, waking up the dog. It began howling back from the bedroom to match him.

"SHUT THE FUCK UP, GOMER. SHUT THE *FUCK* UP. I NEVER LIKED YOU. YOU PIECE OF SHIT, *SHUT UP*."

The howling stopped.

The couple waited in limbo for a few moments. The house was silent, besides the sporadic sniffles and grunts Frank emitted as he pulled at his hair, thinking of any other last requests. Finally, his wife broke the seal. "Look, we both know you're not gonna do it. You're gonna sit out here and cry and moan for a few hours, wake up the neighbors, and go out and get drunk before they call the cops. You can't expect me to hold your goddamn hand every time you can't handle life."

The sniffles and grunts slowly dissolved into weak laughter as Frank decided that all his demands had been heard. He was smiling with tears in his eyes. "I hope I have cancer then. Yeah ha ha. I got this lump here under my jaw—see?" He rolled his index finger around the area beneath his ear as if she could feel it as well. "I'm probably dying anyway. That way you won't have to worry about the cleanup. I'll just crawl into a ditch somewhere and wait for the wolves to eat me. I just don't care anymore, Barbara. I just don't... care anymore."

That final revelation calmed Frank down considerably. He shook his head, recognizing defeat, leaned his back against the wall and released a deep breath.

Barbara stood there in her curlers and her pink robe and her clean face. Frank always thought she looked most beautiful at night when she wore no makeup—when he was having his episodes. He would look up at her through the blurred lens of his depressive fit and become all too aware of what he was destroying, unable to stop it. "I hate myself and I think you're beautiful," he would say. She never believed him. At least the latter part.

Barbara's eyes began to well up. She had been through these sorts of empty threats before but she was only human and did still love him in some way—she could admit that. "I wish I never married you, Frank," she whimpered.

"I wish I was never born," said Frank, unperturbed by his wife's admission. He threw up his hands. "I just never could catch a break, y'know? That motherfucker upstairs—ha ha—he just didn't see it fit for me to enjoy this ride. It's all fucked isn't it?"

Barbara wiped away the tears before they could fall from her crooked nose and injected the strength back into her voice. "I'm going to bed."

She turned around to leave and Frank scrambled to think of something to say, anything to keep from being alone for a few more seconds. "Barbara?"

She stopped but didn't turn around, didn't respond.

"Do you think there's a Hell?" he asked.

She waited a moment before speaking. "If there is, you're going there."

Frank seemed unfazed. He agreed with her. "But, do you think there *is* a Hell?"

"No, I don't," she said.

Barbara walked down the hall and returned to the bedroom alone.

Frank sat there in the corner for a few hours, crying and moaning, until the neighbors started calling and someone outside threatened to call the cops, so he went out to get drunk.

The bar was full. It must have been a Thursday. It was happy hour at the Yacht Tavern all night on Thursdays. Frank found a seat at the end of the bar, ordered a beer, and stared into a chip in the wood counter that must have been made with a dull knife.

He was never going to do it. He knew that. He really did want to get sick; that way he wouldn't have to grow the courage to do it himself. Or he thought he did. When Frank got like this, all the fear would rush out of him like blood draining from his veins. When it would come back—which it always did—the heat and nausea of anxiety would collapse in on him, and any death wish he had so hoped for before, if granted, would elicit such existential dread that he might cling to life desperately as if the previous night had never existed.

Frank was a coward. Frank hated himself for being a coward. An act that an overwhelming majority of the human population, if asked, would label an irreprehensible and cowardly act, was the single most courageous thing Frank thought a person could ever do.

Death and the unknown are the two greatest fears of almost every person on Earth who can grasp such a concept. And what greater unknown is there than death—the great leap into the one thing that no one in all of time has ever come back from to tell about? There are neither comforting statistics, nor methods of understanding that don't involve some sort of religious dogma that can never be proven. There are no case studies definitively involving what comes after that leap.

To Frank, the bravest act a person could commit, would be to stand defiantly in the face of the universe that had forsaken and beaten them down so relentlessly, and leap into the black confines of death before existence slowly sucked the life out of them on its own cold terms. But Frank wasn't going to do that. Frank was a coward.

The first beer had gone down, and a Def Leppard cover band was onstage playing a song Frank never wanted to hear again. The band was bad. The crowd was trying their best to talk over the faux hair metal. A young woman sitting next to him looked up and made eye contact with Frank in the mirror. She appeared as though at one time she was quite fat but had recently lost a great deal of weight in an unhealthy manner. Loose jowls hung down from her neck and chin, and stretch marks were visible behind the thin spaghetti straps of her pink tank top. Her nose was wide and hooked like a beak. Her eyes were black.

"Hey, mister."

Frank waved his hand around over the crowded bar to get another beer. "Yes?"

"Why you lookin' like that, mister?"

"Like what?" The beer was placed in front of Frank and he answered with his eyes forward and his voice muffled by the mouth of the bottle.

"Like your dick don't work or your hair's goin' or your wife's fuckin' the pool boy or somethin'."

"My dick works, my hair's goin', and if I had a pool my wife would probably be fuckin' the pool boy right now. But I don't care about that."

"Well shit, mister. What you got to be sad about then?"

Frank thought about it. He didn't really have an answer.

"I just am," he said.

The young woman giggled. She was one of those people who snort when they laugh. "Well, that's no reason! Hell, we're alive ain't we?"

"That's the problem," Frank mumbled behind his beer. The young lady didn't hear him.

"My mother—rest her soul—always said—you wanna know what she said? She said the strongest people are the ones who can still smile when there's shit on their face. Ha ha!" She waited for Frank to react in some way but he didn't. "You can always just wipe that shit off, but you won't always be able to smile. And mister, I think that's a blessing. My mother—rest her soul—told me that and she's the bravest lady I ever seen, so I trust her on that one. Life's got a lot of shit and a lot of it's gon' fly in your face, but life also gave you that mouth to smile with anyway. Now I don't believe that was an accident, mister."

The young lady flashed him the biggest grin she could produce, revealing a mouth full of crooked, cracked and yellow teeth. But she looked happy. There was beauty there because of that. Frank could see the beauty in that.

Frank finished the second beer and went to piss in the bathroom. It was a small room the size of a jail cell with a single rusted and shit-stained toilet in the corner. He read the graffiti on the wall while he relieved himself. One read: *"I FUCKED YOUR MOM IN HERE,"* and below that: *"GO HOME DAD YOU'RE DRUNK."*

After shaking off and forgetting to zip up, Frank walked out and sat back down at the end of the bar. The bar was very quiet now; in fact, no one was speaking. The band had stopped playing. Frank liked that. He broke the silence when he asked for a whiskey, and looked down the bar to realize that the bartender was preoccupied. The bartender was pulling wads of bills out of the cash register and placing them on the bar in front of a man. The man was wearing a black ski mask. He had a gun, and the gun was pointed at the bartender. Oh.

The pistol in the masked man's hand was trembling violently as he struggled to stuff all the bills into a small backpack he'd placed on the barstool next to him. He wasn't very tall. Frank couldn't really make out anything about the man other than that.

When the bills were successfully tucked away, the man turned his attention to the room of people. "NOW... EVERYBODY. EVERYBODY TAKE OUT YOUR WALLETS. ALRIGHT? TAKE OUT YOUR FUCKING WALLETS." He swung the pistol around recklessly, trying to appear as though he was in control of the situation. His voice was high and cracked to a falsetto when he said "alright". People seemed scared. The really timid ones whipped their hands to their wallets immediately. Frank was frustrated because this meant that he probably wasn't going to get another drink any time soon.

The masked man started in on the rounds, going up to each patron and screaming things with the pistol pointed to their heads until they handed him their wallets. It looked like everyone was complying. That made sense. People tend to do what a person says when that person has a gun pointed at their head. Frank tried to get the bartender's attention for a drink, but he wasn't interested.

"Well there goes your tip, man!"

The robber froze as he dropped a wallet into the backpack, and spun around. "WHO THE FUCK WAS THAT? I SAID, WHO THE FUCK WAS THAT?"

The room was static. People were glancing at each other, waiting for someone to point to the middle-aged man in the corner.

"I'LL START WASTING MOTHERFUCKERS. WHO—"

"Relax, kid," came Frank's voice, much lower and more confident than the one behind the gun. "You're the big man. Just get it over with."

The kid bee-lined to Frank and pressed the barrel against the back of his head as he sat facing the mirror. The metal was cold against his skin and the kid smelled strongly of body odor.

"Okay then, old man," the kid said, trying his best to hold his waning composure. "*Wallet.*"

Frank ignored the order and pointed to the bartender shrinking into the opposite corner of the room. "Can you ask this guy to get me a glass of whiskey? He doesn't need to do anything special with it, just pour some whiskey in a glass. Can you do that? He won't listen to me."

The kid paused, trying to register such a peculiar reaction to an armed robbery. "What the fuck is—are you listening to me? Hand me your wallet, old man, or I *swear to God* I'll kill you in your seat." He pressed the end of the pistol harder into the back of Frank's balding scalp.

Frank sucked his teeth and shook his head. "Ah… no."

"What the fuck do you mean 'no'?"

"I mean no. I'm not gonna give you my wallet. So, y'know… do with that what you will."

"What do you got in there that you're willing to lose brains over, old man? You got kids?" The robber's voice was growing more excitable.

"I don't have any kids. There's nothing in my wallet—a couple bucks maybe. It's just a matter of principle. I don't like you. A man's gotta have principles."

"Principles? Man, you're ten seconds away from being a—a… *fucking stain* on the mirror… and you're talking about PRINCIPLES?"

Frank exhaled a long, labored breath. "Ah, just do it."

He could feel the barrel trembling against his skin.

"Motherfucker, I'm serious. Hand me the wallet or you're a FUCKING dead man."

"Yeah. Yeah. I heard you. Just do it. I've been looking for you for a long time, kid. Do it."

"I'm serious." The kid's voice was shaking. A wave of fearful panic was rising up through his body like mercury in a thermometer.

Frank felt nothing. Frank had found his loophole.

The bar remained still as Frank sat quietly, waiting for something to happen. When nothing did, he called over to the bartender again. "Look man, will you just make me a fuckin' drink? The kid says he's gonna kill me, can I just get some goddamn whiskey? I was kidding about the tip, alright?"

The bartender hesitated and looked around the room at the wide-eyed drunks for either some kind of encouragement or naysay.

"It's fine," Frank said. "Just walk over and pour the drink."

He stared briefly at the floor before beginning the long, slow journey to the shelf of alcohol, and like a stray cat reacting to a garbage can falling over in the street, the kid jolted and pivoted to aim the sweat-covered weapon squarely at the bartender's chest.

"No, no, no—hey," said Frank, holding out his hands, watching the kid's movements in the mirror, "you point that thing at me, kid. I'm the risk here. You point that thing at me. He's just doing his job... there you go."

The bartender choked on his breath and laid the entire bottle down on the bar in front of Frank, walked slowly backwards to the corner with his hands in the air. The gun remained pointed at the back of Frank's head.

"That works. Thank you." He took an empty glass sitting next to him, wiped it off with the bottom of his shirt, and poured a healthy amount of the cheap whiskey. "You've never killed someone before, have ya, kid?"

The unstable thief screamed and the pistol grip connected with Frank's temple. A white-hot electric jolt erupted across his skull, buzzing behind his eyes, and his head hit the bar with a dull *thwump*. There was a symphony of horrified gasps. Flashes of light danced across his vision as the blood pooled onto the wood underneath his face. Frank peeled himself off the wet surface and pressed a hand against the wound, drank from the glass with the other, and continued talking: "That's okay, kid, I can help you. Just pull back the hammer right there."

The kid pulled back the hammer. The metallic *click* filled the brief vacuum of silence. He was breathing heavily. His teeth were gritted. His knees were buckling. The stench of body odor had intensified.

"There you go," Frank said, taking a sip from the whiskey. "Now just slide that finger over the trigger—"

"SHUT UP. SHUT UP. SHUT THE FUCK UP." The kid was howling like a primitive animal and kicking the wall next to Frank's seat. "*I'M* IN FUCKING CONTROL. *I'M* IN CONTROL. SHUT THE *FUCK* UP."

"You're right," said Frank. "You're right. You're in control." He took a final, lingering swig from the glass and emptied the drink. Dark scarlet blood was gushing down the left side of his face. "You can do it, kid. You can do this." Frank inhaled hard, exhaled an even breath, and closed his eyes. "*Kill me.*"

He could smell the gunpowder already, could taste it on his tongue. He was that close. A bright white calm came over him as his heartbeat slowed and thumped inside his ears. His mind emptied any regard for past or future; all of time was constricting into a singular moment. His life was not flashing before his eyes. Frank always wondered if that would happen, but was happy it wasn't. He released his final exhale. And then another. And another…

One eye opened.

"…Kid?"

Frank was not dead. Fuck.

"Kid?"

The kid stood shrunken in the mirror, holding back sobs behind the black ski mask. Violent spasms vibrated through his outstretched arm, now barely able to steady the pistol. He had shattered. It wasn't going to happening. The crushing sickness of life thrust itself back inside Frank's chest like an invading spirit.

"Jesus Christ." The words fell out of him, along with the electrifying hope that hummed inside his head just moments earlier.

"I'm sorry. I'm—fuck—I'm sorry." The kid lowered the pistol and sniffed up the snot in his nose. "I'm so sorry. Fuck, I—I can't do this. I just wanna go home." He looked around the bar at the bewildered faces staring at him, his arms thrown awkwardly over his head with the pistol resting sideways against his temple; his body trembling and convulsing like the frightened child that he was. "Please, I just wanna go home."

Unable to hold back the bubbling spite and frustration, Frank shot up out of his seat and snarled: "Who *the fuck* do you think you are? You *coward*. You're a FUCKING COWARD." He stood towering over the faceless robber and pressed his chest against his body, his face an inch away from the black mask. "Do you think life works like this? Do you think you get to just *check out*? You stupid fucking kid, you don't know ANYTHING. YOU'RE FUCKED. *WE*… ARE FUCKED."

The kid was paralyzed with fear, his neck withdrawing into his shoulders. Frank took hold of the pistol, still in the kid's grasp, and pressed the end of the barrel against his own forehead with his hands wrapped around the robber's. "YOU SAY YOU'RE GONNA DO SOMETHING, YOU FUCKING DO IT. YOU *FUCKING* DO IT… *DO IT.*"

The kid was now openly bawling, and let go of the pistol, crumbling to the ground as he threw the backpack full of cash and wallets onto the floor next to him. "JUST PLEASE LET ME GO. LEMME GO LEMME GO LEMME GO! YOU'RE CRAZY!"

Frank kicked him in the ribs and screamed through bared teeth: "JUST GET OUT."

The kid immediately sprung back onto his feet, wailing and sobbing, and took off out through the heavy bar door, leaving behind the pistol and bag full of spoils. And finally, with the sudden rush of the city's noises snuffed out as the door slammed shut, the room returned to a deafening quiet. Frank sat back down at the end of the bar and poured himself another drink.

After the shock subsided, and the drunks and regulars with warrants split for the exit, people began walking up to Frank, offering their thanks as they reached into the bag for their wallets.

"That was crazy, man—Yo! Yo, Maurice! Get this nutjob a shot of whiskey! The nice shit, man, the nice shit!"

"What's your name, fella? …Frank? Frank, you're a fuckin' hero. You're a hero, man. Thank you."

The bar slowly cleared out as the bag's contents were returned to their rightful owners, until all who stayed behind were Frank and the bartender, waiting for the police to arrive. Frank remained seated at the corner barstool with his head down, still clutching onto the gun.

The bartender broke the silence, speaking softly from across the empty floor as he refilled the cash register. "Y'know… that was one of the bravest things I think I've ever seen a man do."

Dancing to Broken Records

Frank traced the chip in the wood counter with his finger, staring at the black pistol in his hand, and mumbled: "Fuck."

Walter

Walter's dump truck had broken down and that cost $7,000 to fix and Walter's girlfriend's dog got cancer and that cost $1,000 for some kind of dog surgery and Walter's girlfriend had just left the bar because he was drinking so much because he was now broke and had an ugly girlfriend yelling at him for drinking so much. So he started talking to me.

"You see this pink pen?"

"Yes," I said.

"You're this pink pen."

"Okay."

Walter reached into the cup full of straws sitting on the bar and pulled out three long green ones. "See these straws?"

"Yeah."

Walter placed the three straws next to the pink pen on the bar. He was swaying on his stool like a thick branch in a storm. "Okay, you see this? This pink pen is you—it's uh, it's the present moment. Alright?"

"Okay."

He took a long drink from the tall glass of vodka next to him. "Now this straw... okay—it's your past: all your cunty ex-girlfriends, your mistakes, your blah blah blah. Right?"

"Sure."

I looked around hoping to see someone I knew come through the door so I had an excuse to walk away, but a thought occurred to me: Walter was a large man, mid-forties, covered in scars and prison-quality tattoos, with the beard and lifeless eyes of a Hell's Angel whose mind was scrambled back when Hunter S.T. made them all anti-heroes. He was already significantly disgruntled and intoxicated by the time I entered the Guilty Sparrow. The point is that I had no interest in talking to this man, but couldn't help but be enticed by the fact that Walter, out of anyone I'd met at this dive, held a solid possibility of stabbing me if I stuck around and let him get drunk enough.

"Okay, this next straw—"

"Right."

"This next straw is… your friends, your family, your cunty ex-girlfriends—hell, how 'bout your girlfriend too… you a faggot?"

"Nah."

"Alright… not saying it's a bad thing or anything; I've seen plenty of straight guys fuck plenty of straight guys in prison and they ain't no faggot."

"Right."

"So y'know, your girlfriend, boyfriend, whatever—that's that straw. Are you following, Harry?"

"Henry."

"Who?"

"Henry. I'm Henry."

"Okay. You got that, Harry?"

"Yeah."

He slapped the third straw back down on the bar, spilling some of the whiskey out of my glass. "Now straw number…three. Yeah. This is the future. Alright? Fuck that straw." He stared into my eyes and pointed to it with palpable malice. "*Fuck* this straw, Harry. It don't exist. It don't… *exist*. Fucking Harry, you handsome fuck, are you listening?"

"Yes."

"This don't exist. It ain't never happened. You don't think about this straw. You hear me? I'll beat the fuck outta you. What're you gonna do, Harry?"

"Not think about that straw."

"Right! Right... right."

Walter, content with the lesson he bestowed upon me, sat back, nearly falling off his stool, and finished the last of the tall vodka-soda.

Walter's barstool philosophies made it difficult to continue listening to him, but it was early in the day and only a handful of morose barflies populated the rest of the space, so he would have to do for now. I could get up and walk over to another seat, but the vague threat of violence kept me where I was, if at least for the subpar entertainment. I would've preferred a voluptuous, aging blonde with daddy issues or perhaps an ex-con celebrating being freshly off parole (they tend to either be the most volatile or most willing to buy your drinks), but you take what you can get.

Walter ordered another vodka and stared at the side of my head. "You understand what I'm trying to say? We could all be gone in a *second*. This is all we got. Right?"

I remained silent, sipped at the whiskey in my glass.

"See, like... I could take you outside and kill you in my truck *right now*. Just break your neck. Like *that*." He snapped his fingers to help drive home the point. "You ain't that big. I could just kill you. And that would be it. No more Harry. You're the pink pen."

I always knew I knew how to pick 'em. The crazies, the drunks, the downtrodden, the weirdos—they always seemed to gravitate towards me all my life.

"I understand," I said.

"You're a little prick, you know that? You probably haven't seen *shit*." He belched before continuing: "You ever fucked a prostitute without a rubber?"

I thought about bringing up some things that may have validated myself in his eyes, but decided against forming any sort of bond between the two of us.

"You wanna know where I got this?" Walter pointed to a long, snake-like scar running down the inside of his forearm. "That's where a six-inch knife went into me. And this." He got up, stumbled for a moment, and lifted up his shirt, revealing a scarred tattoo of the grim reaper fucking a poorly drawn young woman that covered his lower back. He pointed to a small patch of flesh that resembled unhealed eczema. "That's where a .22 bullet went right through me. You ever been shot?"

"No."

"Ever been in a fight?"

"Yeah."

"You think you could take me?"

"If you drink a couple more of those."

"I oughta kill you."

"Truck's right there."

Walter laughed, coughed violently and eyed the unfinished whiskey in front of me. "What're you doing with that drink still there? Harry, you fuck." He hung his head over the counter and yelled down towards the bartender: "HEY. HEY! THIS PUSSYFUCK WANTS A DOUBLE SHOT OF JACK. I'M BUYIN'."

Walter ordered one as well, in the interest of camaraderie. "If you don't drink this," he said as the glasses were placed in front of us, "I'll take you in the back and break your fuckin' spine." He laughed, mumbled something about life being a real bitch, and downed the large drink in a single gulp. Never one to back away from a challenge, I followed suit.

There aren't many talents I possess, but if I do possess any, drinking copious amounts of alcohol is one of them. So I wasn't particularly worried when Walter ordered two more double shots, but did get the feeling that being sober would be the best option in a situation such as this. There was also the small detail that I was waiting at this bar to have a conversation with my ex whom I hadn't seen in long enough that I deemed it necessary to empty a few drinks beforehand. The other small detail was that she had left me because of my drinking. So after draining the second double, I realized that any chance of having a cordial or civil conversation with her was now out the window, bloodied up and twitching on the ground with a broken leg. But it turns out the bitch had been cheating the whole time with her *other* ex, and was just coming down to tell me that to assuage her guilt. If I had known this, I probably would've drunk a few more of those double shots.

Anyway, Walter was beginning to have trouble. He had that far-out look in his eyes where they can't seem to focus on any specific object in front of them—that alcoholic thousand-yard stare. His pale, pockmarked face was turning a bright red. The sizeable gut hanging over the waist of his jeans was heaving up and down like it was a separate entity. I realized he wasn't going to make it. So I ordered two more double whiskeys. I figured if he wasn't going to do me in, then I'd do it myself. David and the biker Goliath. Odysseus and the liquor-drunk Cyclops. The prospect of it being either him or me became more interesting than the possibility of a public assisted suicide.

"You sick fuck," Walter mumbled. A thin line of drool dripped from the corner of his mouth onto his beard. "I love you, man. I… dude. I fuckin' love you. You're a sick fuck AH HAHA."

I nodded and drank it down. The world was spinning and there were now two Walters, but I was there. Walter hesitated for a moment, gulped it, and swallowed a brief urge to vomit.

"You," he said.

"Yes?" I said.

"You're too pretty for jail. HAHA. You... you'd get... fuckin'... you—HAHA."

I figured one more drink would do it. "Hey, barkeep! Oh barkeep! —Ay, these are on you, right?"

Walter nodded and spit on the bar counter. "You're my brother now, we drink. We drink." His hand came down hard on my shoulder. It was the size of my head.

I nodded back and yelled at the irritated bartender, doing my best to focus my vision on the correct one, "Yeah, let's get two double tequila shots over here... thank you. You, uh—you're a man of the people."

We toasted to my cunty ex-girlfriend and downed the drinks. He was about to fall off the stool. One more drink and I might too.

"We should, ah, HAHA—we should fight, man. Blood brothers." Walter belched and spit on the counter again. "My fighting style is like—"

"HEY CUT THE SHIT, WALTER. CUT THE SHIT." The bartender charged down and wiped up the globs of saliva.

Walter ignored the threat and continued as if nothing happened: "My fighting style is like... Krav Maga mixed with prison brawls. Y—you wanna see?"

"More than anything, Walter."

Walter then stood up and without warning, promptly fell flat on his face, taking the barstool down with him. It sounded like a brick had been dropped on the floor. He was snoring.

"GODDAMNIT, WALTER." The bartender came running out from behind the bar and knelt down next to the massive heap of a man as drool pooled beneath his scarred cheek. It was like watching Polyphemus with the wooden stake through his eye. It was like watching Goliath beheaded on the battlefield. I decided he probably wasn't going to die. I liked Walter.

Dancing to Broken Records

I got up and walked outside for a cigarette. The sun was still up and the sky was clear. My phone was vibrating in my pocket. I took it out and squinted to look at the name on the screen: *Kaitlyn*. I declined the call and a bird shit on the car parked next to me.

It was going to be a good day.

Women

I thought about calling her as I had my hand wrapped firmly around my cock. She was sweet, innocent, a good person—much better than me. She suffered from anxiety and PTSD from an incident as a small child involving her scumbag uncle. She never wanted to say much more than that. I got the gist, though. She lived a few hours away and we pretended to have some kind of relationship for about three years, neither one of us willing to gain the courage to drive out and see one another, only communicating over the phone or text every few days.

Eventually I suppose we just grew tired of the anticipation and drifted apart to the point that the calls dried up and turned exclusively to texts, which became less and less frequent until they ended entirely. She lived with her grandfather in a small town. Her mother had died of a brain aneurism a long time ago. She said I calmed her down when she had panic attacks. I liked her.

A big-breasted redhead was taking the brunt of a large cum shot on my screen. I had changed my number so many times out of paranoia that even if she wanted to contact me again, she couldn't. I thought, just as well—I would come soon and the urge to call her would go away anyway.

I looked down at the veiny protuberance and the purple head sticking out above my knuckles. My stomach was slimming down again underneath my stained undershirt. The whole sight was pleasing. Another brunette woman wearing thick-rimmed glasses was on her knees with her tongue out. The title underneath the video read in all caps: CUM GUZZLING SLUTFEST VOL. 2.

The glob of white sperm emptied out onto her tongue. She was wearing a tongue-stud. It reminded me of my first ex-girlfriend. I hadn't seen her in about three years. She broke up with me before I turned twenty. I had bought her a tongue-stud for forty dollars a year and a half into our relationship because I'd heard that it intensifies the pleasure during oral sex—for me, obviously, not her. We met in high school, before I learned how damaged I was. She helped me learn that, and for years after, I both thanked her and hated her for it.

She was mixed, coming from a black, alcoholic father and a white, Jewish mother. She was beautiful and extremely volatile. Looking back on it now, we were obviously too much for each other. Separately, we may have stood a shot at being people, but together we were doomed from the beginning. One of the women on the screen was being far too vocal about her excitement for getting ejaculated on, so I turned down the volume a bit. It pays to watch the overenthusiasm, in porn as well as in life.

I think I started cheating on her around four months into the relationship. It may have been sooner, but that whole era has been largely blocked out of my memory now. I didn't know at the time, but I now understand it as the darkest and most mentally unstable period of my life up until now; a time culminating in a brief stint in jail, multiple fights with other men who had found out I fucked their women, an STD scare, and estrangement from most of those whom I considered friends at the time. And all the while, I was still dating this poor girl.

Everybody thought I was crazy, and that's an idea that I didn't even deny, nor display any evidence to the contrary. But she didn't seem to care. She seemed to really love me, and I didn't understand it. She knew almost the entire time that I was fucking other women—everybody did. It wasn't a secret. People just brushed it off and explained it by saying that I was bat shit insane. They must have pitied her, but she didn't listen to anyone but me.

Years later, I still sit up in bed at night, wondering how I could become that grotesque, that bad. Years later, I still have no answer—my less than picturesque upbringing, my clinical diagnoses, my substance abuse issues? Nothing explained away that behavior that I exhibited for those years, and for a good year or two afterwards. Eventually I just decided that I was inherently evil, and went to work on a serious alcohol problem. I don't think I am anymore, but I'm not sure why.

Sweat was beginning to form on the palms of my hands and on my back. I was still hard. I backed out of CUM GUZZLING SLUTFEST VOL. 2 and started perusing the thumbnails of wet pussies and anal penetration. One thumbnail brought back the memory of an old friend from a couple years back. It was of a pregnant woman getting fucked by an ugly man with a mustache.

She was a good fuck. She was petite, tight, and curved in all the places one would wish a woman to be. She was two years younger than me, about nineteen or twenty I think. She found me online after having read some of my poetry. She decided that I was an artist and a beautiful, tortured soul. I told her that she was only half right. She lived a few towns over but said she would come and visit me in a few days. I looked over some of her pictures a second time and then accepted.

She picked me up on a hot summer day. She wore a thin blue sundress and sandals. Her hair was short and red-blonde. She had freckles covering her face and thick pink lips. She looked like pure sex. I was already drunk, wearing a sweat-stained t-shirt around my head like a turban, and letting my pants sag too low. I hadn't shaved in a week. I smelled like body odor and liquor. She told me I looked like just how she'd imagined I would in person. I apologized.

We drove to a park to lay in the grass and talk. I don't remember much of what we talked about, mostly my writing and a bit of her life. I remember her father was a tattoo artist who lived in San Francisco, but she didn't live with him. She worked at a fast food restaurant and lived with her adoptive parents, and had been since the age of five or six. I don't remember why she was given up for adoption. I think her mother had died of a drug overdose. It probably had something to do with that.

We ended up back at my apartment and lay in bed together, making images out of the shapes in the ceiling tiles. I remember being astounded by how soft her lips were when we first kissed. They were warm and smooth and full. It was deeply sexual and innocent at the same time. It was more intimate than fucking. We never left the bed, kissing for hours until she realized she had to leave. I hadn't even thought about sex until that moment, too perfectly wrapped up in an act that felt so pure and real. I wasn't used to my encounters with women being anything but shameful. I reacted like a child as she got up to leave, shyly asking if I could see her again. She said yes.

The next time we saw each other we jumped right into fucking, unable to hold off as soon as she sat down on my bed. The sex was good. She seemed to like doing most of the work, reaching behind to tickle my balls as she rode me with her back arched up, giving me violent, primal looks like a lioness in heat, talking to me and urging me to come inside her once she felt me getting close. She had an unfinished tattoo of the Hyrule Crest from *The Legend of Zelda* on her stomach. I would watch it bend and twist as she pumped on top of me, and wonder when she would get it finished. It felt empty.

I remember once after we'd been seeing each other for a while, I had just finished inside of her from behind and left my hands on either side of her hips, commenting on the accentuated curves of her body. She let me slide out and stood up, then told me how once her grandmother had told her she had "child-bearing hips." I made sure to check that the condom hadn't broken every time we fucked after that.

Eventually we grew apart, as all good things tend to, and I moved away and she moved away again. It wasn't until about a year after I had last seen her that I decided to text her on a whim one drunken, lonely night. I asked her how she was, and she responded: "Fat, miserable and pregnant." I assumed she was kidding. She said she wasn't. I told her to stop fucking with me. I couldn't imagine that perfect, petite body stretched out with a baby inside it. She sent me a picture of the ultrasound. She was pregnant, all right. She told me she was due in four months. She said she hadn't planned on keeping the baby, but tripped acid with it as it slept and formed in her womb. This created an unbreakable spiritual bond between the two of them, and as the acid peaked it came to her like a golden sunrise that she was going to be a mother. I congratulated her and sat back, took a long pull from the pint of whiskey in my lap, and silently acknowledged that I had dodged a bullet. We talked a couple times after that. I even saw pictures of her baby. He's happy and healthy. I think she lives with the father now. Once I changed my number, we never talked again.

So as I lay there, sweating into the sheets on my bed, stroking my cock to anal whores and glory hole bukkake, I came on my dirty undershirt while thinking about women from my past—women who probably never thought about me and certainly not while doing what I was doing while thinking about them. And I sat there in my cum and sweat, and realized that they had dodged a bullet far bigger than any bullet of theirs that I ever thought was fired at me. And I was happy for them. It was better for those women that I didn't text any of them. They were beautiful creatures.

I wiped off my hand on my undershirt and tried to go back to sleep.

The Beast

The first time I cheated on my high school girlfriend was with an emaciated blonde with acne covering her chest and back. I don't remember her name or how we met. We fucked in the back of my car with a condom that she said had been in her purse for three years. I pulled down my pants and she slid the old thing over my cock, and pulled a pair of frilly pink panties to the side. She wasn't particularly attractive. There wasn't any life in her eyes. She seemed bored by the whole event.

Just before she sat on top of me, hovering over my waist with her legs resting on either side of my thighs, her knees touching the odorless leather of the '97 Volvo, she exhaled the words: "Why do you wanna do this?"

Her clit was oversized. The lips resembled deli meat.

"I just do," I said.

I hadn't really thought about it. It was just instinct. There was sex to be had and she was an opportunity for more of it.

"But what about your girl?" she asked. "Why do you wanna do this to her?"

The moral arbiter that she was.

I don't remember giving her an answer. Obviously I didn't have one.

Her mouth tasted like expired mayonnaise and morning breath. I came in under a minute. The disappointment was painted in striking colors across the dull emotions in her facial features. I pushed her off, opened the car door, and tossed the used condom onto the cement of the cul-de-sac we'd parked at.

The only way that she was allowed to leave the house was if she told her mother she was bringing home a friend, and that she would be back soon. So after this supremely disappointing sexual encounter, I had to pull up my pants, get back into the driver's seat, and endure a silent, fifteen-minute drive to her apartment, where we sat on an uncomfortable couch watching daytime television while her mother lay drunk in the adjacent bedroom behind a locked door. We didn't say a word to each other until I decided I had stayed in this emotional prison for long enough to corroborate her alibi, and then stood up to go, mumbling: "So... I'm gonna leave now."

"Okay," she said without eye contact, eyes shamefully glued to Judge Judy reprimanding a fat bald man for failing to pay his child support.

I made my way out, noticed her mother's pack of cigarettes resting on the kitchen counter by the door—Parliaments—took one out of the pack along with the pink lighter sitting next to it, and walked outside with the pilfered Menthol between my chapped lips, still stained with the lingering scent of rotting eggs and halitosis.

I squinted through the midday sun, lit the cigarette as I sat on the hood of my Volvo, and waited for the regret to rush through me like freezing water. Nothing came.

This was maybe a few months before the invention of Tinder—or at least a few months before I learned of its existence. This app opened up the floodgates.

For some, Tinder was a legitimate and beneficial addition to the increasingly normalized realm of online dating. For me, it was the key to the locked cage within me where I harbored a beast.

Without realizing what I'd done, I unlocked the cage and unleashed the ugliest, scarred, damaged aspect of my being that until this revelation, had remained dormant; blissfully unaware of the reasonably sensible man that lived a daily life at the helm of my consciousness—and vice versa.

Look, I'm sure there are fairytale stories as a result of the creation of Tinder—my older sister met the guy she's been with for three years through the app, for example—but something about the opportunities this app provided, along with my morally absent, shattered psyche proved to be a combination on par with ammonia and bleach.

There was Annie. I don't even remember saying hello. It went something like, "Do you wanna fuck?" and, "Yeah. Where do you live?"

Two hours later she was at my house, lying naked on my bed next to me.

Earlier that day, I had broken into a neighbor's house with my girlfriend to drink forties and fuck in their pool. She sat on the steps under the water while I floated with the tops of my feet at an angle against the cement, my hands grasping onto the edge of the pool, hammering into her so every time I thrust, the skin rubbed violently against the bottom step until it ripped open so badly that a faint red tint began to rise up to the top of the water like a freed soul. Before I noticed that all the skin from the tops of both feet was gone, we moved out of the pool and into the house through the sliding glass door, and finished fucking on their bed. There were bloodstains everywhere. I'm sure they had to throw out the sheets and pillows (and steam-clean the carpet). So I remember having two large bandages wrapped around my feet while I fucked Annie that night.

She was overweight with enormous breasts. Her pussy smelled like vinegar. I remember a friend later told me during an unrelated conversation that if a girl's pussy smells bad, it means she has a disease. I never got anything, but I was wearing a condom. So who knows. No one's ever proved or disproved that fact for me.

Then there was Monica. Monica was the Moroccan with the big ass. She contacted me first after we matched. She was interesting.

"We're going to fuck," is how she started the conversation.

"Yeah?" I replied. "Why?"

"Because I wanna get fucked. And I've decided that you're going to do it."

I was in between vomiting fits due to a prolonged, abnormally fierce anxiety attack that lasted for a few weeks, but my swollen libido took over as it tended to, and I allowed her to come over.

She was violent in bed, forceful. She dug nails into me, slapped me, screamed in a language I didn't recognize while I bent her over and pulled at the curled, black hair extending down to her waist.

When we finished, I loaded a bowl and offered her a hit. She wasn't used to smoking weed, and descended immediately into a paranoid panic attack, leaning against the wall of my bedroom with her knees tucked up against her chest, babbling about her hatred of people and her vehement distrust of the way the light hit my face. Her nose and cheeks were sharp and angular. There was no humanity in the way she looked. She was cold and frightening with bloodshot eyes. I lay on my back with my hands pressed against the sour pain striking my insides, trying desperately to breath through the sickness and growing anxiety that this stranger's rants were bringing upon me. Eventually I snapped, and squeezed out, "Just get the fuck out. I can't handle you, you crazy bitch."

She laughed, her eyes wild and so brown that they appeared black, and without a word, jumped out my first-floor window, disappearing into the shadows of the trees and the moonless night. I never talked to her again. She was interesting.

And Tiffany. Tiffany was an airy, beautiful Mexican girl with an innocent face. She wore a brightly colored blouse with flowers on it. We began kissing before we first spoke. The sex was above average. We went a couple times, and then lay together in bed for three hours, watching horror movies. We both liked horror movies. And sex. We bonded on that. There was nothing wrong with Tiffany. She wasn't damaged. She wasn't cold. She was sweet. I got lucky with her. When she left, we had plans to see each other the next day.

She picked me up and we went to a park. It was summer. The sky was blue and bright and she wore a perpetual smile. We held hands. It felt like the beginning of something.

I took her under a tree and we fucked there on the grass with the crickets and ants and people walking their dogs. She was screaming so loud that one of the neighbors in the houses adjacent to the park yelled from his porch: "I DON'T KNOW WHAT YOU THINK YOU'RE DOING, BUT SHUT THE *FUCK* UP. I'LL CALL THE FUCKIN' COPS."

We burst into laughter and came together. I left the condom on the top of an anthill.

Before she dropped me off, Tiffany parked the car and climbed on top of me to go again. I slid inside her without a condom. The windows were up and the sun cooked our naked bodies as we wriggled and humped like the carefree teenagers that that moment in time allowed us to be. The sweat glistened and ran down our chests and legs. She drew in sharp breaths and her lips parted wide. I stuck my tongue in her mouth and she pressed her hands against the fogged windows and I came inside her. She told me she loved me. The poor girl.

After this encounter, the paranoiac burst out of me. I ignored her texts for a week, convinced that I'd contracted a disease from her for no reason other than the fact that we'd gone unprotected. When I finally responded to her increasingly stern messages, I told her I couldn't see her anymore, that she could have infected me, that I could be dying now thanks to her, that I felt sick to my stomach at the thought of having unprotected sex with a stranger like her. Fucking hypocrite. She didn't take this well, told me to fuck off, told me I'd ruined the male species for her forever, told me she thought we had something, told me to never contact her again. I didn't contract anything from her. I never contacted her again. I had squashed one of the most beautiful flowers I'd ever picked.

A few months later, I was downtown wasting my days with a blunt and a forty, and down the street she came, with a tall, tattooed boyfriend on her arm. She was wearing the blouse with the flowers on it. We made eye contact, and for a moment there was recognition in her eyes. Then she turned her head and walked past as I watched her back fade into the crowd of people. And that was it.

Jade. Jade wasn't a stripper; that was her real name. Jade was a Filipino with the body of a porn star, skin like untouched soil, and straight, black hair down to her ass that sucked the light out of any room she stood in. She was far too beautiful to be fucking me, but was a bona fide sex addict, so I just happened to come in at the right time. She was an engineering major at the college I attempted to go to for a week or so before quickly bailing out to instead drink myself toward addiction in a house full of friends who opted to take college life more seriously than I did.

I was so whiskey-bloated and out of shape that by the time we'd finished after fifteen or twenty minutes of the first workout I'd gotten in weeks, I leapt up from the bed, leaving her covered in my sweat in the prone position, and excused myself to the bathroom to vomit into the toilet, leaving the sink faucet on to mask the sounds of the pint of Old Crow expelling itself from my body.

For reasons that weren't lost on me, Jade never returned any of my texts after our first encounter. The fact that I couldn't have her increased my attraction to her to the point where I was despondent for weeks. I stared at her name in my phone every night, drunkenly wrestling with the urge to contact her for the fifth day in a row, drinking in those precious moments with her when I had gotten my fix. I didn't realize that what I was experiencing was withdrawal.

For the first time since my sex addiction came to the forefront of my mind and began to control me, I finally found myself on the other side of these sexual encounters—the side that until now, was reserved for the opposite party. I finally knew what it felt like to be abandoned after allowing a human being inside the hole I'd been trying to fill. This vulnerability sickened me. I didn't understand why it had to exist. There was this empathy bubbling inside my chest like boiling water. It had never occurred to me until this point that I was hurting people; that they were in fact people, and not sex dolls to be used and done away with. It became morbidly fascinating to me that I'd been able to suppress such a basic human emotion until then. It was as if the months of drug-like, numbing apathy had worn off, and with a single epiphany, every emotion and reaction that any normal person would have felt during that span of time suddenly came flooding into me like a heroin overdose.

The beast was tranquilized and thrown back inside its cage. For the time being.

I'd like to say that this was the defining moment where I recognized my sex addiction, but it took darker, more traumatic events before the consequences of my actions weighed so heavily on my soul that I had to give in out of desperation, and like the true self-destructor that I was, I simply traded it in wholeheartedly for the bottle and took out my self-hatred on myself rather than those around me.

But that's another story.

It always is, isn't it?

Ex

Black hair. Caramel-brown skin. The faint scent of organic perfume bought from some new-age hippie shop on the east end. *No fucking way. It's not her.* I kept my eyes forward, fixed in disbelief, sipped at the glass of well whiskey burning through my wallet and stomach lining. *She didn't recognize you. No way she recognized you. You're hiding behind the beard, and the twenty extra pounds clinging to your gut. She doesn't know what you look like anymore. It's been three years. Has it been that long? Yes, yes it's been three years.* Her hand was still slender, manicured and covered in blue and green and purple rings. *That's her hand. It must be.* I didn't dare look again until I finished my drink and gained the courage. Dark brown eyes, large brown eyes. Puffy lips with deep red lipstick applied just correctly, hugging the lines between the soft tissue and her upper lip. She was talking to somebody, laughing with somebody. *She never used to laugh like that with me. She must be happier now. Well, of course she's happier now. She's your ex. Your ex-anything is bound to be happier now than when they knew you. Shit, your ex-mailman must be prospering by now.*

I hesitated before calling out to the bartender, wary that she may recognize my voice. I could only hope that the years of cigarette and alcohol abuse had damaged my vocal chords to the point where it was no longer the same. Wishful thinking. *This is my fucking luck. What is she doing here? The place is nearly empty. The place is a shit dive bar. It's MY shit dive bar. How dare she come into my one place of solace? That bitch. I could pay the tab and walk out now, and she may never know that I was ever sitting next to her. I could avoid the whole unpleasant situation if I handle it deftly.*

I forced myself to take another peek: bright red dress ending halfway up her thigh—skin tight, grasping against her hips and her breasts and her stomach. *Fuck. She looks good. I won't lie to myself. She looks good. Lost weight, gained an honest smile. Time away from me did her a hell of a favor.* She was drinking a low-calorie microbrew. The woman laughing with her on her left was drinking something pink and iridescent. I didn't recognize her but there was something undeniably familiar about her features, even just from the brief peripheral glimpse that I allowed myself. *Who the fuck is that? How do I know her?*

I began to get antsy. Something had to give. The moment demanded action. I made eye contact with the bartender at the end of the counter, smiled weakly with the empty glass raised up in my hand.

"Another one, Henry?"

Fuck. She said my name. Of course she said your name, you idiot. She knows you. All these bartenders know you. Didn't think about that, did you? I hung my head in defeat, too afraid to peer over to my left.

"Yes. Another one, Anna. Thank you."

Everything has to die eventually.

I could feel her eyes on me. Penetrating. Frozen in as much shock as I was. *Okay, she recognizes you. Just relax. Keep all hands and feet inside the ride.* It was apparent that neither of us wanted this interaction to become a reality. But it was too late. The gentle *clink* of the fresh glass laid in front of me broke the tension growing between our two barstools. My hand shot towards the drink and I put it to my mouth as if it were an oxygen mask, during which I made the mistake of glancing over as she was studying the pickled monstrosity I'd become in her absence. There. It was done. Her light-brown skin flushed pale, deep brown eyes like muddied reflective pools. Her friend stopped laughing. She must have recognized me too. The time we spent looking into each other's eyes in animalistic terror could have been ten seconds or ten years. Finally, it was her that broke the silence, always the braver of the two of us.

"Hi, Henry."

"Hi, Adrienne."

Her voice was delicate and calm. It was the result of years of mental agony that finally gave way into a Zen-like acceptance. Talking to me would probably set her back half a decade.

"How have you been?"

"Fresh as a fuckin' daisy." I heard the words come out of my mouth as if someone else had said them, like I was hearing it from across the room. *Are you kidding me? Who fucking says that? When have you ever heard someone say that?* I scrambled, trying to salvage my response, and quickly let out, "And you?"

Unaffected by my complete inability to be a social creature, she answered, "Good, I'm good."

Then came a solid thirty seconds of silence as the both of us struggled with the expectation to be cordial versus our shrieking desire to abandon the conversation entirely. I decided I would get something out of the way that was bound to happen eventually.

"Look… I'm sorry."

"About what?" she said with a straight face, as if expecting it, requiring it to continue the interaction any further.

"About everything. You know why."

"I do. But I'd like to hear *you* say it."

She had officially taken control of the conversation. She had the upper hand now. I shrunk back into my seat and thought about how best to say what I was about to.

"About being crazy," I guessed, but I knew that was the easy answer, the blanket term for my sociopathic treatment of my ex-girlfriend for two years.

"You don't need to apologize for being crazy. You can't help the way your mind works."

"Then I apologize for everything else," I relented. "For cheating, for lying, for scaring you, for being unable to stop."

"It's okay," she said. "I forgive you."

"You do?"

"Yes. I deserve that. I deserve to not hold any contempt for you any longer."

"Do you still?"

"I did for a long time. But then I decided to get better. I forgave you, for me."

That stung as bad as if she hadn't forgiven me at all. That meant that all I was something to be overcome so that she could be happy. She wasn't forgiving me. She was forgiving herself for ever putting up with me. But before I could produce a knee-jerk reaction to being cast as the villain in her life, I realized that she was probably right.

"I understand," I said. "You know... I tried to get better after you left. I really did. I went on pills. I got a shrink and everything. All that shit. I feel terrible, Adrienne."

"Well, I'm glad you're trying to be a better person," she spat out.

What she didn't understand was that I didn't just mean I felt terrible about her, I felt terrible about everything. In the drunken depression that I had spiraled into over the last three years, you could have blamed me for war, famine and cancer, and I would've gladly taken the blame for all of it. What I also didn't tell her was that I wasn't taking any pills or seeing any shrink anymore. I had given up on that months after it began. She didn't know that I'd been sitting at that barstool punishing myself every night, doing my penance like the good little ex-Catholic that I was. That she always could have found me there alone, too drunk to speak if she had ever gone looking.

It was then that I finally recognized the shy face hiding behind Adrienne, the one drinking the alcoholic candy-drink, the one who hadn't said a word since the interaction began. It was the face of Cindy Lawrence, one of the many women with whom I had cheated on Adrienne. Apparently now they were great friends. I'm sure that was only because Cindy had never told her that one small detail. She was short and blonde, on the pudgy side, but was mostly filled out only in the areas where it could work to her advantage. The look of shock and fear was barely concealed behind the flood of crimson blossoming across her face. But I had no reason to blow her cover at this point. One of us had to take the arrow to the heart and I was by far the most deserving candidate between the two of our restless souls.

Upon seeing that I wasn't the only guilty person in attendance, I eased up a bit and called out to the bartender for another whiskey. "What have you been doing?" I asked, hoping to skate the conversation away from our marred past.

"Working," she said. "At a yoga and meditation studio in northeast."

Of course she was. After ending our tumultuous relationship, Adrienne and I reacted in very different ways to cope with the pain and detachment of losing a human being who was once close to you. I went the masochistic, self-pitying route; involving staggering amounts of alcohol consumption and many hours a day in bed with the lights off, phone off. Adrienne reacted how a healthier human being might: she joined a gym, became a vegan, adopted a sudden interest in spirituality, and began running with a group of poncho-clad hippies who had orgies on acid and worshipped the magical healing property of crystals. Now, I'm not saying *my* approach was one that I would recommend to people, but if you ever find me sitting in a drum circle in the city park, humming *ooooooooommmmm* while some Timothy Leary knock-off in a dashiki rambles on about the law of attraction, just please shoot me in the fuckin' head.

"That's cool," I said.

"What about you?"

"I'm going for the Guinness World Record for most consecutive hours spent on a barstool." I picked up the new glass in front of me, drank down enough to feel it burn inside my chest. "So things are really lookin' up. Y'know."

Adrienne nodded, ignoring my sarcasm. "I have a boyfriend now." She said it like she was ripping off a Band-Aid.

"Oh, do ya?" I said as nonchalantly as I could. "Where'd you meet him?"

"At the yoga studio. We had a kundalini yoga class together."

Ah, yeah. I could picture him now: tall, blonde, pristine sculpted body underneath his deep V-neck sweater and locally made, cruelty-free scarf. Moccasins. No, Birkenstocks. Yeah. I hated his guts already.

"So, how's that going?" I asked. "He rub magic crystals over your pussy while you're fucking to increase the orgasm? I bet that's really spiritual." I could no longer hide the spite coming through my words, egged on by the liquor swimming around in my stomach. I was taking the low road again, freeing Adrienne to take the high road as it always was. We were back in our old positions once more. Or I suppose we'd never left.

She just laughed at me, like a princess conveying false pity to a beggar who would never be what she was. "I knew you wouldn't change. You're still an asshole." She said it with a smile. It was what she wanted all along and had finally gotten her proof.

I finished my drink and slammed it down on the bar as she got up to leave.

"C'mon, Cindy, let's get outta here."

I turned to look at Cindy, her face redder now than it was when she first recognized me. She sat still, eyes focused on the floor, apparently mulling over something of importance underneath those blonde curls.

"Cindy, LET'S GO. I don't wanna be here anymore," Adrienne snapped.

Then it came out, like a sudden burst of vomit:

"I FUCKED HENRY. I'M SORRY."

The silence that followed was something I'd best equate to the vacuum of space. Cindy looked up at Adrienne as a dog would that just shit on the rug. Adrienne stood frozen, mouth agape, staring at me. I burst into laughter.

Before Cindy could say anything else, Adrienne spun around and stormed out the bar without a word to either of us. The door slammed shut, and a red-nosed drunk who had seen the whole thing asked me if I had fire insurance. Cindy then pivoted on her barstool, at a loss for words and embarrassed, and looked at me with eyes that screamed for me to say something. The crimson was draining from her face and becoming a pale white—the shame of the secret now replaced by the realization that she might've fucked up by confessing it. Finally, from her lips came the shaky sentence: "What do I do now?"

I shrugged.

Her eyes darted back and forth, scanning the expression on my face for an answer, knowing I'd already gone through this with

Adrienne. But I didn't know what to say. It never got easier. It felt like stabbing your loved one in the heart every time you came clean. It made you feel evil. Like you were the villain, the antagonist. The one people rooted against in private conversations. And you were. You were all those things. It drove you to drink because you didn't know why you couldn't stop. It drove you to drink because you couldn't figure out why you would hurt people like that. It drove you to drink because you didn't want to hurt people. And you kept drinking because then at least you'd hurt too. So I shrugged. If I had an answer for her, then I wouldn't have been slumped over that bar with a pint of liquor in my veins. I wouldn't have been a lot of things. So Cindy stood up and walked outside alone like a lost child.

I watched her leave, called over to the bartender; ordered a double whiskey—the cheap stuff. On the rocks.

The Devil's Breath

Harry walked alone into the nearest pharmacy to his apartment. He was picking up anti-depressants—good ones too. A nosy coworker at the insurance company he worked at had told him all about them.

"Look, Harry," he said over the thin wall separating their cubicles, "you know it, I know it: you're down in the dumps. You're blue. You're sad. You're really sad, Harry. In fact, I don't think I can stand it anymore, being your cubicle-mate and all. Hell, you're making *me* depressed. Now, you need to go down to your doctor after work today—march the hell in there—and tell him all about it. Tell him your buddy Hector thinks you should be on something for depression. You tell him that."

Harry didn't know how to tell Hector no—he didn't know why Hector thought telling a doctor that Hector thought he was depressed had anything to do with anything—but he was never very good at speaking up for himself, and besides, he *was* feeling a little down lately. There was no reason for it, nothing wild or depressing that had occurred recently, but he couldn't shake the feeling. So Harry took Hector's advice, and what do you know it, his doctor prescribed him some shiny new anti-depressants for him to pick up later that day.

This particular pharmacy was new to the neighborhood, but it got good reviews and Harry trusted what people had to say about things like this. A bell rang as the door opened, and Harry walked right up to the counter as confidently as he could. The place was empty, so Harry delicately rang the call bell and waited patiently, growing a bit uncomfortable, as he knew that soon he would have to ring the call bell again. He began to tremble, letting his hand hover over the call bell, unwilling to ring it again as it could possibly irritate the pharmacist whom he was sure was coming, but this was suddenly becoming quite an urgent matter—he needed these pills desperately, he realized—but he was sure this pharmacist was coming, wasn't he? He (or she! Sorry, sorry!) was no doubt a hard-working person and would come s—oh.

"Can I help you?"

The pharmacist had appeared—a sharp-eyed, short man with a crooked nose. He stunk of cologne, but that was no business of Harry's. Long blonde hair hung over his forehead, almost but not quite hiding a rather large scar jutting down the man's forehead and ending just above his blue eye—the left one. He smiled a little too much.

"Yes... hello. I'm, uh... oh, here." Harry averted his gaze and handed the prescription slip to the pharmacist with his eyes trained on the tiled floor.

"Of course," smiled the pharmacist. "I'll get that for you right away... wait here, please."

Harry exhaled with relief, now that that social interaction was over. "It's, uh, a little empty in here... isn't it?" he said.

The pharmacist had disappeared behind a wall of pill bottles, unable to hear him—or perhaps he hated him? Did he not want to talk to him? Did he do something wrong?

"Hey," Harry stammered, "I was just, y'know, I—"

"Here you are." The pharmacist appeared back behind the counter. "Now, make sure you take one of these every night, around seven. Take it with food—dinner perhaps. I'm sure this will help. You just need to make sure to take it every night…" he looked down at the name on the orange pill bottle. "…Harry."

"Thank you, um…" Harry peered at the nametag on the pharmacist's white uniform. "Franklin?"

Franklin smiled.

That night, Harry sat back into his favorite chair in his little apartment with a glass of scotch, dropped one of the little white pills into his hand, and swallowed it down with a gulp of Dewar's—and then another gulp… and another… and another…

Harry woke up seven hours later on the floor of his apartment with vomit on his chest, a throbbing headache, and the bottle of scotch spilled over on his brand new carpet. This wasn't an entirely new experience for Harry—it's not that he was an alcoholic or anything; Harry could stop any time he wanted, he just—anyway, so he got back up to his feet, showered and got ready for work.

His day at work wasn't awful—maybe even all right, if Harry thought about it. Did those anti-depressants work that fast? Even Hector noticed.

"Say Harry, you saw the doctor didn't you? I noticed. This is good. This is great. I feel less depressed today, on account of you not being depressed—on account of this newfound pep in your step, Harry."

So that helped. In fact, if it weren't for the rather pernicious hangover, Harry might have even dared to say it was a good day.

On that second night, Harry settled back into his favorite chair with a glass of newly bought scotch, dropped a little white pill into his hand with a smile, and drank it down with a gulp of Dewar's. And you know what? Harry had a few more drinks. Hell, why not? He had a good day! He deserved a few drinks!

The following morning, Harry woke up on the floor. He forgot how comfortable his carpet was. Maybe he just wanted to take a nap, take in all that money he spent on the furry thing. Ignoring the headache, Harry struggled to his feet, showered and dressed. It was Friday today. He was getting paid today. That's two good days in a row! He felt like celebrating. Harry opened up his bank account on the computer to decide how much he would spend tonight, on account of having two good days and all. And that's about when he wasn't having a good day anymore. Harry's bank account was down about two thousand dollars. He didn't remember spending all that. Harry didn't do too bad or anything— he thought he actually did pretty well, thank you very much—but to lose two thousand in what couldn't have been more than two nights was...problematic. What had he done while blacked out? Was he partying a little too hard thanks to the new lease on life these pills were giving him? Hell, Harry never partied at all, let alone enough to blow through two grand in two nights. This was troubling. Nevertheless, he went on his way to work, vowing not to drink that night.

And what do you know, he didn't. Harry sat down that night in his favorite chair with a glass of *water*—thank you very much— and swallowed down the little white pill while he listened to a jazz record he bought once because it made him feel cultured. Without much to do, Harry just went right to bed.

The next morning did not feel like the past two nights. Harry did not feel well at all. He woke up on the floor with an awful headache, just awful. How in the fuck did he get down there? Without the excuse of a hangover, Harry began to worry. Something was not right. Harry sat down at his computer, logged into his bank account, and saw exactly what he hoped he wouldn't: THREE thousand dollars had been taken out. Now, Harry was a decent earner—thank you very much—but FIVE thousand gone in under a week? Harry was soon to be running on fumes at this rate. Had it finally happened? Had he gone mad? Were these pills to blame? No, no, he wasn't going to panic but... he better call the doctor...

On Sunday, Harry awoke feeling sicker than the day before. He struggled to dress himself, failed to shave or shower, and drove down to the office of the doctor who had prescribed him the anti-depressants in the first damn place.

The florescent lights on the ceiling made Harry want to vomit. His thoughts were not those of a sane man, neither was his appearance—and the doctor seemed to recognize both of these irregularities.

"How are you feeling?" the doctor said.

"I am insane."

"Alright... have you... have you been taking those pills, Harry? They should be helping you soon, as long as you take them regularly."

"Yes. Yes, Doctor. I am... taking them. They are... the devil. Black outs... money... Hector... I—"

"Look, Harry, you just gotta stick with it. The side effects may be rough for a few days, that's all. But these pills are top of the line when it comes to people with your... conditions."

"But..."

"It's important right now that you keep taking the pills—fight through the side effects that you may feel for the time being. Most likely, these are just symptoms of disorders you may have never known about, but are exactly why you should be taking this medication in the first place."

Harry felt like throwing his head through the wall but was unable to articulate himself quite well enough to explain that. The doctor smiled with a full mouth of jagged, tobacco-stained teeth.

"So just keep it up, son. I think this will be the best thing for you if you just keep taking them every day."

Harry went home that night and did not settle into his favorite chair, did not take the little white pill. What he did do was drink an entire bottle of vodka on the floor next to the scotch stain. He decided he would like to aim for a blackout, as opposed to having it forced upon him. This goal was met.

Monday came, and Harry trudged into work, feeling quite unhappy, quite unhappy indeed. In fact, he felt awful. Hector noticed.

"Harry, what're you *doing*? Here you were, all happy, all happy-go-lucky, bringing me up with you—look at me! I look ten years younger, Harry! And what do you do? You come into work all down in the mouth, all blue around the gills—I can feel my life expectancy dropping already! Have you been taking those pills?"

Harry, wild-eyed and unshaven, explained the situation to his cubicle-neighbor.

"Well, goddamnit Harry, what'd the doctor tell you? You gotta take that stuff every day or else it won't work! You go home tonight Harry, and you start taking your pills again! Look at me; I'm about to have a conniption over here! Look what you're doing to me, Harry!"

It was then that Harry did something he was not used to. He spoke for himself.

"Hector," he said. "I am insane. People are after me." Harry peered in either direction over the top of his cubicle wall, eyeing the tops of the heads of his coworkers. "Do you hear me? They are TAKING... my MONEY. I am a PEACOCK! A STOOGE! A FACELESS RAT IN A DARK ALLEY! THEY *HAVE* ME—DON'T YOU SEE? YOU FOOL, HECTOR, YOU FOOL!"

Hector immediately shrunk back into his cubicle as the heads of Harry's coworkers across the room turned towards the sudden commotion.

"THE NAZIS ARE POLAR BEARS AND THE PHONES TALK TO EACH OTHER. I WON'T STAND FOR THIS, HECTOR. I WON'T STAND FOR IT. THE POPE SPIKED MY WHISKEY AND THE VATICAN IS BUYING WHORES WITH MY MONEY... *MY* MONEY, HECTOR."

Harry jumped up and attempted to climb the thin cubicle wall between them, knocking it over and falling onto Hector's desk. Security was on their way. They scooped him up and escorted Harry out of the building, his legs limp, feet dragging on the floor, screaming about the sixth Reich and the fallibility of chaos.

Well, that night it was safe to assume that Harry had lost his job. He sat in the center of his apartment, cross-legged, twitching at any slight noise, drinking out of a bottle of whiskey. He pulled out the orange pill bottle and dropped a single pill into his hand, drank it down. He then dropped two more pills into his hand, drank those down too. If one pill wasn't working yet, then certainly three would work three times faster. This was brilliant logic, and Harry congratulated himself on this ingenious idea.

Two weeks later, Harry had not left the apartment. In fact, he had hardly left his position on the center of the floor. He was blacking out every single night, sometimes for days at a time. Or was he? Some nights felt merely like an extended state of haze. He couldn't remember anymore. Oh, fuck it. He was up to about five pills a day, and despite his ingenious logic and the counsel of his physician, things did not appear to be looking up for Harry. He crawled across the room in his underwear, over to the computer. He logged into his bank account—a relic of a time long passed. He read the statement on the screen with a manic smile: two hundred dollars. That's how much was left. Two hundred dollars. Don't worry about how much he'd lost.

Henry crawled back into the center of the stained carpet and opened up the orange pill bottle. Inside were two little white pills. Two. That wasn't even enough for him to pretend it would help. He popped them into his mouth regardless, swallowing dry, and sat back to wait for the anti-depressants to finally work. It had been long enough, sure it had. He just needed to finish the bottle for the pills to truly take effect, that's all it was. Realizing this, Harry smiled and lay back onto the carpet, as his vision slowly grew blurry and his mind grew hazy...

Harry did not wake up seven hours later. He was jostled awake by a knock on the door. It was still dark out. He immediately leapt to his feet, without any thought at all. He was acutely aware that he was unable to act on his own accord, but equally aware that he was unable to do anything about it. What in the flying fuck was happening?

Harry opened the door, and standing before him in civilian clothes was the pharmacist. The same overpowering scent of cologne permeated through his sweater, the same violent scar extended down over his sharp, blue eye—the left one. Harry was not surprised to see him, but not... unsurprised? He felt an uncomfortable familiarity to the man that he couldn't quite place.

"Lovely to see you, Harry," he said with a smile. "Aren't you going to invite me in?"

"Yes," said Harry. "Come in."

Franklin walked inside and sat down in Harry's favorite chair. Harry didn't mind this.

"Glad to see you've been staying well. You look well," Franklin joked.

"Thank you," said Harry.

Franklin reached over to the empty pill bottle on the floor. "I see you've been abusing your medication…"

"Yes," Harry said. "If I take more, it'll help me get better faster."

"No it won't," said Franklin. "Given how long it's been, I'm not quite sure how it hasn't killed you. You must have grown quite a tolerance for the scopolamine by now. That's remarkable, really. I'm genuinely… surprised you're still alive."

"Scopolamine? Is that what the medication is called?" asked Harry.

"No. No, it's not. It's what I put inside those little capsules instead of whatever your doctor wanted you to take. By the looks of you, you genuinely needed it too. I hadn't counted on finding a real head case. You're crazier than you looked, Harry."

"I don't understand…" Harry heard himself saying.

"Well, of course you don't," said Franklin. "Do you know what they call scopolamine—the thieves that use it?"

"No."

"They call it Devil's Breathe. Do you know why, Harry?"

"No."

"Because it steals your soul. It's a thing of beauty watching you like this every night. Having you as a slave. I almost wish it weren't this easy. But anyway—down to business, my friend. I'd like you to go to the nearest ATM machine, and empty out what's left of your bank account. Can you do that for me, Harry?"

"Yes," he heard himself saying. He wanted to tell Franklin that "ATM machine" was redundant, but this didn't feel like the right time.

"Wonderful," Franklin said. "Seeing as you've exhausted the extent of the scopolamine, I won't be seeing you anymore, friend. It's been a lovely ride, though. Hasn't it?"

"Yes," said Harry.

"Great. And hey, think of it this way: *you're* no longer going to black out and rob yourself blind every night, and *I*... get all your money! So, really it's win-win isn't it, Harry?"

"Yes," said Harry.

"This was a very mutually beneficial partnership, if I do say so myself."

"Yes."

"Now... go. Bring me my money, Harry."

"Yes."

Harry woke up the next morning on the floor. He felt, well, awful—but he was used to that now. He had a horrible dream the night before: a man was drugging him and making him his slave and taking all his money while the whole time he believed he was going cra—hold the fuck on...

Harry dragged himself to his feet and walked over to the computer, logged into his bank account. His face fell into the bottom of his stomach: zero dollars. It read zero dollars. This wasn't a dream; this was zero real-life dollars.

Harry fell to the floor, scrambling towards the empty pill bottle. He picked it up and looked at it: everything was on it—his name, his address, his phone number... and that pharmacist had access to all of it. He had been robbed. Well, shit. He *had* been robbed. Harry felt disgusting, violated. He ran into the bathroom, vomited, threw on the clothes nearest to him, and charged out of his apartment, on his way back to the pharmacy.

Harry burst through the door, his shirt backwards, his pants unzipped, his face unshaven, his eyes bloodshot red, his lips dried and cracked, his hair wildly long and uncombed, twenty pounds lighter and aged by ten years in two and a half weeks. A young woman stood behind the counter, nervously eyeing this absolute wreck who had just come careening through the entrance.

"Um, can I... help you, sir?"

"You goddamn well better," said Harry, any and all semblance of reservation now gone from his demeanor. "There's a man that works here—he drugged me, he stole all my money, and he *thinks* I don't know about it, but LADY... I *do*. Now where's FRANKLIN?"

"Excuse me?" she asked.

"FRANK...LIN!" Harry screamed. "The short man with the blonde hair and the scar on his face... blue eyes? The man smells like he emptied an entire FUCKING bottle of cologne on himself, for *Christ's sake*! ...FRANKLIN! I NEED TO TALK TO HIM... NOW."

The poor woman behind the counter looked as if she thought she was experiencing her last moments on Earth. "I'm sorry... sir... there's no one that works here named Franklin... or anyone near that description."

Harry froze. There was nothing left to say.

The woman behind the counter hesitated for a moment then said, "Sir... you really don't look so well... maybe you should go to a doctor and... get some medication."

Conspiracy at the Guilty Sparrow

It was a regular night, besides a violent case of the hiccups that had been plaguing me since two days previous. Probably an unnecessary detail, all considering, but it was really the only thing I remember about that night besides the woman.

I sat alone at a table at the Guilty Sparrow. My two friends had just left to play pool in another room, leaving me to the ghosts and barflies who haunt these sorts of establishments on a slow Friday night. I sipped at a low-quality beer, surveying my surroundings, as I tend to, when my eyes caught those of a woman at the end of the bar. Just fucking staring at me. Unnerved, I averted my gaze, back towards the drink in front of me. I'm generally quite a paranoid and anxious person, so furtively I glanced back again in the direction of the woman to see if she had looked away. But there she was. Just fucking staring. She was an older woman, maybe middle-aged with some wear and tear, swaying slightly from her visible drunkenness, and appeared to pose no threat to me, so I shook off the anxiety and turned back to watch the bubbles rising to the top of my glass.

It was once I finished my beer that I heard the slurred words twisted into a distinct stench of whiskey just right of my ear.

"You were lookin' a'mme, huh? *Huh?*"

I turned slowly and saw the same dulled brown eyes staring at me from the bar just before. I could see in her soulless gaze that she was one of the ghosts, the type that'll live and die on those barstools with their face in their drink. The type it's best to avoid. Unless you're into that kind of thing. She was not attractive. Her hair was graying and tangled. Wrinkles were cemented into sagging flesh. Makeup was smudged across her face that had probably been left there from the night before. She wore a red rain jacket.

"I said, you were lookin' a'mme. Weren't you? I know what you want."

I slid my barstool back a ways from her.

"You got the wrong idea, lady."

"Mmmm," she said, "you wan' my number, dontchoo."

"Is that what this is?"

She sat down uncomfortably close to me.

"Are youuuu… one'a *them*?"

"Who?" I asked.

"You don't look like the type… I trus' you."

"Okay. The type to what?"

"I'm gonna blow this place… WIDE OPEN!" She threw her arms out to mimic an explosion.

I looked around.

"What, this place?"

"Ohhhh yeeeeah. They're all in onnit… the bartenders, the… bartenders… *everyone*."

I decided at this point to keep the conversation going for my own entertainment.

"Oh yeah? What're they in on?"

She looked at me like I was a fuckin' idiot.

"Oh. Wouldn't *you* like to know."

Before I could answer she continued, leaning in close to me so I could taste the death and rot on her breath.

"They're RUFIEING women customers. They've been doing it… for YEARS."

"That makes no sense," I said.

"Oh YEAH it does. They RUFIE 'em then charge 'em extra for drinks to get all the... the MONEY!"

"Okay," I said.

I could have made a joke but was beginning to feel bad for her. She reeled back, disgusted by my lack of a reaction.

"Oh, WHAT? You don't BELIEVE me? They did it to *ME*! I'm gonna get 'em BACK. I'm a travel writer—fer yer information—and I'm gonna blow this whole thing WIDE OPEN!"

She threw her arms out again to illustrate the point.

It was then that I realized she wasn't just heavily intoxicated, but also possibly mentally ill. I began looking around a bit nervously for my friends.

"Look, lady, hear me out," I said. "If they're really rufieing women customers here, that would make them *more* drunk, maybe even knock 'em out. Right?"

She nodded. She was with me so far.

"So... wouldn't that make them buy *fewer* drinks? On account of being all fucked up and everything?"

She mulled it over.

"Yes. YES. EXACTLY."

I squinted my eyes at her, looking for any evidence of a lobotomy scar.

"You see the flaw in this logic, right?"

This elicited a particularly hostile reaction. The heads of bystanders close to us whipped around like deer that had just heard a gunshot. "WHAT DON'T YOU UNDERSTAND? IT'S SIMPLE. THEY BUY THE DRINKS... THEY RUFIE 'EM... THEY GET ALL THE—THE *MONEY*... OKAY?"

I sat quietly for a moment. There was no getting through to this bitch.

"Fuck it—yeah, I got it."

"So," she said, "you wan' my number?"

I stood up to get another drink. This didn't play well. She became irate and started screaming.

"FINE. I DIDN'T... REALLY WAN' IT ANYWAY. I'DDA SUCKED YOUR DICK LIKE A... SNOWBLOWER... FAGGOT!"

I sat down at the bar and ordered a whiskey neat.

"Don't worry about her," said the young brunette bartender, sliding the glass into my hand. "She's always doing this."

"I'LL BLOW THIS WHOLE THING... WIDE OPEN!" the woman shrieked behind us.

She was then hoisted over the shoulder of a large bouncer in a black shirt and escorted out, still howling as she scratched at the man's face.

"PUT ME THE FUCK DOWN, YOU FASCIST APE. I'LL BLOW THIS PLACE WIDE OPEN! *WIDE OPEN!*"

The doors closed behind the ghost and her handler, and the room erupted in applause. I was sure she'd be back. They always come back. Getting rid of a person like that from a dive like this would require a priest and an exorcism. I finished my drink and placed the glass back down on the bar.

"Lemme get you another one," said the brunette. "It's on me."

She smiled and handed me a fresh full glass. I forced a smile back, took a sip and returned to studying my environment. The bar was abuzz with lilting murmurs and muffled laughter. It wasn't often that anything interesting happened in this place. I guess that was the point, though. There was the time a PTA meeting came to the bar for whatever reason, and some dad broke a bottle over another dad's head because that dad's kid hated the other dad's kid, and then the dad with the shitty kid got arrested while the dad with the other shitty kid lay out cold in a pool of his own blood. But I wasn't there for that.

After a few minutes of attempting moral integrity, I gave in and glued my eyes to the bartender's ass as she turned around—really a wonderful example of the human form. I followed her ass back to the beer taps, where she and her ass filled up a glass with something more expensive than I was used to drinking. I watched the glass sit underneath the tap for a moment as the bartender and her ass walked behind the cash register and reached underneath the bar for something. She emerged with her right hand in a closed fist, walked softly back to the waiting beer glass, and dropped a little white pill into the golden liquid. She then picked up the glass and slid it down the bar towards a young woman sitting alone on a barstool. The young woman picked it up, smiled, and drank deep.

Dumb Luck

"Oh, I've got a bunch of knives," he said.

The blurred lights of buildings we passed illuminated the interior of the car in dull waves.

"Why?" I asked, paying attention to the speeding traffic on my left as I drove through downtown. "Where'd you get 'em?"

"They're box cutters. Here, I got one on me right now. I even have the holster for it."

He produced a pink plastic box cutter with a rusted straight razor inside it, and slid out the blade with his thumb. It was covered with dried, dark red splatters of something.

"They give us a bunch of these at my work. Here, take this one—it's left-handed. I don't even need it. I got three more at home."

I examined it. "Is that blood?"

"Where?"

"There."

"I don't think so."

"Uh…" I hesitated and took it out of his hand without answering properly.

A blue Cadillac with a dented fender took a sharp left turn in front of us to outrun the yellow light. Some bubbly pop song that I didn't care to recognize fizzled through the Pontiac's damaged speakers. I slid the sheathed blade into my tuxedo jacket.

"It's better for slashing than stabbing, so don't try to poke a guy when you're in trouble, just slash his face and run."

The car was stopped at the red light. On our right was a corner store with half the neon letters burnt out on its sign:

3 th RKET

A FRIE D   N   BORH D PL CE !

A group of hooded teenagers lurked around the building on the sidewalk, filming excitedly as one of the hoodlums dropkicked a spilling garbage can. I couldn't hear the clamor over the pop ballad exploding out my vehicle, courtesy of 93.6 fm. The light turned green and I took off toward the wooded side street that would take us out of the city. I switched the radio over to the jazz station. Herbie Hancock was playing.

"So, it's sharp?" I asked. "It'll work for self-defense?"

"Oh yeah," he said. "That'll fucking kill someone."

"I don't wanna *kill* anyone, Randy. I just don't wanna *get killed*. Defense. Like, incapacitate 'em, y'know?"

"Yeah, yeah, yeah. Just don't... swing hard."

"I probably won't even need to use this fuckin' thing."

"Yeah, well—hey, hey, WOAH! SLOW DOWN!"

We were coming around an abrupt curve hidden under a row of bowing conifer trees. The only light at all, provided by the crescent moon, barely reached through the dense canopy of Douglas Firs and Hemlocks.

"Hey, HEY! CHILL! CHILL." I was as much speaking to myself as I was to him.

The vehicle soared around the corner onto a narrow straightaway with a lone streetlight glowing maybe a hundred meters down the road.

"I'm sorry, dude." Randall exhaled hard and stared at his hands. "I think those drugs are really working."

"That's what drugs do," I answered, and lit a cigarette with both hands while he leaned over from the passenger seat and piloted the station wagon with one palm on the wheel.

"How're you feeling? We should park, right?"

Randall's chest was heaving anxiously and I could feel his eyes digging deep into the side of my skull.

"Oh no, no," I said and exhaled smoke. "It's all good, buddy boy. Just breathe it out, just *breeeeeathe* it out. There you go."

I was too high to realize that I was driving thirty miles over the speed limit and ashing on myself. Randall opened the passenger window and hung his head over the side, before returning to his seat in an apparent state of wide-eyed delirium.

"What do you think were in those capsules?"

I shrugged and spit out the window. The glob of white mucous flew straight back and splatted across the side of the car.

"Tuinal, Dilaudid, Oxy, Speed… shit, Ecstasy—I don't know. There was probably a lot of shit in those things."

My revelation didn't seem to help Randall's mounting panic. I cut in before he had further time to voice his concern.

"Well, we'll know in like fifteen minutes. Give it a second. *I* feel good, if that helps."

"You do?"

"Oh yeah! Like a million bucks, buddy. Just float downstream, like Tim Leary said."

He sat back in his seat and closed his eyes, repeating "Timothy Leary" over and over like a mantra between labored breaths.

We passed through a tunnel and the howling wind was traded for muffled echoes of the Pontiac's engine bouncing off cracked cement walls. Any car unable to speed up once I accelerated behind it was quickly passed and honked at. Speed seems to help open the floodgates when on the verge of something good kicking in. The veins widen and increase blood flow as the adrenaline is injected into the bloodstream... something like that. I've always liked to move fast when I shouldn't. It's like that old chestnut kleptomaniacs are always spewing to rationalize their behavior: stolen candy just tastes better.

Randall's sweaty hand found its way onto the top of my head and stayed there for longer than I appreciated.

"I don't fucking trust that guy... I don't trust him, Jim."

"Who?"

"That fucking guy! The dealer!" he shouted, waving his arms around like wet noodles.

"The dealer? The dealer who *we* just ripped off? You know how stupid you sound?"

"Well, I just don't trust him."

"What the hell is he gonna do that we don't already know? And that's if he even does anything. Randy, we got away with it. That guy is gonna be looking up his ass for a month before he gets a fuckin' clue who got over on him. We don't need to trust him. He was the one who shouldn't have been trusting *us*."

"I mean the drugs, man. I don't trust his drugs. I don't feel so good."

"The drugs are fine, Randy. Stop that shit. You're making me nervous."

Randall sunk back in his seat again and sulked quietly. The hyperventilating had slowed down, though. Timothy Leary seemed to have helped.

Meanwhile, the woods weren't letting up. Ours was now the sole vehicle on the winding road, outrunning only the growing darkness and narcotics in our systems. In a few hours we would be home free. I switched the radio to the classical station and left it on Camille Saint-Saens' *Danse Macabre*.

"Do you think we're gonna die?" he asked me.

"Everyone dies," I answered, keeping my eyes on the yellow lines ahead of me.

"I know, but like, our souls. Do you think that dies with us?"

I searched for a hint of comedy in his face, but saw that he was serious. I wanted to ask why it fucking mattered, but stifled my bluntness.

"Being dead probably isn't so bad. Do you remember what it was like before you were born?"

"I don't remember much of anything."

"Well, being dead is probably a lot like that. Think of the billions of years of violent, destructive existence that you skated through as calm as a cucumber. Right? That all might as well have not mattered, as far as your direct living experience is concerned, when you really get down to it."

The drugs were taking hold all at once. I could hear my own voice slowing and elongating as it escaped my vocal chords. My limbs and head were expanding, filling with a pleasant, tingling warmth. I turned and Randall was smiling now, which made me smile too. We must have looked like insane asylum patients together. The road was driving itself. I let go of the wheel as I continued speaking.

"So death is just going back into the static, only you don't hear it."

"That's not comforting at all," he replied flatly. "But what happens to *your soul*?"

At once, both of our grins fell, hoisted in by reality.

"Well, how in the fuck should I know?" I snapped, pulling out another cigarette from the pack tucked behind my handkerchief in the front pocket. "Maybe you don't have a soul. Maybe we're all just slabs of breathing meat, stumbling around in blind fear until collapsing of a heart attack at age fifty. Of course, we'd all like to think we're more special than that. I don't know either way. I don't fucking care."

He caught the raw bitterness in my voice and silenced the topic.

The blood in my veins was vibrating. Abstract colors and shapes were melding before me gently through the windshield. I was about to inform my passenger but decided against it, not wanting to alarm him. I glanced at the rear view mirror and saw headlights following us closely enough to make me uncomfortable.

"Do you see that?"

"See what?"

"Never mind."

I could feel my eyes twitching inside their sockets. The haunting string section pouring out of the car speakers dropped a few octaves and bounced around on either side of my head. It tickled.

"So, this drunk middle-aged guy told me there's gonna be a planetary alignment this week."

Randall looked at me in a perplexed state of horror, eyes glassy and red. "Are you for real?"

"Yeah," I said. "Then he told me how sexy the moon looked that night. It sounded like he knew what he was talking about."

"What does it mean? Are we okay?"

"Mars, Venus and Jupiter will all be visible right next to each other in a line in the sky. It hasn't happened in something like a thousand years, I guess."

"OH JESUS FUCK! Well, what do we do?"

"What do you mean?"

"*To prepare.*"

The glare from one of the streetlights hit me in the face and I blinked hard as flashing red splotches danced around on my windshield. The headlights were still following us.

"How much farther is this place?" I asked, eyes jutting back and forth between the rear view mirror and the poltergeist road. The arrow on the speedometer quivered to the right and I felt the pedal touch the floor.

"Please don't ask me that," he whimpered, pressing the soles of his black dress shoes against the glove box.

"Get your fuckin' shoes off the dash, were you raised by animals?"

"Sorry, Jim. Sorry."

A dense fog was moving in from deep in the woods, encompassing the road in a thick gray veil. I reached out timidly to feel it on my skin and recoiled after bashing my hand into the windshield I forgot was there, startling the both of us. The vehicle then skidded to a halt as I panicked and pressed down abruptly on the brake. I heard the headlights screech and stop just behind us, but the sudden jolt of fear kept me from looking up and seeing for myself. A chorus of chirping crickets deafened the low growl of its engine. My whole being pulsated as we remained transfixed inside the Pontiac. The drugs were coursing through me. My heart was palpitating. I felt paralyzed. Something wasn't right.

Just don't be what you think it is. Just don't be—

"What're you waiting for?" Randall asked.

The headlights lit up the inside of our car with a sickening, pale yellow. I averted my eyes toward the driver's side window to avoid the blinding flashes in the mirror. The fog outside was turning a translucent blue around the ferns and tree trunks.

"GO!" he screamed, and punched me hard on the shoulder.

The force of the blow shook me from my trance—but just as I pressed my foot down on the gas pedal, the blue and red lights came on.

Fuck fuck FUCK.

The Pontiac squealed as we picked up speed, leaving a cloud of smoke and the stench of burnt rubber, and slid around a curve hanging over a steep drop into a pit of dead foliage. The police car's lights filtered my vision and I heard the all too familiar *whoop whoop* and the revving of a much more powerful engine than the one chugging under the hood of my '86 station wagon.

"Where's the shit?" I tersely inquired.

"What?" Randall astutely responded.

"THE SHIT, DUDE. THE DRUGS. WHERE DID YOU PUT THE FUCKING DRUGS?"

"TUNK—I MEAN TRUNK. UNDERNEATH THE SPARE TIRE."

"ALL OF IT?"

"ALL OF IT," he promised.

I switched the radio over to a local alternative station that was playing The Misfits' *Last Caress*. I turned it up to drown out the fear.

WELL I GOT SOMETHING TO SAY. I KILLED A BABY TODAY...

The flashing colors were burning my eyes and creating a dazzling lightshow behind my eyelids every time I blinked. Adrenaline was overtaking the cocktail of narcotics in my bloodstream. I could feel every inch of my body violently trembling beneath my rented tuxedo.

"We're fucked, *we are fuckin' fucked*," Randall babbled, as he stuffed a large nugget of marijuana from his slacks pocket into his mouth and began chewing.

I thought that was hysterical. We had a pound of coke and a pharmacy's-worth of stolen opiates in the trunk, and here was Randy, choking down a dime bag of weed like that would make any fucking difference.

"Where do we tell them we got the pills?" he asked, after swallowing the last of it.

"We're not gonna tell them anything, because we are not getting pulled over," I assured him.

"You're gonna fucking kill us, man!"

"THEY'RE gonna fucking kill us!"

The farther the road twisted us onward, the deeper into the woods we appeared to be. There were streetlights only every half-mile at the most, and any light from the moon was no longer getting through at all. The only real constant glow came from the ominous blue and red lights following us closely like a shark after a bleeding sea lion. Something was going to have to give.

"Do you believe in God?"

"*Shut up*," I barked.

I was starting to have trouble differentiating between my hands on the wheel and the road in front of me. Whatever was reacting inside me was working wonders. It wasn't until this point that the cops' patience evaporated and they turned the sirens on. It screamed at us through the open windows. I rolled them up and cranked the music as far as it could go—a familiar Pixies song that I couldn't recognize in my current state of panic and delirium. I was too busy trying to think of how many years was average for felony class-A drug possession.

Randall turned to me intently and spoke, suit and tie dirtied from our celebration earlier in the night. It was a hell of a lot of drugs to steal, more than we had anticipated on finding.

"Well, I believe in God. I think we all have a—a path. Maybe this was supposed to happen—like a sign. We're on the path to Hell, you and me, for all the shit we did and—and… this is it! This is the moment we either follow the tunnel down or—or—or give up and absolve ourselves, man!"

This was too much. I was out of my mind on an indeterminable amount of illegal substances and alcohol, driving a hurdling station wagon at seventy miles an hour down a nearly pitch-black winding forest road with a police car in pursuit, and now my drug-soaked passenger was firing off like a fucking Evangelist preacher six inches away from my ear. The woods were growing closer and closer to the aged pavement as I drove on. Much farther, and those cops would call in backup or ID my license plate, if they hadn't already. For now, all there was behind us was the single patrol car steadily gaining on our ass. One I could maybe handle, but any more than that…

The gas light flickered on in the corner of my eye. Well, we weren't driving to Mexico. I think at this point one of the cops was talking to us through their car's loudspeaker, but it was hard to tell over the Pixies. Randall was hitting himself and pulling on his matted black hair like a deranged schizophrenic.

"DO SOMETHING, FUCK!"

"Who? What?" I looked to my right to see Randall staring at the ceiling.

"Please! I'm sorry. I'm sorry…"

"Would you stop that shit? You're buggin' me out. I need to focus."

"Oh Father, please forgive me for I have si—"

"WOULD YOU SHUT THE FUCK UP?"

A nauseating mixture of adrenaline, fear and anger surged through me and took my eyes off the wheel to berate the neurotic wreck in my passenger seat.

"GOD ISN'T GOING TO FUCKING HELP YOU, OKAY? *I'M* THE ONE DRIVING, *I'M* THE ONE IN CONTROL OF OUR LIVES, AND *I* NEED YOU TO HELP ME BY SHUTTING THE F—"

"DEER!" Randall interrupted me, throwing out his arms in terror, and pointed at the windshield.

"WHAT?" I yelled, and caught sight of a solid brown object rapidly growing larger as it came into focus in front of our vehicle.

"OH FUCK!"

Spinning the wheel to the left like a sea captain avoiding an iceberg, the station wagon swerved at the absolute last second, veering around a clueless, full-grown buck that decided to stop moving at the worst possible fucking place in the woods. I felt the back wheels slip off the edge of the road, above a twenty-foot drop into the wilderness, as we skidded in a full circle and screamed. My head hit the front of the wheel and honked the horn as we came to a sudden stop, facing the same direction that we'd been driving.

That's when the cop car hit the buck.

It was one of those painful, surreal moments where time slows down to let you appreciate the little things. I craned my neck to the right, head still resting on the wheel, to see the gash dripping red over Randall's eyebrow. His face had smashed into the dashboard. The buck was visible through the passenger window, staring at us with complete indifference. There was a fantastic colorful blur coming upon us, followed by the shrill *WEEEEOOOOO* of the siren. They were going too fast. They weren't going to see it coming.

I heard the sound of the animal getting hit before I saw it happen, which seems scientifically impossible and I attribute to the drugs. It was like a shotgun blast in close proximity without wearing ear protection, or if someone dropped a large cinder block down onto the street from atop a skyscraper.

BAM.

I was reminded of how water can feel like cement if made contact with at a high enough velocity.

I don't think the buck made a noise. It hit the ground and skidded ten yards in front of us. I could see the blood collecting in a pool around the body. Then there was the shrill, cacophonous whining of exploded metal and twisted machinery. The police car was stopped dead, completely destroyed in the front. Headlights were shattered, axles beaten and warped, the engine exposed and leaking underneath the hood that was smashed in like an accordion. The siren was crying erratically, fading in and out to a soft grumble. The deer had decimated this police car.

We sat in silent awe for a moment, stalled a few meters away from the crumpled wreckage, before I regained composure and slammed my foot down on the gas. We were gone before they had a chance to get out of the cruiser—if they weren't killed. I didn't want to think about that. Randall threw up his fist to the dead animal as we tore off into the growing fog.

Once we were clear of the scene I vomited out the window. Randy was grinning like an idiot, dilated pupils filling up the whites of his eyes.

"What did I tell you?"

"Don't fucking say it."

"He did it." Randall widened his smile, showing off his chipped front tooth, and raised his eyebrows, expecting me to rejoice or something.

"You're not pinning this shit on God," I said, after sticking my head into the wind and gagging loudly. "You—you were just moaning how we were sinners and needed to be taken down to eternal damnation, you fucking Judas! Now you and God are homies, and you can just call in a favor, huh?"

"Yes. Yes, that's right. Did you not see what just happened?" He wiped the stream of blood out of his eye and smeared it on his tuxedo jacket.

The forest was beginning to thin out and slivers of moonlight were beaming through the cracks onto the road. I was checking the rear view mirror every minute or so to see if they'd gotten anyone on our tail. I figured there wasn't much time to get out of their path before more found us. We must have been going over 90 mph but I couldn't read the speedometer any longer.

"Yes, I saw. That doesn't constitute divine intervention just because you were mumbling something in the corner over there before a cop car hit a fuckin' deer."

"I think it does."

"Yeah, okay." I exhaled and shook out the nerves tingling their way up my arms. "You're not gonna give me any credit for this? Did you not see that maneuver I pulled? Like James fucking Bond? Nothing?"

I lit another cigarette and sped up around the next curve. I started to think I was seeing city lights, but after the evening's previous events, anything could have been a hallucination. After a few minutes of rigid silence, Randall started back up again.

"Look, man. I've done wrong, but I prayed and asked for forgiveness. He could have rejected me and let us crash into a tree trunk or spend our lives in a cell, but He didn't. He gave us another chance, and that deer was the almighty sign. This is our chance to do better. I'm going straight after this, Jim. I fucking swear. No more booze, no more pills, no more stealing—I'm going clean, Jim."

I rolled my eyes and looked up at the rear view mirror: nothing but dense fog and trees. Where were they?

"Alright, buddy. Maybe give your mind a rest right now. You got a lot of drugs in you. Sleep this off."

"I'm not gonna sleep this off." He turned off the humming Sonic Youth record on the radio to help illustrate how serious he was. "That was a divine wakeup call, what just happened. I think not to recognize that would be squandering the gift we've just been given."

I laughed.

There was a brightly lit clearing at the end of the straightaway we had turned onto. I could make out the streetlights.

"If you're so sure this wasn't a miracle," Randall continued, "then what could it possibly have been, Jim?"

We had almost reached the clearing. I could hear the life of the countryside through my open window. I glanced up at the rear view mirror one last time: the murky blue existence behind us was empty.

"Well?" he reiterated. "Don't dodge the question: what else could that have *possibly* been?"

It was then that I realized they weren't streetlights. A swarm of disorienting blues and reds and bright white flashlight beams swirled around us like exploding fireworks. A small brigade of armed policemen and patrol cars erupted out of the darkness and descended upon us on either side the second we burst out of the woods. I heard the apocalyptic *BANG BANG* as we hit the tire shredders before my wrecked nervous system had time to react. The Pontiac lost control and veered off the road, going airborne at well over the speed limit.

There was the sound of Randall's eardrum-shattering yelp, the smell of leaking oil; and as the brief, peaceful image of the open night sky shrunk into a black wall of solid ground; the dull, crunching *THUD* of our 4,000 lbs. vehicle colliding with a muddy ditch.

I waited for my double vision to focus in on the cracked speedometer in front of my nose, wiped the blood out of my eyes, and was greeted with the barrels of a dozen assault rifles. Men in black Kevlar suits were screaming orders that faded behind the high-pitched ringing in my ears. They sounded like they were underwater. Randall spit up a mouthful of blood on himself and choked on a weak laugh that devolved into a sob. We put our hands in the air.

In our last moment of freedom, as the car doors were being pried open and a fire emerged underneath the demolished hood, I turned to Randall's mangled face with the broken cigarette still between my lips.

"Dumb fucking luck."

Therapy

"Good morning, Henry. I'm glad to see you showed up today."

"Yeah, I'm here. I told you I wasn't going anywhere."

"Good… good. So, how are you feeling?"

"What do you want me to say?"

"How you feel."

"Fine. I'm fine."

"Henry, what have I told you every day we talk?"

"Take your pills?"

"No… well, yes. But I tell you to be honest with me. If you don't do that, I can't help you. Are you taking your pills, though?"

"I'm weaning off them. I tried cold turkey but it didn't work."

"You need to be careful. You can't just go off your medication without talking to a doctor."

"I don't trust any doctor. All they do is sling bullshit at me. Nothing they've ever said has been right."

"Well, what about me? I'm a doctor."

"I don't listen to you."

"Then why are you here?"

"For my mom. She can pretend I'm getting better if I sit here once a week."

"So, you don't want to be here?"

"Of course not. How long have we been talking?"

"About two years. On and off."

"And nothing has changed. I still can't get out of bed until it's dark out. I'm still drinking a fifth of liquor a day. I'm still paranoid that people are following me everywhere I go. I still have panic attacks every time I get a call from a fucking number I don't recognize. I still think about suicide every day. You were supposed to fix this shit. What the fuck do you think you've changed?"

"I'm trying my best, Henry."

"Yeah, me too, Doc."

"You really need to come in every week. The more times you don't show up and decide to quit then decide to try again, the higher the chance is that I just can't help you."

"No one can help me."

"You know that's not true."

"You know what helps me? Getting drunk. That's the only time I ever feel better."

"Until you wake up sick and feel even worse."

"Yeah, then I get drunk again. Problem solved."

"You see the issue here, don't you?"

"Yeah, but it's probably not the same issue that you do."

"Why are you so hostile towards me, Henry?"

"I don't mean to be, alright? I don't hate you."

"I don't hate you either. I want you to feel better."

"No, you want my money. My depression pays your salary. If you actually magically fixed me, you'd be out of a client. You'd lose your salary. You want me sick."

"Do you really believe that?"

"Yes."

"So, I'm your enemy?"

"In some ways, yes. You want me sick. How is it in your interest to help me in any way?"

"Because, contradictory to what you may believe, I got into this line of work to help people. Not for the paycheck."

"The paycheck ain't bad though, right?"

"No, it's not. It lets me take care of my family. Everything isn't about money, though, Henry."

"Whatever you say, Doc."

"Speaking of which, how is the job hunt going?"

"It's not. I don't want a job. I hate people. I don't wanna be around them."

"What about the writing?"

"I still write."

"Are you getting published?"

"No."

"Well, if you like doing it, then keep it up. But you need to start thinking about a real job."

"A real job?"

"Yes. Like something that will bring you a real income."

"This will."

"What will?"

"Writing. I didn't expect you to believe in me. No one else does."

"That's not what I mean. I mean you need a way to support yourself in the meantime. How are you paying for all the alcohol you drink? How do you live?"

"I'm still running through the paycheck from the last job."

"And how much longer do you think that'll last?"

"Long enough to drink myself to death."

"Henry, have you thought about rehab? Somewhere people could help you get through what you're dealing with better than I could?"

"What, you gonna pay for it?"

"Some places will work with what you have to cover as much as possible. Would you be willing to go if that was an option?"

"I don't know."

"Why not?"

"I like drinking."

"It won't help you handle these feelings you're dealing with forever. Eventually this kind of behavior is just going to kill you."

"That's the plan."

"Well, you say that now. People care about you, Henry. Do you ever think about how that would make them feel?"

"No one gives a shit about me but my mom. And she knows this is coming."

"That seems awfully selfish."

"The world is selfish. No one cares about anyone. Sometimes I wish a big asteroid would come down and destroy this whole fucking planet. Just kill us all. Suck out the poison. And you know what the worst part of it all is? We still pretend that we're good people. We still pretend that we want what's best for everyone else. But it's about feeling superior. People are so fast to go up in arms about some fucking dentist putting a bullet through a lion, but they're pulling that holier-than-thou bullshit while choking down the carcass of an animal that was just tortured and slaughtered in a fucking death factory. It's all fake. People love judging people, when those same people are beating their wives and raping their children. It's fucking sick. I hate people. I fucking hate them. Hypocrites."

"It makes me sad to see how angry you are, Henry. Honestly."

"Maybe anger is the only honest reaction someone could have to the world we live in. Maybe I'm the only sane one."

"I'm sorry that I can't help you more."

"Are you really? Or are you just happy that you're not as fucked up as I am? People like me make people like you feel better about being alive."

"Not everyone is as disillusioned as you are. Believe it or not, many people are happy with their lives and believe in the goodness of this world."

"Yeah, well, those people are fucking stupid."

"Okay. Why don't you want to take your medication anymore?"

"It doesn't work. And it makes me fat."

"What about trying a different SSRI?"

"I don't wanna do that."

"Why?"

"I don't wanna go through this whole thing over again with another pill. No one told me how hard it would be to get off this fucking thing when they gave it to me. I don't like being dependent on something that doesn't even work."

"How long have you been on the Lexapro?"

"Two years."

"Did it ever work?"

"Maybe at first. But it's not worth it."

"Try upping the dose?"

"And make it even harder to get off of? Hell no."

"But it might help. Your body has probably just grown a tolerance for it."

"So what, I just keep upping the dose every few years until my blood is half anti-depressant? No thanks, Doc."

"We'll figure something out, Henry."

"How much time is left?"

"Don't focus on the clock. Tell me about your family. How're they doing?"

"Fine. I don't see them much. I make sure to check in with my mom, though. I owe her that."

"What about your father?"

"I think he's doing okay. He's working less, talks a bit more I think. He's not such a zonked-out vegetable anymore. Whatever pills he takes now are working better."

"Do you want to talk about your—"

"No. I forgave him. Okay? Just drop it."

"Do you two have a relationship?"

"No, we don't talk. I don't come around much. I think he's ashamed of me. I think he thinks I'm a loser. He talks more to that fuckin' dog than to me. I can't blame him, though. I'd be ashamed of me too. He's like this super genius whose life got ruined by a couple worthless kids he had to support way longer than he should have. Well, I shouldn't say that. Carmen is doing fine."

"Tell me about your sister."

"She's good. She's fine. She lives upstate with the boyfriend, has a decent job and a house and everything. When she crashed her car and got dragged off to rehab, the doctors just threw a bunch of pills at her until the lithium stuck. That's how they found out she's bipolar like my dad. It explained a lot. The lithium worked like fuckin' magic, though. It's crazy. She's a totally different person now. In a good way. She got lucky."

"That's good to hear. I understand that she caused you to have a difficult childhood."

"I don't wanna talk about that. I don't remember much anyway. It wasn't just her fault, though. How much time do we have left?"

"We're almost done, Henry, but just try to stay focused, alright?"

"Okay."

"You're doing fine, just relax. Now... would you like to talk about the incident?"

"No."

"Are you sure?"

"Yes."

"Alright, but it's very important that we talk about the recent trauma that's caused this new behavior."

"What behavior?"

"The alcoholism, the fear of people, your trust issues, suicidal tendencies, the nightmares."

"What do you want me to say?"

"I want you to tell me about the incident that caused this behavior."

"And I told you no."

"Henry, there's no shame in what you're feeling. There are millions of people struggling with PTSD that are going through the same things you are."

"I told you that I don't wanna fucking talk about it."

"Okay. One day I really hope that you can talk about it. Maybe not with me, but healing from something like this can't happen without facing it. I know that sounds hard, so I won't push you anymore, but I want you to know that. You can't suppress this with alcohol forever. Eventually it just won't work anymore. And all you'll be left with is you and your memories. And I don't want that to happen to you. I wish you could be helped, Henry. If you refuse for now, I understand. But please believe me that I don't want to see you in pain. People do have empathy, despite what your life seems to have taught you."

"Just let me leave."

"Fine, Henry. Time's up."

Father of Mine

So, it was the night before I got arrested. I don't think I'll go into that part here. Or maybe I will. We'll see how this goes.

I was in my late teens. By this time my older sister was out of the house, hidden away in the annals of some eating disorder clinic or rehab or off trying to become a rock star in California—it's hard to remember the chronology of the events, but each of these life paths were reoccurring and tossed her back into the same shitty destination so it hardly matters—and so in her absence, it was now upon me to don the crown and devil horns and take on the title of The Resident Black Sheep of the Family. And let me tell you, I lived up to the task. If it were something to be proud of, Carmen would have been fucking beaming. Plus I'm sure she appreciated the weight off after holding the championship belt for as long as she did. You're welcome, Sis.

My father and I never got along once I became old enough to disappoint him. I had failed him as a son and human being far too many times for him to look at me and see any semblance of the man he wanted me to become when I was first ripped out of my mother's stomach. I was a pot smoking, school skipping, morally bankrupt, fucked-in-the-head, lying little shit with a serious issue with authority. Of course, I would blame most—if not all—of my shortcomings on my father, whether because of his trashed, inbred Irish genetics, or his abusive and shit parenting. So we were at a bit of a standoff throughout my formative years.

Dad has not had an easy life. He's diagnosed bipolar—
something that none of us were really aware of until I had already
nurtured a healthy level of contempt for him. His father died when
he was very young, and he then proceeded through the haze of his
childhood years with a rotating cast of two-bit step-dads who did
nothing to alleviate the loss of a real parent. He overcame a serious
problem with alcoholism in his thirties; still goes to meetings
twice a week. He worked a shit job for three long decades; a job
that by the end of it he hated so much he was vomiting in the
bathroom every morning, unable to bear the idea of going back
into that office another day, but knew he had to. His brother is a
drug-dealing schizophrenic who harbors a roomful of stolen
military hardware, a secret basement that contains a surprisingly
advanced and extensive hydroponic weed grow-op, and who once
stole $60,000 from their cancer-riddled sister who was about to
use that money for chemotherapy treatments (shout-out Uncle
Morgan). There's also something that happened to him as a child,
a something that would violently shake up *anyone's* brain
chemistry, I don't care who you are—a something that I will not
go into here out of respect to a man who didn't deserve it. No one
deserves that. (Also he's not dead and I can't afford to be sued for
libel.)

I'm not trying to slather a turd in glitter before forcing it down
your throat, I suppose I'm just trying to provide some context
ahead of time for why my father treated his young children like a
four year-old left alone with the family cat. In fact it was a lot like
that. He wouldn't bat an eyelash, wouldn't say a word while our
mom was in the room. He couldn't afford to lose her (years later,
my mother would tell me the only reason she never left him was
because he said he would kill himself if she tried). He would just
sit there silent, un-medicated, gritting his teeth—a jagged, yellow

wall surrounded by reddening flesh, violent eyes—stewing in the manic delusions his brain had convinced him were valid.

It wasn't until my mother left for the grocery store, to the hair salon, to the anywhere, to get out and drive to relieve the pressure of living with a family of fucking nutjobs. It wasn't until then that the man my sister and I—little kids, little little kids—feared like death itself came out from his stupor. He would corner us—mostly me, ever the disappointing male figure—and release a mighty hurricane of emotional and psychological abuse for whatever failures we had stockpiled in his eyes in the days or weeks since he was last allowed to be left alone with us. The roars that came hurdling out his mouth, the eyes like daggers and skin like the Devil's and the spittle flying like ash and lava from an erupting volcano. Screaming and breaking objects and pushing his horrible, twitching face into yours so you can smell the disdain for life, his fists clenched up to your chin, demanding a response to his nonsensical ramblings. The openhanded slaps that sent a ringing through your ear like an electric ZAP when your shaken mind couldn't force words into the back of your throat and and and...

Though to be honest, the physical abuse isn't at all what ended up affecting me later in life. The physical abuse could hardly even be considered that. When it happened it was sporadic and I'd hesitate to call them beatings. Most red-blooded Americans would've considered that aspect of the parenting as well within his rights, and I'm not spiteful about the times he ever did put a hand to me. And never to my sister. Never a hand to my sister. I think he could tell she was already too fucked in the head to lay down any more trauma than what she was already guaranteed in the life ahead of her. I was simply too young for my father to recognize the extent of the damage he'd already dealt upon me. Subtle, chronic abuse like that is a slow poison.

Really, I went the rest of my life not thinking much about the effect a mentally ill, erratic father would have on the developing mind of a child, not seeing anything particularly wrong with it. All I knew was that I was growing to hate him. It was this dull white nausea that expanded at the base of my stomach whenever I looked at him. I despised him for making me afraid, for making the place I lived feel like a prison. Always looking over my back, finding ways to get my mom alone so I could ask her not to go to work that day, unable to tell her what Dad did whenever she left for fear of the word getting back to the source.

But maybe I'm going too far back.

I should make this all fair.

By the time I was seventeen I was insane. Truly truly truly. Insane. I would routinely fly into feral rages; collapse into mindless, frightening psychotic episodes like I'd been possessed by a demon. The walls of my isolated basement room were covered in holes from punches. Death punches. Get-the-demon-out punches. Like craters on the moon, everywhere. Between this sort of behavior was debilitating stretches of manic paranoia (I once tore the entire back of my car apart for two hours because I believed somebody had planted drugs in there to get me arrested. For no reason.), abrupt serious-but-not-too-serious suicide attempts; or just plain, good ol' American major depressive episodes where I would fail to eat, drink, or get out of bed for a week or so. I was placed on many medications (never took any of them), taken to many different therapists (never talked to any of them), and diagnosed with many different disorders (I doubt the accuracy of most of them). My family was legitimately worried I was schizophrenic. Like in two years you're going to be yelling at lampposts schizophrenic. I suppose I would have been too if I wasn't too busy cheating on my girlfriend with anything that had a pussy, and stealing my parents' money to afford my excessive and oddly intense weed habit—a habit which I'm sure did nothing to curb the psychosis and paranoia.

So I guess all I'm trying to say is that the night I'm about to talk about was neither my father's fault nor mine. Or more accurately, I guess, it was both our faults. A lot of things lead up to the present moment. As obvious as it is, I forget that sometimes.

The problem is that whatever I did or didn't do to lead to me hurling my fist into the refrigerator, shattering my hand and smearing blood across its white surface, I really can't remember. I'm not trying to save face—I'd rather make myself look even worse than give you some *but I'm still the hero* answer—but when in that unstable of a mental space, it can be hard to un-blur the moments later in life. It's probably best I don't remember. It was probably an awful reason. I was probably just hungry. There probably wasn't any food. Who knows.

But anyway, there I was: stupid crazy teenager, fed up with life, angry at the world, angry at my father for still having power over me, angry at the fucking fridge for breaking my hand.

Enter: Father. Dad. Pops. Roger.

I could hear the footsteps coming down the hallway next to me like the marching of an enemy armada. Like a herd of wild animals. Then the familiar bellow:

"WHAT THE FUCK ARE YOU DOING. WHAT DID YOU DO? YOU LITTLE SHIT. *YOU LITTLE SHIT, GODDAMNIT! FUCK!*"

He was more wary around me at this point in my life, toning down his gale-force rage, careful not to fuck with me too much since I was crazy now and all. And plus I had been boxing the last year or so and could easily knock him out if I wanted and he knew this and I guess I knew this, but the psychological effect of his particular brand of parenting (let's call it that) was still deeply engrained in me. I was still Pavlov's dog. Ring the bell and my mouth watered. Or something to that effect. I couldn't seem to shake that deep-seated fear of my father even after it was long passed useful as a survival mechanism.

So I just stood there waiting to get punched in the face. Mind racing, adrenaline spiking, lungs hyperventilating, eyes dilating, legs giving out like rubber stilts, hand pulsing, hand bleeding, the all-too-familiar passive impotency forcing its way up my chest like a dry heave. Fear. Fear. Fear.

Now see, I could have thrown a punch instead of what I did, even just held my fists up like "okay let's do this old man, you and me"—that alone could've scared him off. But the anger spilled out of me. The resentment. The bubbling insanity. The memories I didn't realize had so fucked with me.

I thought of the day my dad had an anxiety attack while driving me to school when I was fourteen. We'd been riding in silence the whole way before he abruptly stopped the car about a block away from the building, and without saying a word, opened the door and collapsed on the street. Cars were driving past. Other kids walking by with their backpacks watched timidly from the sidewalk, deciding if intervening was worth their trouble. I sat there with the seatbelt still harnessed over me yelling, "Dad, get up! Is this a heart attack? Dad? Do I call an ambulance?" He didn't answer. He just gave up. Choking on shallow, fluttering breaths. Staring blankly into the bleak and sunless sky. He didn't want it anymore. He never wanted any of it. He never asked for it. He was just a man. A man overcome with and forever molded by, fear. A man like me.

As my father rounded the corner with those dagger eyes, that protruding stomach, those big hairy fists, I thought of that memory. As my father rounded that corner to hurt me, to scream out all the disappointment and despair of his life, I thought of that memory, and I grabbed a kitchen knife. A big one. Like seven inches. And I held it out in front of me. Bleeding, shaking, insane.

My father took one look at the knife, one look at me. And froze. Every ounce of the beast that had frightened me into submission for years drained out of him with the cherry red in his face until it was nothing but ghost white. Dead white. He looked up at me... and turned right the fuck around. Didn't say a word. Ran right out the front door. Just ran.

That was the moment I was no longer afraid of my father. That was the moment I forgave my father. In that moment, for the first time in fourteen years, I didn't see a beast. I didn't feel hatred. I saw a beaten down, scared, flawed human being. I saw me. I saw his son.

Obviously, the story doesn't end there. You don't break your hand, hold a knife up to a family member, and run from the cops for a half-mile without some kind of repercussion. Things were not all good after that. I didn't truly recognize how important of a moment that time in the kitchen was right away. It took me a while. My father and I's relationship took a few more years, a few more medications, a few more drastic life changes before we started to see each other with love again. But we did. It just had to start somewhere.

I remember when I was really little, maybe four or five, I would sneak into the bathroom while my dad was taking a shower and I'd flush the toilet. I'd heard somewhere that flushing the toilet while someone showers turns the water boiling hot. It sounds sadistic but I promise my intent was innocent. Anyway, our water system didn't work like that. Flushing the toilet didn't do anything. But every time I did it, my dad would recognize the soft pitter-patter of my footsteps, wait for the flush, and go, "AGGGGHHHHH! YOU GOT ME! AGGGGHHH!" And I'd double over in laughter. It was the funniest thing I'd ever seen. He really sold it. "AGGGHHHHH! IT'S SO HOT. AGGGHHHH!" And once I'd wiped the tears out of my eyes and gotten back onto my feet, my dad and I would stare at each other like runners waiting for the starting gun; him peeking his head around the curtain, his hair all black and slathered white with shampoo, and he'd say, "Now, Henry... I know what you're thinking... Don't you—" And I'd pounce on the toilet flusher, and my dad would scream all over again: "AGGHHHH! AGGGHHHH! I TOLD YOU NOT TO, YOU LITTLE STINKER! YOU GOT ME!" And goddamn I would laugh so hard I thought my lungs would burst.

I'm glad I remember that.

Oh. And well, shit. As for jail, I don't recommend it. The food sucks.

The Old German I Fucked Over

I met the German at my father's 60-somethingeth birthday dinner party. I don't remember his name so don't ask me. Apparently he knew my father from AA. My father has been sober for, what, 30 years? Who knows how long the old German had.

By some stroke of fate, I ended up seated next to the thick-accented octogenarian. I was twenty-one, stinking of whiskey from the flask resting underneath my car seat I had drained in the parking lot before going in—in retrospect not the best idea, given that I was then heading into a room filled almost exclusively with ex-alcoholics, but if the rest of this story will tell you anything, it's that this sort of behavior was mild compared to the rest of my decisions during that time in my life.

The German was old enough to have been a ten year-old boy during the 1944 bombings of Berlin by the RAF. I know this because he told me his entire life story—unsolicited—within ten minutes of me sitting down next to him. His brother was a Hitler Youth, and was killed when the train station they were waiting at to get out of the city collapsed under the explosion of a half-ton bomb. Our German lost his left leg in the blast. I don't feel much like going into the rest of the story, already bored by the prospect of stretching this thing out longer than it needs to go. And if I didn't write it then, I'm not going to write it now.

Basically, the old man had the most tried and true American Dream, pull-yourself-up-by-the-bootstraps, rags to riches immigrant story that you'd ever be hard-pressed to find. The cliff notes: He survived the war, got a nice fake leg (through some fluke, paid for by the German government. Like for life. Like every five years the German government sends him a new fake leg as part of some form of war-injury reparations), moved to America with literally 65 cents or some such and no understanding of the English language, then fast-forward to our German owning his own lucrative business in... locksmithing? Or something? And now he was traveling the world with his wife—I forget her name too—happily spending all that hard-earned American Dream money and presumably not drinking.

Well, after telling me all this shit, through the haze of a fading hangover and a building drunk, I heard him say, "And now I eem looking for a vriter, to tell dis shtory before I eem dead. I have diabeetus, and soon I veel be dead." Or however a German accent sounds—I'm a writer, not a fuckin' linguist.

I'd hardly been writing seriously—let alone, writing—for more than six months at this time, but was already more than determined to be the millennials' answer to Bukowski, an unfortunate but understandable first influence on me and—more unfortunately—my lifestyle, so I almost leapt out of my chair when I told him, "Yes! I'm a writer! I do that! I'll write it!"

The old man's eyes lit up. "You vill? Excellent! Vunderbar! Vee schall get started immediately! Yes?"

"Yes!" I shouted.

"I vill make you... Fayymous! Like Steeephen King! You vill vrite my life, and I vill pay you money! Five zousand dollars! Yes?"

My jaw dropped. I had never seen that much money in my life—never imagined ever making that much money through anything but illegal avenues. This was unprecedented. This was life altering. This sober, one-legged German would change my life without me ever showing him a single word of prose. This must have been what the BIG TIME felt like. It was as if I had conned my way into the pants of the Queen of Fucking England.

"Yes! That's fine! That's FINE!" I could have kissed him if his mouth wasn't dripping with schnitzel and non-alcoholic wine.

After basking in the glow of my newfound artistic genius and grifting talent, the two of us exchanged information and planned to meet at his estate—ESTATE, what a country—for me to begin the interviews that I had no idea how in the hell to conduct. But that didn't matter. I was a writer now! I made the BIG TIME. 5,000 BUCKS, baby!

I remember going home that night and polishing off a fifth of cheap whiskey, feeling very pleased with myself.

Once interviewing time came around, I strolled into the old German's castle on the outside of town with a pint of Old Crow in my stomach, absentmindedly chewing a piece of gum. He didn't seem to notice; more interested in regaling me with tales that, even in my drunken and virginal state as a biographer, I knew were completely useless. Essentially the entire story that could at all fill this imaginary book was already told in fifteen minutes at a dinner party. The old German was wasting away mentally and could hardly reiterate the only useable anecdotes.

Nonetheless, I continued with the notion that I would write his story—help him with the honor of dying a known man or whatever it was he wanted. That is, until I was handed the check before I left.

He rolled forward on his wheelchair (there's only so much a fake leg on an eighty-something year-old can do) and handed me the crisp piece of paper with a liver-spotted hand, smiling. "You vill vrite my shtory. I trust zis. You vill make us faymous. I pay you now, for inspirayschun! Yes?"

I just stared at it: $5,000. Pay to the order of Henry Gallagher. Signed with barely legible chicken scratch from an unsteady hand.

"Yes," I said.

"You vill vrite zee first chapter tonight, yes?"

I took the check and slid it carefully into my back pocket. "Yes."

At that moment, I no longer had any intention of writing a single word.

So, the deadline rolled through. Days passed. Weeks passed. Phone calls came constantly. I ignored everything, assuming they would eventually stop. They did. I didn't know how to tell him I wasn't going to do it. But mostly I just didn't want to give him the money back. The old motherfucker was rich! Shit, he could afford to hand out thousands like you or I would hand spare change to a homeless person. He wouldn't miss it. And maybe that was right. But in truth, I didn't want to give him back that money because within three weeks I had already blown through $1,500 of it. Oh, on what, you ask?

On booze.

Lots.

And lots.

Of booze.

Heroic amounts of it.

This was at the peak of my desperate issue with alcoholism and the absolute worst time to step into such a large sum of money. I spent every day at the bar—hours and hours of fucking off and drowning my liver with cash I hadn't earned. Not writing. Not calling him back. Not thinking about it. Just drinking.

Then I really fucked up. One night during one of my many blackouts, I lost the portfolio that he entrusted me with to use for research—the only material thing left in the world that he cared about—full of photographs and documents he'd saved since the late-thirties. Pictures of his dead brother. News articles from the day he was killed. Awards he'd been presented with for his businesses. Hand-written notes from his father before the war. The first dollar he ever made on American soil. AA chips spanning decades back. I got drunk and misplaced his entire life.

I never talked to that German again. And that $5,000 was gone within four months.

Four months.

So effectively, I stole a small fortune from an old man, failed to fulfill his one—mutually beneficial—dying wish, lost every memento of his past that he'd ever held dear in his life, and proceeded to drink through that small fortune within the span of time it takes to finish a semester of college. For all I know, that old German is dead now. Dead and forgotten, his story never told. And that's on me. That one's definitely on me.

But wouldn't it be a hell of a thing if one day, maybe soon, I'm walking down the street and happen upon a quaint little bookstore, and I decide to go in—just to see if there are any cute bookworms hanging around in the dusty aisles of literature. And after perusing the aisles for a minute or so, I happen upon the shelf of the newly released stuff—no, the Best-Sellers. Yeah. And there on one of the shiny book covers, staring at me, is the old German's face: the thinning white hair, the deep wrinkles indented into the skin hanging loosely around the gray light of the eyes, the unmistakable glow of a man with morals; proud and healthy-looking—on account of the Photoshop. And beneath that is the name of some other author, now wildly famous—that writer I've heard about with all the movie deals, the numerous awards and accolades. I've probably seen him on Jimmy Kimmel by now. And at the top of the shiny book cover: MILLIONS SOLD. THE STORY OF A GENERATION.

Yeah.
I'd probably deserve that.

Fuck, that would make me happy.

Death and a Funeral

I had never talked to a man on one day who was dead on the next. As far as I know. It was a peculiar feeling. We stood outside the pub together—the regulars; the bartenders; me, the tourist— and watched as his funeral procession passed by. Eamon, one of the bartenders, closed the blinds and locked the door behind us as an act of respect for the deceased. And there we stood together smoking cigarettes, them solemn and quiet, me quite confused by the whole thing—death, Ireland, everything. I must have been six pints deep by the time I realized what was happening. It was silent that morning when I came down from my small room on the upper floor of O'Phelan's pub. The wrinkled regulars were dressed in black, mumbling over their pints of Guinness. I was still drunk from the previous night.

First came the crowd of whom I could only assume were close friends and family. Small towns in Ireland kept a close-knit community. They held bouquets of flowers and tall cans of beer— some pouring them out on the cement, some drinking them. Then came the long black hearse, complete with the corpse and coffin resting upon a bed of red and blue flowers. There he was, dead as dead could be. The procession hit a left and turned towards St. John's Cathedral for the preemptive ceremony. I forget the name for it. Once the car passed, we all tossed our cigarettes and hobbled back into the bar for another drink.

I think his name was Mickey. Or Michael. Something like that. We were playing pool together on a Sunday night. The Irish call it snooker. I don't know why. I remember he won. I bought him a pint, we drank together, and then he left. He walked out the door, into the street, walked about another half-mile, then collapsed on the cement, dead from a sudden brain aneurism. We didn't find out until Tuesday. He wasn't even that old. He looked it, but so did every Irishman who spent their afternoons drinking at the same pub every day. People would tell me that I was the last person to have a proper conversation with the man before he passed on. I'm not sure what to do with that information. I suppose it doesn't change much. I don't even remember what we talked about. At this point I'm sure it's inconsequential.

Someone had laid out his pool cue stick on the snooker table to honor his memory. It was the stick he had always used at O'Phelan's, every day since he had been old enough to drink. Or probably even before that. Eamon informed us that today, no one would play snooker as a sign of reverence to our fallen companion. A particularly drunk regular then promptly picked up the stick and knocked the balls every which way, laughing hysterically. The people were not amused. But it would take much more than disrespecting the dead to get 86'd from an Irish pub, so the lad was given a second chance, albeit shunned—but not cut off. If he had murdered the man himself, I believe he'd still be sitting at the bar downing pints until the cops arrived. I'd once seen a man break a glass over his own head, vomit on the patron next to him, collapse on the floor, stumble back to his feet, take a punch from the vomit-drenched Irishman, shake his hand, and order another shot of whiskey as blood ran down his face, only to then get served again.

So after some harsh words exchanged in thick tongues I had trouble deciphering, the pub fizzled back into a mournful lull. Then someone turned on the television.

There were immediate flashes of screaming and bloodied faces, shots of rubble and dust clouds, crowds of frightened people running in tandem towards the same direction, away from something awful. The bar became silent once more. We all watched together. I ordered another pint. I would need it. A newscaster came on the screen. She explained that Brussels was under attack; the city had been bombed and hundreds were dead or missing. Someone near me slammed his fist down on the bar counter. It was too much death for one day. In seconds, the sheer force of life jamming its way down our throats exhausted the lot of us. The terrorists had struck again. Fresh pints were ordered all around. We drank to peace, silently watching the death unfold across our faces and the television screen before us.

That night, I broke the nose of a drunken local who made a joke about how it was America's fault that the Belgians were slaughtered. If he had given me a day or two, I wouldn't have reacted so harshly, maybe even agreed with him for the sake of nihilistic comedy, but wounds were too fresh that night and I was too drunk. Frankly, I was looking to do harm to someone anyway. There was too much darkness distorting my vision. Death will do that to a man, I realized that.

The next morning, I was invited by the regulars to join them for the official funeral at the cathedral. I promised them I would go, and then immediately ran away to the nearest bar that wasn't O'Phelan's and drank myself into a stupor. I still don't know why I did that. I suppose I am just a coward, and that much death was something I couldn't face with my chin up. Looking back on it, though, I realize that none of those men's chins were up, but they went anyway. These were better men than me. I'm proud to have met them. I imagine that the ceremony was beautiful: angelic choirs, a priestly sermon, sudden admissions of love from former girlfriends, the whole shebang—life flashing before the eyes of the dead, and vice versa.

Meanwhile, I was slumped over a foaming pint of Irish beer in the loneliest pub I could find in all of Kilkenny, thinking over the meaning of death and life, waiting for a moment to change the chemical imbalance inside my brain that made me such a pussy. But no such luck. Mickey (Michael?) was in the ground, terrorists had killed hundreds in a country 600 miles away from me, and fear still shook me to the very core of my flimsy being. The world was on fire and I felt every goddamned molecule of it brushing against my thin skin. And yet, there I was, still breathing. Still drinking away the thoughts slamming into the walls of my skull.

I don't know what to say any longer. I am now back in the United States and slumped over a bottle of cheap wine. It tastes like a sweet death and I'm reminded of those days I spent nursing my alcoholism in the best place in the world to do it. Mickey (Michael) is still in the ground, decomposing for no one but the worms in the dirt and I feel no different. The bombs were still detonated, the man is still dead of an event very few can or will understand, the pints are empty, my bottle is nearly so. These words are meaningless. Few people will understand the complexities of what goes on in the mind during a situation such as death. Many will experience it but few will understand. I find myself among the ignorant majority. Life is still too empty. Life is still too intricate to analyze. Perhaps a greater mind could turn my experience into a truly great work of art. But that mind does not belong to me. Death is simply an excuse to live with urgency. The drink is simply an escape. My mind is simply a vessel. And the vessel is simply afraid. One thing I know how to do: run.

Dancing to Broken Records

I still hear his voice from time to time, mostly when I'm too drunk to speak myself. He speaks in tongues of which I can't understand. But his voice is there, imprinted into my nothingness. I wish I could remember his face. The details, you know? Something solid to grasp at when his voice comes to me in the night. Maybe then I could believe in some sort of purpose for it all. But I can only keep up my charade of sincerity for so long. Death is meaningless, as meaningless as life, and another body in the dirt is just another body that isn't me.

Sometimes I can't write a happy ending to a story. Not every story has one.

I Love You

That's the hardest part about having such a tolerance for alcohol. You just keep getting drunker and the words come out as eloquently as they did eight whiskey-sodas ago. There's no slur in your voice so the bartender doesn't know to stop serving you. The only indication is in the actual words you use. They spill out like black tar, venomous and toxic. Angry, depressed, spiteful words, spoken so fluidly that instead of a drunk, you just look like an asshole. A piece of shit, really. You don't look like someone with a problem, or a few.

And then you just get quiet. You get so drunk that any words spoken would just be another nail in your coffin. You stare into the mirror in front of you and look at that bloated, depressed bastard swirling around his glass, staring back at you, and you hate him. You fucking hate him. You're eye-to-eye with your worst fucking enemy. That cocksucker is the reason for every terrible thing that's ever happened in your life. He's stolen girlfriends from you, lost you jobs, robbed you of a future. And he just drinks and stares back like he did nothing wrong. You hate him.

And then you hear a voice. You forgot you came here with people. Not people—a someone. A girl. Her voice sounds like what you hear when someone tries to talk to you while your head is underwater. It's dulled and distant and all you can hear are soft waves of vowels.

"What?"

"I said, are you okay?"

You have two options now and both end in failure, so really it doesn't matter which one you pick. You can lie, say you're fine, feign a weak smile and turn back to the death glare in the mirror. Or you can tell her the truth. And that normally is the best option. But when you're at this point, there's only so many times you can tell her that you're depressed and don't want to talk to anybody, and you want to go home or kill yourself or keep drinking until the world doesn't exist anymore. She tells you to be honest with her, but you know that sometimes honesty is unnecessary and simply self-defeating. Because eventually she'll get the message that wow, you really are damaged goods, and someone this depressed and sick and drunk and angry probably will never not be depressed and sick and drunk and angry, and she'll realize she should really just get out now.

So you choose option one.

"I'm fine," you say.

And you feign a weak smile, turn back towards the man in the mirror, and you watch him finish the whiskey in that glass he's got. And she knows you're lying. And she's almost angry. Almost.

She gives you another chance, one last life preserver to cling to before you sink. She reaches in and kisses your cheek, and grabs your hand with a charitable amount of grace and empathy that you know you don't deserve. And she waits.

You feel her eyes on the side of your head, those big blue eyes that were the first thing you noticed about her; that dragged you across the room like a rope was tied around your ankle and yanked you towards her. Those big blue eyes that you love but don't want to tell her because she doesn't want to love a self-destructor, and you just want another day to look at her and pretend it's not fleeting like everything else.

And what the fuck do you do? You idiot. You ignore her. You let those perfect, big blue lights dim and turn away, and it's like every light in the fucking world just went out.

And now she's angry. She gets up and walks over to your friends whom you forgot were here, and flirts with the one friend you really wish she wouldn't. And the fucked up thing is, a part of you is relieved. Relieved, because now you have an excuse to be a drunken mess, to be sad, to be angry, to get another drink.

"Anna, another one."

The bartender smiles. She knows you. She trusts you. She's never seen you scream or fight or throw food or break a glass. She just watches you sit alone and look at the mirror and drink your booze, and she doesn't know you're the drunkest motherfucker in the goddamn bar.

It clinks when it's placed on the bar in front of you. You crane your neck back and drain the whole thing. It tastes like ash. Not like gasoline or turpentine. It tastes like you swallowed a handful of ash.

But you're too drunk to care and you look over at her, and Jesus she's beautiful. She's laughing and talking about something people talk about and rubbing his bicep. He looks at you and gets uncomfortable. You hear him say your name to her and it sounds like you've sunk another 10,000 feet. You can't see the life preserver anymore. The water's surface is probably on fire and you're better off down here anyway.

"Anna. Anna? I'll have another one."

You never had to care before. You always hated yourself, but you were free to drink and smoke and disregard any bright future because that was your right. You liked killing yourself. You became your own entertainment, like that worm you found in your backyard when you were four, and you got a knife from the kitchen and you cut it into little pieces to see if it'd grow back. It didn't, and you won't, but that didn't seem to matter.

But now it's different. You aren't alone anymore. There's that little voice calling from above the water and those big blue eyes, and drinking and smoking and killing yourself doesn't feel good anymore because you're not the only victim. There's this girl here and you're hurting her and that doesn't feel good. It feels awful. It feels fucking awful. She wants you to care about yourself, but you care about her and that's the closest thing to it that you've had in four years.

"Hey, Bukowski."

It's Chris' girlfriend, Frida. Like Frida Kahlo. You're not feeling humorous enough to ask her when she shaved the unibrow, like you always do. She calls you that because you write and you're an alcoholic, and you're never quite sure if she means it as a compliment when she says it.

"Yes?" you say.

"How you doin'?"

They're drunk and she's giggling because Chris is rubbing his hands over her ass and hips as he hugs her from behind. They look happy. They always look happy.

"I'm fine, Frida. Thank you."

"Kaitlyn just left. Everything alright?"

"Everything's perfect, Frida. Everything's peachy."

But it's not and you must be too drunk to identify objects in your peripheries, because it's true—she left and you didn't notice.

"Go to her, man… go to her."

Chris is joking and it makes you not want to, but you know if you don't, you probably won't see her again. And as much as you're inclined towards masochism, you can't press the red button on this one. You can't seem to drive your happiness off the cliff this time. They're kissing now and whispering into each other's ears, and it makes you sick so you get up to leave.

It's cold out and there's no moon and the only stars you can find are making up the Big Dipper. She's sitting on the bench next to the window smoking a cigarette. She never smokes cigarettes, and she's talking to a kid with torn jeans and hair that looks like a dead animal resting atop his head. You sit down next to her and say nothing because you know anything you say won't come out how you want, and you start to feel bad that you're this drunk. She glares at you and drags the cigarette like she's kicking you in the stomach.

The kid with the dead animal on his head is talking about how gnarly the powder is on Mt. Whateverthefuck. She doesn't care and you know she doesn't care, but she's trying to pretend that he's more interesting than you are. You bum a cigarette off the kid and you realize it looks like a possum, a dead possum. On his head, you mean. You light the cigarette and inhale, and the smoke is blue when it touches the sparse light of the stars.

Then it's quiet for a while. The wind is as loud as your thoughts and there are three words floating around the oblivion inside your head. You're afraid to say them but you realize there really aren't any other options.

You used to have an intimacy problem. The problem being that you didn't want any. A switch would flip the second you came. You would roll off whatever woman of the week you bedded this time, look at her face, study the lines and contours and the glimmer of life in the eyes you at one time found attractive, and like a bright light had suddenly focused on her, you would see every disgusting, unfixable flaw popping out and oozing from her being. You would kick her out in shame, delete her number, open a bottle of whiskey and drink until the black sky turned purple and orange.

Sex was an ugly and disturbing phenomenon that you had to endure, like that next hit of heroin an addict desperately doesn't want to put in his vein but fucking has to. Sex was performed behind closed doors and shut blinds, and you wouldn't ever let yourself be seen in the light of day with one of your conquests. It was announcing to the world that your addiction existed.

Now, alcoholism was simple. Alcoholism was a shared addiction, celebrated and appreciated by the community and culture. You were among kin when you walked into any bar in the goddamn country, slowly disintegrating together with mile-wide grins on your faces. Billboards of pretty, 50-foot models pouring glasses of scotch like swimming pools plastered the streets you drove down with a bottle tucked under your seat. The world wanted you to drink. Your heroes drank. They drank because they had the same problems you did. Depressed people drank. That's what they did. You decided it was expected of you. Your parents were alcoholics. They met at AA. You would always joke that if it weren't for alcoholism, you would never have existed. And that meant you could keep drinking. Then you would laugh and throw up that shot of tequila.

Sex was different. Sex was for dirty perverts and deviants. There was no romanticism in it, like there was in killing yourself with the bottle. Every second was bloated with paranoia and shame and utter disgust. You weren't the only one hurt in this kind of addiction. Women were slabs of meat, thrown away when they reached their all-too-soon expiration date. With each one gone, each door closed, each ringing silence once you were alone again in an empty room, you could feel another piece of your soul chipped off and buried deep in the black hole somewhere within you that could never fill.

So you cut yourself off, vowed to make a change, and you did. You were celibate for over a year and—unwilling to live without a vice—replaced pussy with the bottle.

And then you met her. Maybe it was the time out of the game. Maybe it was the loneliness decaying inside you. But she was perfect. Man, she was fucking perfect. The way her hair fell down around her shoulders when she undid her bun. The way her freckles came out with the sun like they were old friends. The way her eyes looked for yours in the room before anyone else's. You wanted to write entire books of poetry for her, write stories about her, and you did; stories you were too embarrassed to show her because you thought she might laugh. You hoped to God you were better because you wanted to be perfect for her, because that's what she deserved. You never wanted to leave her. You fucked, and you still never wanted to leave her. You were hooked. And you were scared shitless because of it, but you didn't care. This felt better than liquor.

So those three words are tumbling around in your head, and you think if you say them, she'll only react exactly how *you* would've fifteen months ago. It's a cosmic, karmic fuck you for the lives you damaged. The last thing you'll see is her ass running for the road, and the last thing you'll hear is that now she's fucking your friend.

But she's still sitting here and that kid with the possum on his head is still talking about gnarly powder, and you still have three goddamn words at the tip of your mind that might implode if you don't get them out.

And then, there it is. The words pour out like the spirit from a dead body. Like the universe collapsing in on itself. Like the words aren't just words but an ancient, mystic incantation that has to be uttered to keep the world spinning:

"Hey. Fuck, uh. You make me happy. It may not look like it...
but life doesn't seem so awful when you're around. You make me
not wanna drink so much. You make me wanna be... decent.
Which is saying a lot. I'm sorry this still happens, I really am. But
I'm trying. And I didn't used to wanna try. That's gotta mean
something. I'm not asking you to fix me or even help me. I'm not
even saying I'm broken—I just... I like this. I like sitting next to
you. Everything doesn't hurt so much when we talk. I uh, I... love
you."

That wasn't three words.

You sit in silence. Possum Kid says, "Oh. My bad," then tosses
his cigarette and walks inside. She looks at you and those big blue
eyes are like lakes of placid water. The cigarette is burning at the
filter in her right hand. You inhale the last drag of yours like it's
your dying breath. And you wait.

Damned

It started with a drunk at the Rusty Saloon who told me I could talk to a man who knew the Devil if I had any business with him. He told me the man hung around on the corner of 30th and Winslow at around two in the morning but I could catch him if I hurried.

"Don't call him 'him' though," he said. "He won't like that."

"What do I call him then?" I asked.

"Call him Madam. He likes that better. One of those pre-ops— the cock is still there but you're looking for a woman. Madam."

"Alright, thanks."

I made my way down to the cross street and found myself among a wavering line of catcalling prostitutes. Fat ones mostly; bellies hanging out under fishnet crop-tops, herpes sores dotting their mouths, broken teeth, missing teeth, missing souls. I knew the Madam was around here somewhere.

I began walking from one pro to another, inquiring about his whereabouts, starting with a green-haired lady with the sharp features and track marks to suggest that she knew these sorts of things.

"Hey, honey. You know where I could find—"

"You a cop?"

"Uh, no."

"Because you know you have to tell me. That's the law."

"I'm not sure that's actually true. You probably shouldn't stick by that."

"You sound like a cop."

"I'm not. Look, I'm looking for—"

"A date. Well I'm right here, baby. Twenty bucks'll get you started, fifty will get you just about anything that pretty little head can think of. 'Cept no scat-play. That's extra, for the cleanup."

"Well, that's good to know, but I'm actually looking for the Madam."

"The Madam? Shit, I ain't tellin' you that."

I continued down the line of sex workers to similar results. One told me I looked like her dead boyfriend and tearfully offered to give it away free if she could call me Trevor. But no word on the Madam. Everyone either played dumb or shut me down as soon as I said the word. The women were loyal.

The street grew darker and more decayed the farther down I headed, stepping over nodding junkies and following the line of prostitutes like I was crawling up the back of a great coiling snake until reaching the head. The moon was dimming behind thick clouds and the streets were growing quiet. Shadows danced underneath flickering streetlights. The herd was thinning, but an intangible force was breathing down my neck, propelling me forward. I had pertinent business that night and wasn't going to give up without being granted an audience.

It felt like I had been walking in circles for hours before I noticed the purple light hanging over the doorway of a foreclosed building. The windows were smashed in and repaired with crisscrossing 2x4s. A pregnant rat ejected itself from a storm drain by my feet and took off into a small crack in the wall of the looming structure. The light was full and replaced the lost glow of the moon. It tinted my skin blue as I came closer, following the pregnant rat's rapid footsteps. The wind was talking to me, urging me—cool against my skin like wet lips. I was here. I could feel that much.

I tentatively approached the makeshift cardboard door and waited for a moment before knocking, pondering whether I really wanted to ask the Devil what I thought I wanted to ask. I was raised a Catholic—not by choice but nonetheless—and the Irish guilt was well instilled in me by the time I was old enough to reject the whole zeitgeist. If on the off chance those kid-touchers and Jesus-lovers were right, certainly a meeting with Old Nick himself would bar me from the pearly gates, if I hadn't already been. But I decided, as I stood bathed in the ominous purple glow at the doorway of a dilapidated building off skid row, that the business I had was worth it.

So with that I knocked on the flimsy door. The purple light bulb hung over my head, swaying from a thin electrical cord like a metronome. I waited.

Nothing happened for a few minutes. But I knew from enough shitty pulp fiction stories that the second I left the door would open. I had that kind of luck; the twisted kind of luck that most people wouldn't call lucky.

I knocked again. "Hey! Madam! …Madam?"

Then, without the precursor of light footsteps or angry grumbling, the door burst open, nearly flying off its rusted hinges. A tall, thin older woman stood over me with a ring-covered hand placed on a left hip that jutted out unnaturally. The other hand grasped a black pistol aimed at my forehead. Her eyes were bright green and narrow, and they stared into me as if she could see everything I'd ever done in my life and was disgusted by it. Thick layers of eyeliner were painted over the bags making her resemble a malnourished raccoon. She wore a black negligee, lazily left askew, revealing small fake breasts with the surgery scars visible underneath. Her skin wrapped tightly around her rib cage like an anorexic. A purple wig hung down to her shoulders. A tuft of pubic hair was visible above black panties that crawled up her stomach into a happy trail. One testicle was hanging out the bottom. She was angry.

"Who the fuck are you? And WHY are you so LOUD?" Her voice was deep and forceful and I instinctually recoiled from the abrasiveness of it all. She cocked the pistol and I threw up my hands, blurting out, "I'M HERE TO TALK TO THE DEVIL." And then respectfully added in a calmer tone, "...Madam."

There was a brief, silent pause, and the Madam's features softened—as much as they could anyway. "Oh. Well, why didn't you say so?" She lowered the handgun and slid it next to her cock, letting the grip hang out of her panties. "Come in. Yeah, come in."

The interior of the house was dark; illuminated only by the faint light provided by a single light bulb on a table in the corner with no lampshade over it. The only furniture was a single pink couch in the center of the room, covered in a thick film of dust with the stuffing billowing out of tears in the cushions like smoke from a forest fire. A young man with wide, paranoid eyes sat upon it next to a large stain that resembled dried blood. He wore nothing but a pair of soiled underwear. Open sores covered his body. They were shiny red and crusted around the edges. He was in the middle of tying a rubber hose around his arm to shoot up with the needle balanced between his teeth.

The Madam directed me around the loose nails jutting out of the floorboards and told me to make myself at home. I sat on the floor.

She noticed me staring at the young man—now plunging the needle directly into the center of a leaking, black abscess—and waved it off nonchalantly. "He minds his own business. Don't mind him either."

"I wasn't."

"So," the Madam redirected my attention, "you came here for a reason. I can help you. You're not the first, and you won't be the last."

She didn't seem to care how I had come upon this information or how I had found her. This apparently was a casual and frequent service. Like a tour guide.

"I don't care why you want this, or what business you have with him. I don't care about the content of your soul, or if you have one." She stood over me; her hairy, sinewy legs at eye-level. "What I care about is how much you can pay me."

I watched as the young man slowly nodded and sunk into the couch, dropping the needle on the ground with a soft *clink*. A thin stream of blood and yellow pus began trickling down from the infected hole on the inside crease of his arm. "How much do you want?"

"How much do you have?"

I opened my wallet and handed her everything that was in there. She counted the bills, walked over to the dim light bulb and held each bill under the orange glow to see if they were in fact legal tender. They checked out.

She stuffed the money into her panties next to the handgun and sat down on the bloodstained part of the couch. "That'll work. Are you ready?"

I nodded.

She stared at me for a moment, trying to gauge the sincerity of my answer. "Alright then. I'll be right back."

The Madam got up, letting the heroin addict spread out across the couch like a sunbathing cat, and disappeared up a set of stairs in the opposite corner of the room. The young man and I looked at each other as the silence was broken by the creaking staccato of her footsteps on the tenuous wood. The blood and pus draining from the hole in his arm was mixing into a thick, dark orange as it dripped onto the couch. His limbs no longer served a purpose other than as pale canvasses for the constellations of bruises and abscesses where he'd stabbed and stabbed again in desperate attempts to find the remaining veins that hadn't yet collapsed. His wounds fascinated me.

When the sounds of the footsteps eroded, he spoke suddenly, surprisingly lucid— as if waiting for this opportunity since I walked in. "The big one is coming, y'know."

"What?"

"In the 1906 San Francisco Earthquake, 3,000 people died. Eighty percent of the city was destroyed. It was a 7.8. The landscape of the entire state of California was forever changed. Untold death and destruction."

"Um."

"Every 500 years, the west coast is due for an earthquake of at least a 9.0 magnitude. This is science. This is guaranteed. And we're overdue. By nearly a century. Did you know that? Untold death and destruction. We built some of our largest, most populated cities over two of the most volatile fault lines in the world. Are we sick people? Do we understand this? Do you understand this?"

He paused and stared at me, expecting me to say something.

"Uh, well—"

"Of course you don't. You're a sheep. The face of North America will tear open like fucking confetti paper. The hot core of the planet will engulf entire cities. The screams will be heard from every corner of every civilization. The resulting tsunamis will dwarf the tallest buildings man has ever erected. The planet will flood with the rising sea, and the bodies of millions will float like decaying logs. The world as we know it will forever cease to exist. Untold death and destruction."

"Alright," I said.

There was a brief pause.

"You want some heroin?"

"No, thanks."

The Madam then returned down the stairs with a large book tucked under her arm and a knife in her hand.

"Stand over here," she said.

I got up and stood in the center of the room.

"Now hold out your arm."

I did.

The Madam walked up slowly next to me and traced the veins running underneath my skin with a boney finger. "I'm going to cut you now."

"Ah, okay—what?"

"And then I'm going to read something from this book. That's when you let the blood drip onto the pages. You do that."

My first thought was about how many people had used that knife to summon Satan before me. It obviously hadn't been washed.

Before I had time to voice my concern, however, she sliced the knife across the center of my forearm. I winced as the sting expanded down the length of the wound and became a sharp burn when the flesh split open. It was a dull blade and dug in deep before the blood started running down my skin. The Madam then opened the book to a dog-eared page and began reading in a language I didn't recognize that sounded like animals fucking. But like angry fucking. Angry animals fucking.

Feeling my heart rate increase at the sudden recognition that this was really happening, I rambled over her words to get out my final anxiety: "Wait, wait—what happens next? What do I do? H—how do I get back?" But the Madam only uttered the frightening, inhuman noises louder, drowning out my fear and impulsive regret, as the limp addict on the couch slid up in his seat and began laughing and clapping, cackling at my horror, and as a passing police siren roared across the street outside, the red and blue lights illuminated the entire room, presenting the nightmarish imagery of hundreds of violent words written across the walls like the manic notes of a serial killer in what looked like fresh blood, and just as I felt as if I was about to faint from the pure shock of the insanity I'd been thrust into, the Madam finished her ancient ramblings and screamed at the top of her lungs: "NOW. LET THE BLOOD DRIP ACROSS THE WORDS. LET THE BLOOD SPILL AND MAY HE HAVE MERCY ON YOUR PATHETIC INTENTIONS."

The book was shoved underneath me and I watched as the first dark red drop fell onto the gnarled pages, already stained with the blood of however many had come before me. And then it was done.

I looked up at the Madam, holding my shaking and bloody arm against my chest. She closed the book and stepped back from me. The junkie leaned forward on the couch, watching my face with a look of pure anticipation, beaming with rotting teeth and dulled, penetrating eyes. The static intensity of the event was diminishing. The room was coming back into focus. My ears were ringing. I began to feel calm again. Had we done it wrong? My eyes darted between the two characters watching me like an animal inside the enclosure, silent. Then I realized.

Oh. It was just a scam. Hah! I knew it! Thank fucking God! It was just a fucking sca—

Hell is different than you'd think. Less fire and brimstone, more claustrophobic black nothingness and a lingering and profound sense of existential despair. Not a lot going on. Picture Heaven, with the clouds and blue nothingness and boring and a few naked angels playing harps. Now just replace the clouds with a long, narrow and pitch-dark mineshaft; the blue nothingness with that space you're in when you sleep without dreaming; the boring with horrifying; and the naked angels playing harps with millions of translucent gray souls being tortured for eternity who are all screaming and reaching out with withered limbs through the walls of the shaft like drowning plane crash victims. Now picture that you're falling down the shaft. That's Hell. You're welcome.

In the space that I'd entered, it was impossible to tell whether I'd been falling for hours or days or years. With my back to whatever plane of existence lay underneath me, and the black expanse seemingly infinite in front of my eyes, the only tangible sensory experience was the deafening screams of the damned, filling the entirety of my being like a hive of insects buzzing throughout the inside of my head. Their cries enveloped this dimension; their arms reaching out and brushing my living, human flesh with the desperate urgency of beings still very much in pain and acutely aware of their fate of everlasting suffering. I felt the grasps of their arms like strong gusts of wind, and heard the bloodcurdling cries intensify above me as each forsaken soul failed to cling to my body as I passed. This place was every injustice that was ever committed—every murder, every rape, every broken heart, every lost mind; every sickening memory ever hidden away in the dark corners of the psyches of anything that ever lived, being played and replayed for these fractured creatures on a loop for all of eternity.

Then I hit the ground. I got up, brushed off, realized there was nothing to brush off, and looked around. I was in a small room with a desk. A nice desk. The walls were bright red. That was very "Hell". Nice touch. Simple aesthetic. Straight to the point. Really grabbed you. There was a wooden door behind me. I tried the knob but it was locked. It was cold to the touch. In fact it was fucking

150

freezing in the room. On the other side of the desk there was a fancy armchair, very regal. Red. Naturally. On my side of the desk was a folding chair. Not much. I figured the Prince of the Underworld could've shilled out for more than that, but I was a guest so I sat down and kept my thoughts to myself.

Then came the knock on the door.

I remained frozen, hesitant to turn around and face the creature that my entire life I'd been taught to fear by people I didn't trust. The little Catholic boy inside me gripped at the metal edges of my chair and held back the inexplicable urge to laugh. Whenever I'd gotten myself into trouble as a child, and I realized—as whichever assorted flavor of authoritative figure happened to be scolding me that day—that I'd committed a serious offense, my first instinct was always to burst into laughter. It was that or cry. To my undeveloped child-mind, these were the only two reasonable reactions to visceral dread.

I waited for the sound of the hooves against the floor, the steady thump of the end of a pitchfork, the smell of sulfur. Shit, Robert Johnson did it. Worked out for him. Anton LaVey had a healthy following. Marilyn Manson was yet to overdose, last I checked. This could be all right. I'd gone this far.

As the door opened and I felt the presence of another being enter the room behind me, I was struck with the feeling one gets when they lean back too far in their seat. The familiar cold shock stabbed the center of my chest, filling the vacuum where a heartbeat skipped. Then there was the unmistakable and arousing *clack-clack* of high heels. She walked across the room, dragging her finger along the desk, sat down opposite me, leaned back in her seat and crossed her legs. The skirt withdrew into her hips, revealing full, pure white thighs. My eyes followed the legs up to the stomach; up to the swelling breasts pressing against the black blouse leaving the shoulders bare, the black hair hanging softly over them; up the slender neck, until meeting the face of the Devil. Her nose was pointed and narrow. Her eyes were devoid of color—black orbs like mirrors in a dark room. She looked like the kind of woman who would fuck you after buying her drinks, and leave in the middle of the night with your wallet then block your number. She looked like every bad decision I'd ever made. Fuck, I liked her.

She sat there staring at me staring at her, and smiled. Two fangs hung down where her canines should have been. Like a serpent.

"So," said the Devil.

"You're a woman," is what I blurted out.

She lifted her legs onto the desk and re-crossed them. Open-toed stilettos wrapped around her feet, with sharpened heels like black daggers that dug into the wood. Her nails were painted red.

"Yes," said the Devil. "What were you expecting?" She spoke with a low rasp, dripping of sex. Hell didn't seem like so bad a place all of a sudden.

"I just—I, uh…" My tongue had failed me.

"Have you read the Bible?"

"The Bible?" I squeezed out.

"Yeah. That big book written by the bearded man in the sky."

"No, I haven't."

In Catholic school every Monday morning, we would convene as a class and discuss the homily the priest had given the day before during Sunday mass. I was always the only child in the room who hadn't gone to church. While my classmates gave Father O'Malley's interpretations of Mathew 3:14 or John 21:6 and smiled their wholesome smiles when our former-nun-turned-educator rewarded them for their ability to regurgitate somebody else's words, I sat silent; shrinking into my little wooden chair in embarrassment. I was the outcast.

I was confused why I was the only one who didn't have this connection to religion. My friends had a community that I'd never been a part of. At some point during the mass, all the kids got to go to another room and have their own meeting, and read stories and eat snacks and believe in the same God and they seemed to like it. And worst of all, I heard that after each service everyone got to head to the backroom for donuts. I wanted to believe in God if it meant I could have donuts. This seemed like a fair deal, considering the outcome described to me nearly every day in religion class if I didn't repent for my godless, heathen lifestyle: Hell. The big H-E-Double-Hockey-Sticks. This part didn't bother me too much, though, because despite the gruesome descriptions of rivers of blood and man-eating beasts and being skinned alive and burned and decapitated for eternity, it seemed that every hero of mine happened to reside there—according to the nuns. Hendrix was a dope fiend: Hell. Biggie Smalls was a drug peddler: Hell. Morrison was a pagan fornicator: Hell. I didn't know what a pagan or a fornicator was, but once I heard Jim Morrison was those things, I wanted to be a pagan fornicator too. Some of the kids even got to hang out with Father O'Malley at his house across the street from the church after the services. They were the most special kids. I wanted to be special.

So one Saturday night I asked my father if he'd take me to mass in the morning, because I was pretty sure I didn't want to go to Hell and I was sure I wanted donuts. He told me, "I'm not allowed back there," which I thought was odd because the teachers always talked about how inclusive church was, that God loved everyone, but I didn't love my dad either so I didn't blame God for feeling any different.

"Don't listen to those motherfuckers, Charlie," he said. "It's a house of fuckin' lies. Shit, try to tell ME what to think? You think you're the fuckin' moral arbiter of the Earth, *motherfucker*?"

I wasn't sure if he was talking to me or God or nobody, so I just kept listening.

"Don't let those sick fucks pollute your head with their bullshit, Charlie. You get that good education your mother and I pay for so you can go to law school and pay us back for all the toilet paper and food and medicine we waste on you. You learn your math and history—you pay attention to all that shit—or I will whip your *fucking ass* until you're eighteen. You hear me? Good. But don't listen to that God shit. Block all that out. You think for yourself, Charlie. Like your old man." He threw his head back and guzzled down the whiskey in his glass. "You got that?"

"Yes sir," I said.

So I never went to Sunday mass.

And it turned out my dad wasn't allowed back in the church because once, in a self-pitying drunken stupor, he wandered in to repent for the laundry list of sins he'd committed in his life, and vomited in the confessional booth before he could get to "Forgive me, Father".

And—drumroll—I never became a lawyer.

Oh, and those special kids who came to the priest's house after the services to talk about Jesus? Father O'Malley was raping those special kids. I saw him one day a few years later on the front-page of one of those *BUSTED* magazines that they sell in convenience stores next to the porno mags and condoms. You probably saw that coming, though.

"Well if you had," said the Devil, "you'd know they were hinting at it. They didn't quite get me right, but the character is undeniably feminine."

"You've read the Bible?" I asked, astonished. It was as if hearing a Westboro Baptist had read a gay romance novel.

"I'm a narcissist," she replied, and parted her lips with a smile to reveal her fangs. "So. You have three minutes. Talk."

The abrupt switch to business threw me off guard. My vision lost focus in the void of her eyes as my jaw hung open, the words I'd been preparing to speak lodged in my throat. I balked.

The Devil tilted her head at me, twirled a lock of black hair around her finger and pursed her lips. "It's rude to stare," she snarled.

The bite in her voice cut through the thin layer of composure keeping my little Catholic boy inside. With her tall model figure towering over my eyes, she resembled what I used to imagine the nuns looked like underneath that lifeless garb as they bent over to reprimand me.

"Sorry. Uh—"

"Two minutes," she snapped. "What do you need? Love? Money? Fame? You don't lose points for unoriginality. But I have other things to do. ...Or you could just ask for a pair of balls so we can get this ov—"

"*I want you to kill my ex.*"

The words launched off my tongue like projectile vomit. I was reminded of the moment I met the Madam, what now felt like a lifetime ago: The death-black hole of the pistol's business end staring down at me, the fearful jolt of life it conjured up inside me. The desperate truth that burst forth out of me as an impulse.

I surprised the both of us.

The Devil raised her finely tweezed eyebrows, forming three shallow waves of wrinkles across her forehead. "That's more like it. Okay, yeah."

I paused and inhaled sharply. "And I want you to take her down here with you."

The brief pinch of remorse at the base of my stomach drowned beneath the Devil's approving smirk. I'd take an enabler wherever I could get one.

"I can do that," she cooed.

A tan papyrus scroll appeared in her left hand with a burst of deep crimson smoke. A quill-tip pen appeared in the other. She really had a flare for the theatrics.

"Sign here." She handed me the pen and turned around the contract to face me. It was written in what I could only guess was Latin.

"I can't read this," I said.

"It's just details regarding method of murder, forms of torture once she arrives—basic logistics. You can just sign it right... *here.*" She pointed with a manicured finger to a line at the bottom of the scroll.

"I don't sign it in blood?" I asked.

"Don't trust everything you read."

I let the pen hover over the line, eyeing the dead language printed across the papyrus as if it were anything but pure gibberish to me. I stopped and looked up at her, doing my best to focus on her face. "There must be a catch, though. What's the catch?"

"I'm guessing you never thought you were getting into Heaven. Since you're here."

I figured as much. I had a good twenty, thirty years left? That was worth it well enough. She could have me then. Fuck it.

"Ah. Right," I responded frankly. "Fair enough."

"Honesty is our policy at the Fiery Gates."

"So I sign and get outta here, and you handle the rest?"

"What was your ex's name?" she pivoted. "I'll need that."

I told her. Uttering the syllables tasted like rat poison at the back of my tongue. Every nauseating, fractured memory that was seared into my subconsciousness flooded back into the front of my mind, playing before my eyes like torture porn vignettes displayed on a projector screen. Any reservation I had previously maintained disintegrated into a festering puddle of animosity and hatred. Kill the bitch.

"Pretty name," she said.

"*Ugly bitch*," I corrected her between my teeth.

I wrote my signature in sharp, violent strokes, imagining each letter was another knife being jammed into her abdomen. I handed back the pen and looked down at what I'd done. It looked like the lifeline of a meth addict on a heart monitor.

"Perfect," said the Devil, lowering her chin and glancing up at me. Her eyes glowed in the shadow it created. With another *poof* and a burst of crimson smoke, the pen and contract disappeared. We stared at each other in silence. The walls seemed to be palpitating, throbbing.

"What now?"

"*What now?*" she mirrored my words, a disconcerting grin curling across her face. "I do the ex. I keep my word. Honesty is our policy here at the Fiery Gates."

"You already said that," I mumbled. "How do I get back?"

The Devil's grin widened until it filled the whole of her being, until everything I feared was conveyed perfectly across her face. I was getting that fall-back-in-your-chair-feeling again. My pulse quickened.

"*How do I get back?*" I repeated with more urgency. It was getting hot.

Her fangs presented themselves, and in their glinting reflection I could see a bright red light expanding across the center of the door behind my back. The Devil didn't look so pretty anymore. Purple veins were weaving underneath her skin, pressing up against the flesh as if about to burst out of her. The blacks of her eyes ignited into a deep yellow. The room shook and trembled forcefully like we were inside the stomach of a massive beast.

"HOW DO I GET BACK?" I screamed, but I already knew the answer.

Then from behind me came a low rumble and the deafening *BOOM*, sucking the air out of the room with an overwhelming howl until there was nothing left but a piercing ringing in my ears.

I whipped around in the metal chair now scalding my ass in the searing glow of the light to see that the door had opened, and behind it was an encompassing and blinding energy, red-orange liquid heat spilling out around the frame. A storm of black smoke rose up off the flaming entity, twisting around itself in erratic circles like an orgy of snakes. Thousands of possessed souls caught in the midst of gale force winds. It was screaming and burned through my eyes until I had to look away in terror.

I was staring into Hell itself. The real one. I'd made the VIP list.

"You lying goddamn bitch," I barked. The floor was giving out underneath my feet.

"What did you expect?" she said, rising up from her seat. Her voice had dropped three octaves to a demonic growl. Painted nails grew out of her fingers into curved, yellowed talons. *"I'm taking the ex. But you come with her. You're not going anywhere."*

The walls of the room were melting around me, crumbling away into the hellscape at my back. I felt a magnetic force dragging me into it. The light filled the corners of my vision until the heat grasped at my arms and legs. I didn't bother to fight it.

As I was lifted out of my chair, swooped up into the whirling entity, the Devil's voice rang out behind my eyes, inside my head; buzzing, crying: *"Whatever she did, rest assured that there can't be any worse torture than being locked in a room with you for all of eternity. You're welcome, Charlie. Say hello to Jim for me."*

I was raised up high into the air, enveloped by the incinerating red light; any semblance of a room burnt away into what surrounded it. I screamed as the flames of Hell reached in through my chest and eradicated what was left of a soul. Before my eyes was now a vast inferno, pierced only by the cackling laughter of the Devil somewhere beyond the plane I'd been sucked into.

And then, from somewhere I couldn't place, a new sound began to overtake the delighted howl of the Devil, an enthusiastic and freeing sound; booming, shrieking laughter, drowning out the Devil's in spiteful arrogance: My own laughter.

HAHAHAHA! AH HAHAHA!

It became all I could hear, echoing across the realm of fire as the heat destroyed every invisible molecule of my essence, until the triumphant roar was all that remained, and I fizzled away into the red light.

What idiot would think it would be any different? What did I really think was going to happen? I was going to Hell. But I'd succeeded. I was taking her down with me. Just like old times.

Damned.

Kristine

"Look, it's over. It's done. I need space. This whole thing is—it's too much. I didn't set out to hurt you, but I realized I'm still all fucked up from my last relationship and... I still love him. I like you, but you made this all happen too quickly and I'm not ready for that. And honestly, you drink way too much. I can't stand around watching you kill yourself like this. I hope you can understand, because I don't think we should talk anymore. I don't wanna be with you. I don't know if I wanna be with him, but I don't wanna be with you. ...Henry? You there?"

I thought about hanging up. "Yeah. I understand."

"I'm sorry, I just think—"

I hung up. It was two in the afternoon and I had lost a woman.

The bar was dark and quiet. Two heavy wooden doors blocked the sunlight attempting to shine in from the outside world. I ordered a whiskey and went to work feeling sorry for myself. It went down fast. I ordered another.

Kathy leaned over the bar with the glass in her hand and smiled at me. Kathy was the Guilty Sparrow's regular bartender during the dayshifts. She was white-haired, in her mid-fifties; a caring woman with a motherly instinct and a pronounced snaggletooth that I found endearing, perhaps because of the relationship we had formed after years of seeing each other during hours when most people wouldn't choose to drink. She said something, slid over my refilled glass, and continued a conversation she'd been having with a young woman I hadn't noticed at the end of the bar. I made an effort not to look over at her, letting the cathartic heartache instead take over my chest and swim down to my extremities.

For those who have had the good fortune not to experience it, heartache is a real thing—physically as well as emotionally. It starts in the center of your chest, a tightness similar to severe anxiety, but more akin to a 40 lbs. weight pressing down on your sternum. Then the sharp burn emanating from the weight spiders out like a poison entering your bloodstream. The pain nearly forces you to double over. The most troubling aspect of it, though, is that the sensation can be invigorating—possibly only to those who take a sort of twisted joy in self-inflicted pain, but it could also be the simple realization that you are alive and are feeling something.

After draining most of the next drink, I worked up the courage to glance at the young woman, if only to fuel my self-loathing with the knowledge that I would never know her. She had her nose buried in her cell phone, only looking up from whatever she was so immersed in to nurse the bottle of High Life in front of her and respond to Kathy. I returned to my glass, thinking about if ants killed themselves over their women.

I heard the young woman speak—a confident voice with a soft and traveled tone—then noticed Kathy point over to me as they talked. She walked over to my side of the bar.

"Henry, this is Kristine." Kathy pointed over to the young woman who was already looking at me. She was pretty. "She's not from here and she's looking for a place to stay. I told her there's hostels up on Shattuck, but d'ya know any other hostels closer to the bar?"

I tried to make it less obvious that I was staring. "Yeah, I mean, downtown there's a lot."

"I know, but I don't want her staying downtown by herself, it's too dangerous down there. She's traveling alone."

"Oh, okay."

She looked back over at Kristine. "Sweetie, this is Henry. He's safe. You can trust him. He'll help you out."

I got up without thinking and sat down next to her. She looked better up close. Her face was perfectly constructed: high cheek bones sat above red, parted lips; her eyes were bright green and placed just right on her face—eyes a centimeter too apart or together can ruin the features of an otherwise beautiful person. Brown hair with faint blonde highlights hung over her head in a loose bun, with two thick bangs hanging down in front of each of her ears.

I needed to say something fast.

"You could try Airbnb or one of those things. I used that to stay when I was in New Orleans. My room ended up being on the top floor of a twenty-four hour karaoke bar on the edge of the ghetto. They should really tell you that kind of shit ahead of time. I hate karaoke. Awful singers. A few songs I can tolerate, but after 48 hours of Journey covers you just wanna put your head through a fuckin' wall. A crackhead told me he was gonna break my neck 'cause I wouldn't give him a dollar—but, I mean, I'm sure yours'll be better."

I stopped talking when I realized I was rambling, and finished the whiskey hovering under my nose. Kristine's lips parted farther like a blooming flower, opening up into a wide grin, and she laughed. I was glad for that.

"I know. I'm checking right now, but it looks like no one is gonna let me in on this short of notice."

I wanted to tell her she could stay with me, but I was a freelance (unsuccessful) writer crashing on a friend's couch. All the money

I did make from dead-end jobs and the occasional publication was quickly blown on a single meal a day and multiple drinks.

"Are you hitch-hiking or something? That's sort of dangerous, isn't it?"

"No," she said, "I'm driving my car. It's been fine so far. I just spent a week camping alone in the woods, and right now all I wanna do is shower and sleep in a real bed for a few days."

I ordered another drink for the both of us and cursed myself for not having a real bed.

We continued talking for hours; mostly her but I didn't mind. There was something undeniably interesting about her—this light glowing inside her that for most people I'd met had long been extinguished. How she'd managed to hold onto it I didn't know, but I wanted to. Her mannerisms were combative but approachable. She spoke loudly and enthusiastically about her life and perspectives, without being overbearing or over-sharing, taking jabs and poking fun at my awkward demeanor as if we had known each other for years. When she would become particularly excited by a certain topic, her eyes would light up and widen, and her quirky, midwestern twang would come out when she spoke words with hard A's. Kristine was sure of herself and unafraid to tell the truth without hesitation. I was drawn to her immediately. She fascinated me.

Kristine was born and raised in a small town of about 5,000 outside of Cleveland, and had been working a string of blue-collar jobs to support her and her family since she was fourteen: bartender, waitress, mail clerk, dishwasher; and once she became desperate, a member of a cleanup crew for a local nuclear power plant that she worked at for six months at fifteen dollars an hour, seventy hours a week, in order to save up enough to jump in her car and drive. I couldn't imagine that petite, 22-year-old body hidden inside one of those anonymous HAZMAT suits—the suffocation of beauty.

She had been on the road for two months before wandering into the bar I happened to be at; stopping in Kansas City, Missoula, Olympia, etc., etc. She was only planning on being in the city for a night or two, but I already knew I had to convince her to stay longer.

By the time she left to go to a cheap motel, I had her number and plans to see her the next day to hear a band she knew that happened to be coming to town. Kristine smiled and waved as she walked out the wooden doors into the moonlight. I had forgotten completely about the other woman. She was it.

That night she texted me. "This motel seems really creepy. I don't know if I feel safe."

"Where are you?" I texted back.

"What do you mean? I have no idea where the fuck I am."

"Oh, right. Well, what's the address?"

She sent it to me. She was staying on 104th—the street on the edge of the city where the hookers and drug dealers hung out. We were always taught as kids never to go there. I did out of curiosity originally and later for drugs, but never had the street smarts enough to avoid trouble each time I went. One night, a friend of mine got drunk and drove down 104th street throwing eggs at the rows of prostitutes like an arcade game, until one of their pimps saw it happen and drove his car into my friend's passenger side window, got out, walked up and stabbed him to death.

"Yeah, that's not a good area," I said. "What creeped you out?"

"This shirtless guy with tattoos all over him kept telling me I could make a lot of money and he's been following me around. I think he's waiting outside my motel room right now."

"Well, I'm sure you could."

"Could what?"

"Make a lot of money."

"That's not funny. Should I leave?"

"I would. But I'm sure you'll be fine."

"No, I wanna leave."

"Okay. Find a place closer to the city."

"Okay. I'll text you tomorrow."

The next day we met at a bookstore in the southeast end. She had moved to a nicer hotel next to the local college campus. I found her browsing through the philosophy section. She had a stack of books by Nietzsche and Kierkegaard under one arm and a small cup of coffee in her free hand. Her hair was down. It hung down around her breasts over a tattered jean jacket. She looked beautiful. She looked too good to be seen in public with me. I felt lucky, something that didn't happen often.

"I always end up buying too many books when I go to stores," she said.

"Have you tried the library?"

"I never end up bringing them back. I think I still owe my old high school library about 500 bucks. It feels good to own them."

I followed loyally behind her as she glided between the aisles of books. Her ass was pristine. It was large and well shaped and her hips were wide. I was reminded of a woman I hadn't seen in years who once told me after sex that she had childbearing hips. The last time I talked to her, she was pregnant. I assumed it wasn't mine. She never said anything.

Kristine turned around and stood very close to me. "Have any suggestions? I need more shit to read when I'm alone in the woods. Or for tinder if you have bad taste."

I knelt down and looked through the stacks of dead old white men. "Have you ever read Camus? He gave up on the universe but wrote a little more happily than most."

165

I handed her a copy of *The Stranger*. "The art of not giving a fuck."

"It's easier than you think," she said. "I like that it's short. You don't need to say much."

Kristine checked out and we wandered outside into the rain and smog. She wanted food and beer, and I told her I'd show her around the city.

The day went smooth enough. I'd forgotten how little of my hometown I really knew, and got us lost multiple times attempting to take us to spots I would never go but assumed a tourist would want to see. She quickly became as bored as I was.

"Hank, this is lame. Just take me to a fuckin' dive bar. Let's get a drink."

No one ever called me Hank. I liked when she did it.

"I know a place," I said.

I took her to a local biker bar called The Dead Rabbit. I figured it would do the trick. Motorcycles hung from metal wires over the inside of the bar. I always wondered when one would fall and kill a bartender. I wanted to be there when it happened. Kristine ordered a High Life. I ordered the same.

We sat in silence for about three beers. I didn't mind. She didn't seem to either. I liked that. People talk too much. They get uncomfortable when bathed in silence, feeling like they need to fill the space with idle words to avoid the existential anxiety from setting in. I never understood that. I don't normally talk unless I have something to say, and that intangible sense of dread is pervasive whether or not I choose to speak so it hardly matters. In that moment it just felt good to sit next to a beautiful creature like her. I was proud that life sometimes threw you moments like these. I could feel the stares of the old men in leather jackets, wondering how I pulled this one off. If I had an answer, I would have told them.

After a crippled man with a lazy eye and a wart on his nose approached Kristine to tell her how a blood clot in his chest almost killed him a week earlier, I made with the conversation to shake off his presence.

"Why did you decide to just drive? A lot of people talk about that, but I've never met anyone who actually did it. Especially our age."

"Why does anyone do anything?" she said. "I just got bored. It was something to do." She took a sip from her beer. "Why'd you brush off that old guy? He was interesting."

"He was rambling. He just thought you were cute."

"Jesus. You're not one of those people that think they're too good to talk to strangers, are you? Let me guess: you don't like people? Don't be such a cliché."

"People are fine. I like some of them. I like you, anyway."

"But not him."

"Most of them, yes."

"Don't be that guy."

"I'm not. People interest me from a distance. I get too close and I see what they are."

"And what's that?"

"Waiting to die. Desperate for something to help them forget what's gonna happen."

"You don't like people. I think everyone has something interesting to say if you listen."

"People scare me. We're sick. I try to avoid them."

"That's no way to go about life."

"Probably."

"You're pretty boring. Has anyone ever told you that?"

"Probably."

I ordered two more beers and asked the bartender if he was worried one of the motorcycles would ever fall on him. He showed us a video on his cellphone from the security camera of a light fixture narrowly missing him as it smashed on the floor just left of his shoulder.

"Holy shit, man."

"Yep. I dove the fuck outta the way, but my homie told me I should've just taken the hit and copped that fat worker's comp check. Could've been sitting on a beach in Mexico right now if that fight or flight instinct hadn't kicked in. Eh, fuck it. Next time."

After a few more drinks the sun had gone down. Kristine ordered an Uber and we piled in the back to head towards the venue for the show.

The show was playing at a dive called the West Street Saloon in the heart of downtown. We paid a five dollar cover to get in, and were greeted by about five hipsters watching a band comprised of three elderly men with beer guts and short, white hair who looked like they'd have to wake up early to get to the office the next day. They were playing a cover of the Star Wars cantina theme. Evidently they were the openers.

Kristine mumbled into my ear: "You're not making me watch this shit. C'mon. I promise the other guys are better."

We walked into what I thought was a diner I knew of down the street to pass the time until the real band came on. It was a high-end restaurant. Everyone was dressed in expensive suits and cocktail dresses, having quiet discussions over candlelight. A man was seated in the corner playing something delicate on a piano. It immediately set in that I'd made a mistake. We sat down at the bar and ordered frighteningly over-priced drinks. Kristine had been chain-smoking cigarettes and was wearing clothes that obviously hadn't been washed in some time. My hair was long and untamed beneath a black beanie, and my hand-me-down army jacket reeked from various liquor stains that never came out. We looked like homeless kids who had accidentally wandered into the wrong establishment. Which, come to think of it, would be an accurate assessment.

Kristine's mouth gaped as she looked at the prices on the menu, and leaned into me so the bartender wouldn't hear. "You didn't mean to take me here, did you?"

"No. I thought this was... not this."

"You said you've lived here your whole life?"

"Yeah."

"How do you always not know where the hell you are?"

"I guess I don't pay attention."

"You must be an awful writer."

The bartender was eyeing us warily from down the room.

"Should we bail?" I asked.

"Not yet. We get the food first. Then we bail. I hope you're fast." She looked around the restaurant, watching the drapes on the walls, the antique paintings, the waiting staff donned in rented tuxedos, the rich clientele eating steaks and drinking wine. "These people won't miss a few dozen bucks. They've spent their whole lives getting over on other people to be where they are. We can do the same."

"You don't like the rich?" I asked.

"No one likes the rich but the rich. And they probably don't even really like themselves. I never wanted to be anything but a real person. Genuine. But these people... these people aren't *people*. They're caricatures of what they think they should be. That guy at the bar, with the blood clot—that was a real person. Just trying to live his life, not pretending for anybody. I don't have respect for these people."

"What about the waiters? What did they ever do to you?"

"They chose to work in a place like this. They'll make more in tips off a glass of champagne from one of these entitled assholes than we'll make in two weeks."

I was about to say something until the bartender shuffled back over to us and Kristine kicked me in the shin.

"Have you decided what you'd like?" he asked. He was a gangly man with a curled mustache and beady eyes, wrinkles running across his face despite his apparent young age.

"Yes," Kristine chirped in a mocking, snobby drawl, studying the menu like a SkyMall catalogue. "I believe we'll have the porterhouse steak. And the filet mignon. And—oh! How about the risotto? And..." she turned to me. "What else sounds good, darling?" Now turning back to the bartender, beaming: "We're celebrating. James just closed the Whitman deal." Grabbing my hand: "Isn't that right, darling? I'm so proud of him."

I held back the smirk and got into character. "Yes, yes. Big day, sweetheart. Big day. Yes, I'll have the... what's the most expensive thing you've got?"

"That would be the lobster frittata, sir."

"Yes, that sounds delightful... I'll get two of those."

There was a palpable moment of discernment as the bartender's eyes darted between the two dirty twenty-somethings with shit-eating grins on their faces.

"...Very good, sir. Ma'am. That'll be right out."

We turned to each other about to burst into laughter when the bartender did an about-face and stared at me, his mustache twitching beneath his bulbous nose. "And sir... congratulations. On the deal."

I nodded silently, doing everything in my power to keep a straight face.

Once he left to the kitchen, Kristine slumped forward in her seat, covering her face with her hands to mute the giggling.

"There's no way they're bringing us that food," I whispered.

She shot back up and looked at me, and said in complete seriousness, "It's all about the confidence, Henry. You just gotta sell it."

"I look like I should be pumping his gas."

"You probably should be. But you could be one of those millennial tech millionaire douchebags for all he knows. You created Tinder for dogs and made it big."

"And what the fuck is the Whitman deal?"

"I don't know, man. I hear rich people on TV say that kinda shit all the time. Don't blow this."

After thirty minutes and six drinks between the both of us, the food was brought out by three waiters and laid out on the bar. A grand feast. Kristine dove into the meals, cycling through enormous bites of each plate like a starved POW.

"Slow down. Jesus," I laughed. "Eat like you're rich."

"But we are," she smiled and winked, stuffing a lump of risotto in her mouth. "I've never eaten anything like this in my life! Try some!"

Once she'd slowed down on gorging herself, I called over to the bartender, who bounded towards us and stood at attention.

"Yes, sir. Is the meal not to your liking?"

"No, no. It's lovely. Just exquisite. I'd like to get all this to go."

He hesitated, glancing at Kristine cleaning the plate of filet mignon. "Of course, sir. One moment."

He came back with two others who boxed the food and stacked them in bags, and placed the check daintily in front of me before walking away. I didn't bother looking at the price. No one had said anything.

"Okay, what now?" I mumbled through my teeth.

She put down her fork and exhaled, staking out the room. "Ready to run?"

I didn't have a problem with the rich more than I did any other person, but when the opportunity for chaos presents itself I have difficulty turning it down. "Yeah. Fuck, okay. Yeah."

"On three," she said.

I glanced at the exit. It was a straight shot.

"One…"

A fat couple at the other end was distracting the bartender. He was pouring a martini in a long stream into a glass from above his head while they applauded.

"Two…"

The pianist was playing a piece by Chopin that I recognized.

"…"

"…Three?"

"…Three!"

Both at once we launched out of our seats, each taking a bag under our arms, and sprinted out the building, crashing through the door as the bartender's voice faded into the harsh noises of the city outside: "OH GODDAMNIT! HEY! SOME*one go get them…!*"

We made it down a few blocks, lungs on fire and still sprinting, then turned the corner and skidded to a halt at a walk signal before a speeding car nearly hit us. I spun around and put my hands on my knees to catch my breath, peering around the corner for any sign of pursuers. I didn't see anyone.

Kristine was coughing up phlegm, attempting to breathe between chokes of laughter. "THEY DIDN'T—*AGH*—HAHAHA—THEY DIDN'T EVEN COME AFTER US! HAHA! I DIDN'T THINK THAT WOULD WORK. *AGGHHH…PHOO.*"

I sat down on the cement, spit into a drainpipe and grinned at her.

Kristine wasn't used to the amount of homeless people scattered throughout the streets, and felt obligated to deliver our pilfered dinner to one of the poor bastards. So as we walked back, it became a game of sorts to determine who was to be blessed with a week's worth of meals. The point was you couldn't give the food away to just any old homeless person. They had to be crazy, but not crazy enough that you might get spit on or screamed at if you were to approach them. It felt like we were perusing the animal shelter for a traumatized dog to save, but one that still wouldn't shit the rug or eat the toddler if we took it home. Eventually, Kristine gave up and started handing out boxes to whomever we passed, until a mob of homeless people began forming around us like we were the Red Cross, all scratching at their sores and smoking cigarette butts. Within five minutes the food was gone and we'd reached the venue, leaving behind a small village with eighty-dollar cuisine in their hands.

We both moved onto whiskey, starting in at the bar as the last opener was finishing up. Kristine was matching me drink for drink. I'd never met anyone able to do that before, man or woman. I found it incredibly attractive. But she was getting drunk, and pressed her leg against mine, smiling and giggling at whatever bullshit came out of my mouth. Kristine did most of the talking, allowing me to let the drunk really fill me without worrying about whether I was saying the right things. I realized something was about to happen, and didn't want to fuck it up with my nervous, verbal diarrhea so close to the moment.

The band started playing. We moved up to the front to help fill up the empty room. It was us and about ten old women, and one dirty guy with a backpack who kept whooping like a feral dog during inopportune times. They were good, though. The singer would scream and cry and moan in high octaves, rolling his eyes to the back of his head when he hit certain notes. I was starting to

173

feel good. I kept shooting glances over to Kristine, waiting for eye contact. When she didn't reciprocate I would look up at the band posters lining the ceiling to play it off.

Between songs, Kristine leaned in to say something.

I said, "What?"

She said something again, and she smiled. Her eyes were full and glowing from the stage lights, and looked into me. A loose strand of hair fell onto her forehead and she blew it out of her face. She was still looking at me. The music started up again. It was slow and nocturnal, the bass vibrating up and down my body. I leaned in to kiss her. She backed her face away only an inch, bringing her body closer to mine.

"Uh uh," she said, still smiling with closed lips.

"Uh uh?" I mumbled.

"Uh uh."

Then her lips parted and she reached in. All at once I felt her. I went back in again and she dug deeper, running her tongue along the inside of my mouth. Then tenderly we separated. She reached her arm around my back, placing her other hand on my chest, and laid her head against my shoulder. I rested my arm around her and took a deep swig from the beer in my left hand. That band could really play.

"Give me that." She took the bottle out of my hand and sipped, holding back a laugh.

I kissed her again.

"Take me somewhere else," she said.

"Where?" I asked.

"I don't care."

"What about the band?"

"Fuck the band."

"Okay. Let's go to your hotel."

"Yeah."

We ended up in the middle of the street, making out and groping at each other as the homeless and insane watched. She could really kiss. She would fill up your entire body with her intent, forcing you to let go of intuition and allow her to take you wherever her passion was going. It felt like I had no control whatsoever. We fell into the wall of the saloon. I slid my hands up the curves of her body and pulled at the back of her hair, pushed my tongue into the deepest part of her mouth I could reach, reveling in the wetness and warmth of it. She latched onto my bottom lip with her teeth and bit down hard. My cock rose and she grasped it violently through my jeans. That's around when the next Uber showed up.

We were kicked out a few blocks away from the hotel when I lit a cigarette in the car. On the walk back, Kristine picked up a bottle of wine from a gas station.

The room was already messily decorated with loose clothing and toiletries. She sat down on the bed, popped open the cork and took a drink out the bottle, handed it to me. It tasted cheap. I fell down onto the bed and she climbed on top of me. We started back in on the kissing. I pulled off her shirt and she undid her bra, revealing breasts with pierced nipples. I sucked at them and tasted the cold metal before laying back and taking another drink from the wine. There were no words spoken. I pulled off the rest of her clothes until a perfectly naked woman was lying on the bed next to me. She pulled off my shirt and wrapped her bare thigh around my leg. Her lips were on my earlobe, licking and biting, and I began to moan softly.

Kristine sat up abruptly. "I'm on my period, so you know."

I spoke between heavy breaths, "Yeah, yeah. No sex, okay."

She then slid down against my bare chest, letting me feel the glow of her body, and undid my jeans. Her hair was strewn across her face and I couldn't see her eyes as she pressed the head of my cock against her tongue.

"*Oh fuck, Kristine.*"

"*Mhmm,*" she moaned with it in her mouth.

She sucked up and down, sticking her tongue out and wrapping it around my cock as it pulsed and stiffened. I knew immediately I wasn't going to make it; the alcohol was keeping me from getting hard enough. I could feel her working, really working, bobbing and twisting, trying to get me there. I appreciated the dedication. I took a handful of that long, brown hair and forced her down to the bottom, thrusting it into her throat. She then surfaced and cupped the balls, stuck her tongue out again with her eyes looking up at me, and lapped at them before licking up the length of my shaft. It was a master class. I was happy knowing it was going to last as long as she could do it. She lay prone on the bed between my legs, her ass up in the air like an animal in heat. Her eyes burned green and I let out a whimper. She would moan back when I made noises, wriggling her ass and thrusting her hips against the bed. I took advantage of the moment and reached for the bottle while she continued. But it wasn't going anywhere and she was beginning to realize it. She let my cock reappear from her throat like a magic trick, making a suction-like popping noise when the head was released, glistening with saliva.

"It's not gonna happen, is it?"

"I don't think so," I relented.

"That's okay. I'm tired."

"It's not your fault."

"No shit. We can try again in the morning. You aren't one of those that can't make it hungover, are you?"

"Not at all. When hungover is your default state, you learn to adapt to these conditions."

She laughed and sat back up against the bed. I handed her the wine. We sat naked together, passing the bottle until it was finished.

I woke up the next morning hanging halfway off the bed, not sure of where I was. Kristine was lying naked on her stomach next to me. I checked my phone: it was nine o'clock. I had a dishwashing shift in twenty minutes. Obviously, that wasn't going to happen. I stumbled to my feet, thought about vomiting, shook off the feeling, and drank five glasses of water from the sink. I knew my car was somewhere, but couldn't remember where I'd left it. I walked out into the hotel parking lot to smoke a cigarette and see if somehow miraculously I had brought it back there. I hadn't.

When I returned, Kristine was sitting up in bed with her breasts exposed, drinking the hotel coffee and watching the morning news. It was a segment about the hidden health benefits of eating small amounts of high-end dog food.

I rolled into bed and began kissing down her stomach.

"Hey, watch the coffee!"

"Put it down," I said into her belly button, "I'm busy."

She arched her back and exhaled, dug her nails into my scalp. Kristine seemed like a woman who would haul off and punch you during sex. My fingers found her clit and I rubbed it in slow circles until I could feel her parting for me. She was trembling and moaning loudly. Her mouth opened wide and she grasped at the edge of the mattress like it was keeping her from falling off. I moved up and pressed my tongue between her lips. She bit it and forcefully pushed my head back down to her torso.

The shape of her figure was baffling: a thin, flat stomach bloomed into wildly curved hips and thick flanks that wrapped tight around my head as I sunk my teeth into the inside of her thigh. I couldn't breathe, but I thought, what a way to die this would be.

Just as my tongue was about to touch the edge of her clit, and I was just about to suffocate, Kristine relinquished her grip and slapped the side of my head.

"*Ow*! What the fuck!" I shouted.

"No! Period! Period blood! Gross!"

"Oh shit, that's right. Jesus, why'd you let me go down there? That could have been traumatizing."

"It felt good…"

"Okay. Then I'm going to the store. I'm gonna handle this. Want anything?"

"Nope."

"Booze? Cigs? Tampons?"

"No. Come back."

Kristine pulled me in for a kiss and then pushed me off the bed. I threw on a loosely buttoned shirt, slid a cigarette in my mouth and walked out into the world.

When the sunlight hit my eyes, the full scope of the growing hangover became apparent. I lit the cigarette behind a bush, gagged, and spit a glob of white mucous onto the cement. People in suits passed me by on the street, visibly off-put by my appearance. It was a productive morning for them. They had woken up bright-eyed, eaten breakfast, scanned the morning paper for political scandals and murder sprees; kissed their kids, mistresses and significant others goodbye, and were on their way to well-paying jobs. I was disheveled and messy-haired, stinking of pussy and liquor, walking down the street with squinted eyes, hacking up phlegm between drags of a Camel Blue. I did not envy them. I felt good. I felt great.

A middle easterner with a heavy accent was behind the register of the gas station.

"Condoms?" I asked.

"Condoms?"

"Yeah. You got those?"

He hesitated and looked around, pointed to the assortment of prophylactics on the wall behind him. "You want?"

He took a box of Magnums off the wall.

"Look, I'm flattered but let's not get ahead of ourselves here."

He pointed to another box.

"Yeah, that's fine."

When I got back to the hotel, I got turned around and forgot what the room number was. I knew I was on the right floor, but decided to take a stab at a room that looked familiar enough with the door cracked open. I opened the door, and inside was a fat man lying naked on the bed masturbating to what appeared to be an aerobics infomercial on TV.

"OH JESUS SORRY MAN!"

He turned to look at me, and continued masturbating, straight-faced.

"Hey, it's all good."

"FUCKING OH MAN, WRONG ROOM DUDE SORRY."

"It doesn't have to be. What's your name?"

"WHAT THE FUCK, OH MAN SORRY."

I ran out and slammed the door.

About five minutes later, I found the right room. Kristine was on the bed.

"Do you know what day it is?"

"Ah, I don't know, man."

"What's wrong?"

"Nothing. What day is it?"

"It's Cinco De Mayo! Let's get tacos!"

"Yeah, tacos. Good."

"Are you sure you're alright?"

"Yes. Let's fuck. I wanna have sex with a woman."

"What?" she laughed.

"I don't know. I got condoms."

"Well, I'm busy."

"Are ya?"

"I'm kidding. Come here."

I felt funny putting on the condom. I tried to make it sexy and kiss her while I was doing it, but multitasking can be difficult. I climbed on top of her and watched her expression change as I slid it in.

Having sex with a woman you find truly attractive can be a formative experience. Good sex is the closest thing to spirituality I'll ever feel. When under the right circumstances, sex can be purely the meeting of two souls. Time stops and the Earth spins slower. Entropy of the universe ceases. The vulnerability of it all, the openness and the ecstasy can destroy the deepest of depressions. I understand that it can be explained away as simply a chemical reaction, an instinctual response in the human body as a living organism to elicit procreation, but most all other religions don't make any sense either. You take what you can get. I worship women and whiskey. You worship your God. We'll end up in the same place.

I pumped away on top of her, listening to the moans and screams and the creaks of the shitty hotel bed. Pillows were falling onto the floor, onto her face. She laughed and threw them off. Her nails dug into my back and sliced through the skin, down from my shoulders to my hips. I would pull out to tease her, sliding in my fingers until it evoked a reaction, then jam it back in with forceful thrusts. It drove her crazy. I felt like a wild animal, a god, an immortal. She grinned and I could see the little veins in the whites of her eyes as they rolled back. Her cheeks were flushed red and she pulled me deeper inside her.

"Come inside me! Come inside me!"

I gave her the best ride I could give. I wanted to please this woman. I thought of corpses, grandmothers ramming dildos into each other, tortured puppies, anything to keep this sensation from leaving me. I couldn't hold out any longer.

"*I'm gonna come, fuck.*"

"Do it! Do it, Hank!"

That did it. Hank. I'm not sure why.

I growled and grunted, and spurted it all into the condom as she tightened around me. Kristine grabbed the back of my head and bit down on my lip until I tasted blood.

The resulting scene was a mess. I pulled off the condom and saw that it was doused in crimson. The blood was everywhere. The blanket was covered with a wide spot of dark red between her legs. Bloodstained streaks ran down the top of the bed from where she had grasped at the sheets. It looked like the aftermath of a murder. I got up to wash off my parts in the sink as Kristine lay on the bed laughing.

"I told you!"

"The maids are gonna hate you," I yelled around the corner.

"I'll leave a tip on top of the sheets."

"A tip, shit. Burn those things and pretend it never happened."

"Ahahaha. I'm taking a shower."

She walked behind me and kissed me on the neck before disappearing into the bathroom. I washed off the blood on my fingers with soap and wiped the blood from the corner of my lip. My pubic hair was stained; I couldn't get all of it out. I gave up and tossed the ruined towel on the floor. It was everywhere.

I stood in the mirror looking at my naked body. I felt like a primal beast, drinking and fucking and bloody. Where had my morals gone? Were they ever there? How did I get here? I waited for the familiar rush of Catholic guilt to overtake me, for the self-loathing to take hold, but it didn't. All that was left now was a profound sense of acceptance. Whoever the animal was staring back at me, I liked him. This was all I would ever be. This was all I ever wanted to be. This was success. I didn't care anymore.

Kristine was singing in the shower, still laughing. I could feel myself falling in love again. I was fucked. I felt great.

We spent the rest of the day walking around the city, eating and drinking at every Mexican joint we could find. She would hold my hand and pull me into corners to make out every few blocks. She looked happy.

I tried my best to avoid thinking about the fact that Kristine was leaving the next morning. I would probably never see her again after that. But knowing that felt good in a way. She would leave before I got in too deep, which I certainly would if she stuck around. This way I wouldn't fuck it up. Knowing that I had a short, finite amount of time to spend with Kristine allowed me the ability to be fully present with her. There was no future there, so any thoughts of the future were pointless. I wished it could always be this easy. Sometimes a guy just got lucky.

We came back to the hotel with two bottles of wine before the sun set. At some point she fell asleep. I lay in bed and watched the ceiling as she breathed softly. She didn't snore. That was nice.

I must have fallen asleep eventually. The vibration from my phone on the bed stand forced me back to consciousness.

"H—hello?"

"Are you sleeping?"

"Yes, I'm asleep. Who is this?"

"Rita, you idiot. Where are you?"

"Oh. I'm in a hotel room."

"What? Where?"

I thought about it. "I don't know. Somewhere downtown."

"Okay, I'm not gonna ask. Well, Marcus and I are about to head downtown. Wanna meet us for a drink?"

"Sure." I looked over at the sleeping woman lying next to me. "I'm with someone, though."

"Of course you are. Kaitlyn?"

"No. That didn't work out. Turns out she doesn't like queers."

"Sorry. So who's the new one?"

"No new one. You'll meet her."

"Alright, send me an address. We'll pick you up in an hour. You and your not new one."

I hung up and shook Kristine awake. "Hey. Hey! Wake up. Drink this."

She stirred and groaned, and took the bottle of wine out of my hand. "What's happening?"

"We're drinking. Do you wanna meet a couple of my friends?"

"Can we finish this first?"

"That was my idea."

"Then yes."

We passed the bottle and watched a news segment about a teacher who abducted one of his high school students. He took her to a cabin in the Redwoods to have his way with her. Apparently it was consensual and she did her best to avoid the both of them being caught. But he was, and she went back home to her parents and he went to federal prison for rape and crossing state lines to have sex with a minor.

Kristine was confused. "If she was down, how can this guy be convicted of rape? That's like, the opposite."

"She was a minor," I said, and slugged from the waning bottle. "That's statutory rape, it doesn't matter. The argument is that she didn't know any better on account of not being a legal adult and all."

She took the bottle back and drank it down to the bottom. "I had sex with my teacher."

I coughed. "How'd that go?"

"Not so well. He cried after and took a shower. I still had to go to his class for another six months after it."

"That's a cute story. Did he give you an A at least?"

"C plus."

"Is that wine gone?"

"Yeah."

Once Marcus and Rita arrived we were properly wasted. We spilled out through the revolving doors of the hotel, kissing and holding each other to keep from stumbling over. I collapsed into the backseat next to Kristine. "Guys, this is Kristine. Kristine, this is... the guys."

"Hi," she chirped.

"Hi," said Marcus.

"Hello," said Rita. "You got a cute one this time, Henry."

"I don't know what you're talking about, Rita."

After a few minutes of small talk, we pulled into some bar I had never been to. I lit a cigarette and Kristine took it out of my mouth, so I lit another one. Rita stood awkwardly with Marcus on the sidewalk, watching us, waiting for us to finish and go in. "So... how'd you guys meet?"

"How do you think?" I laughed.

"Tinder?"

Kristine answered before I could. "Yeah, I just travel around the country hitting up dudes on Tinder to fuck."

There was a short silence.

"Well... that's cool."

"We met at a bar," I said.

Marcus attempted to be witty. "Well, what's the difference these days?"

I had no idea what that meant.

Inside, the bar was loud and abrasive. An excess of young people our age stood shoulder to shoulder in a massive, sweat-stained blob extending to each wall, stumbling and yelling over each other's rambling stories of their college majors and relationship woes. It was a sea of blue hair and ear gauges and Pabst cans. A pulsing club anthem currently at the top of the charts blasted through speakers hanging in each corner. I hated the place. I try not to hate these places but I do. Establishments unabashedly meant to cater towards my generation easily disillusion me. I suppose the easy answer is simply that I'm disillusioned by my generation. But that's a me problem.

I ordered a whiskey-soda for far too much money to drown out the feeling of alienation. The wine was getting to me, though. The rotgut shit always had a way of working into the deepest part of my stomach until it dulled my mind and twisted my insides beyond their ability to do so. There wasn't much left to do now but endure the circumstances I'd put myself in.

We all made our way into the basement section of the bar and sat down against the wall. Kristine leaned her head against my shoulder, letting the full glass of beer in her hand hang softly at an angle. "I'm tired. I don't like this place."

"Me neither," I said.

"Let's drink wine and order a pizza at the hotel."

"Alright. We can finish our drinks and we'll get out of here."

"You promise?"

"Why wouldn't I?"

Kristine was falling asleep. I had to shake her awake multiple times to keep her from spilling the beer. Marcus and Rita tried at times to make conversation, but all the words fell away into the abyss of shitty pop music and drunken screams.

185

I began to doubt humanity's ability to survive a nuclear holocaust when I noticed a large dark-haired man staring at me from across the room. He was slouched over on the barstool as if he had a serious issue with his posture as a child that was never corrected. His mouth didn't seem to fit his face—it was too small. In fact, everything on his face appeared as though it was tacked on like a Mr. Potato Head doll. Too much face, not enough eyes, mouth, nose. I didn't like him.

I looked away and laid my hand on Kristine's knee. When I looked again, the odd fellow's gaze had intensified. I stared back. He didn't look away. Finally, I broke the tension: "What the fuck are you looking at?"

"What?"

"I said, what the fuck are you looking at?"

The distance between this confrontation made the whole thing feel juvenile.

"What do you think I'm looking at?" he barked over the music.

"You're looking at *me*, motherfucker. I'm asking why."

We must have been yelling across the room. People were looking at us.

He then got up and walked over. He was larger than I imagined. Sitting at a barstool has a way of distorting a person's size.

"Who's the girl?" he asked.

Kristine shot up out of her stupor. "Who the fuck are *you*, man?"

He was taken aback by this, but composed himself and continued with his noble crusade. "Do you know this guy? Trust me, you don't wanna do this."

"This guy?" she spat, and pointed at me. "Nah, never met him. He told me he'd buy me drinks if I came home and fucked him on his sex swing."

"She's kidding."

"No I'm not."

His face contorted in disgust. "You should come with me. I'll take care of him for you."

She laughed. "Nah. I've always wanted to try a sex swing. I wanna see what it's like to hit that spot in anti-gravity. Like an astronaut. Y'know what I mean? I think I'll go with him."

I began laughing but this was a difficult situation to unfurl myself from. I leaned towards her ear. "What're you trying to do, get me stabbed?"

"Maybe," she grinned. "Give me some chaos. Wake me up."

"Yeah?"

I stood up. The guy had at least half a foot on me. "Look, this ain't your business. The lady wants to go with me. If she wants the sex swing, and I wanna get her a couple drinks to get her there, then that's my right as a GODDAMN AMERICAN. What're you, a COMMUNIST?"

Kristine erupted in laughter behind me.

The ogre-like man puffed out his chest and stepped closer to me. He smelled like cheap cologne you'd get on sale at Wal-Mart. "It *is* my business. *You're* my business. The lady isn't coming with you."

"Then I suggest you invest in a sex swing. It pays for itself."

The blood began rising to his face. His eyes widened. It was coming.

I never knew why I let these things happen, how my life ended up where it did. It would be easy to blame it on alcohol, on family, on genetics, on fate, but then where's the fun in that? Bad decisions feel better when they're your decisions. I could do bad all by myself. And when it really came down to it, I didn't regret a fuckin' thing. It all led me to her.

I leaned in once more next to Kristine. "Are we paid out?"

"Yep."

"Ready to run?"
"Yeah. I think you're cute."
"Tell me that after this."
"On three?"
"On three."

Second Life Replay

Death and I walked into the theater just as the lights dimmed. The trailers were starting. We found our seats close to the back, behind thirty rows of empty chairs. A young woman in high-waisted shorts and white flowers in her hair was screaming at a row of armored policemen on the screen in front of us. She held the hands of two young men in sullied ponchos. Other young men and women were lined up behind her, screaming into cupped hands and megaphones about war. I could make out the pointed tip of the Capitol Building in the background.

Death leaned into me and whispered behind its black cloak, "You used to be quite the activist. Didn't get you anywhere, though."

The woman on the screen reached out to one of the cops and grazed the shield of his riot helmet in a way that I suppose was meant to be peaceful—some sort of "we're not so different, you and I" sentiment—and with a violent immediacy that suggested the cops had been waiting for this moment all along, a hail of rubber bullets then erupted from the wall of government-issue rifles. She dropped to the cement along with a group of hippies unfortunately situated within her proximity. The white flowers fell lightly beside her head and were stained red from the pool of blood emptying out from her left temple. Horrified screams sounded off through the ranks of the protesters like echoes of an explosion. The woman mumbled something to the longhaired fellow lying wounded on the ground next to her, and closed her eyes. The armada of storm troopers charged forward into the sea of their smaller, dirtier counterparts, and her body disappeared under the swarm of sandals and combat boots that followed. The screen faded to black.

"Well, I tried," I said.

"That's nothing," Death replied. "You've lived a long life. Sometimes you even accomplished something."

"Bring it on then. Really give it to me, man. We're already here."

"Shhh… knowing you, the trailers will be the best part."

The screen lit back up, and upon it was a child—an Asian child dressed in brown rags standing alone in a field of dying and shriveled crops. The sun encompassed half the screen and the child was struggling to stand under the weight of its heat.

"Where the hell are my parents?" I asked.

"Dead," said Death. "Congratulations, you're an orphan."

"What am I doing?" I asked.

"You're dying, idiot."

The child reached down slowly and pulled up a plant from the cracked earth. It was gnarled and brown, and provided none of the sustenance that the child seemed to be hoping to reap from it.

"Wait, watch this," Death whispered. "This is the best part."

"I am watching."

The child's eyes were rolling into the back of his head, only to return forward to gaze upon the empty horizon as he wiped the sweat from his brow. His knees were buckling and his head was drooping into the center of his chest. He didn't make a sound, didn't call out for help—although there was no shadow within the frame to suggest that anyone was around to answer if he called.

"What is this?" I asked.

"Rural China, circa 1675 A.D. Back in the bad ol' days, when business was good. Watch."

The sunburnt child lifted the plant over his head and sucked at the roots, coughed up dust, and collapsed upon the dirt like a ragdoll. His dried eyes rolled back a final time, and the screen faded to black. The whole event felt abrupt and I no longer wanted to see whatever would follow.

Death appeared to sense this and slapped me on the leg. "Relax. There's just one more, then you get to bask in your self-indulgence. It'll be great, just sit tight."

I threw up my hands and laughed. "Where am I gonna go?"

"Nowhere," said Death. I could feel the smile curling behind the infinite black inside its hood.

The screen brightened once again.

An elderly man sporting a white beard equal in magnificence to his crown and the jewelry adorning his hands sat upon a golden throne, staring back into me. My eyes lit up.

"Now, THIS is more like it!" I shouted.

"Shut up!" Death howled. "You'll disturb the spirits."

I lowered my voice, "This is what I wanted to see: a leader, a man of the people! Someone who made a difference!"

The man of royalty stroked his beard and clapped his hands, producing a trembling, sharp-eyed man who entered the frame with a plate of roasted duck and a goblet spilling over with purple wine. He took the plate and the jewel-encrusted cup, and kicked the servant as he made his exit, knocking the poor fellow to the ground and out of the frame.

"A man of power!" I whispered through a hoarse breath. "Someone who matters! They showed me respect!"

Death remained silent.

The old man bit into the roasted duck like a wild animal and swallowed the wine in a single gulp, letting the drink spill down his neck and stain the white hair hanging from his face. He clapped his hands once more and a musician out of frame began playing a lute.

I couldn't mask my swelling pride and excitement. "That's really me?" I said. "Finally, somebody who didn't take any SHIT!"

Death laughed, and its breath smelled like the final exhale of my cancer-riddled father.

"Quiet!" I hissed with a cocky smile. "You'll disturb the spirits."

The man of importance stared out upon the unseen crowd and screamed something in a language I couldn't recognize. From out of frame appeared a beautiful redheaded woman with her breasts protruding out from a green corset and a second goblet of wine in her hand. She forced a smile and handed him the drink from as far away as she could reach.

Death tapped me on the shoulder. "Okay, watch this part."

"You're the worst kind of person to watch this with, do you know that?"

"I just get excited."

The king again stroked his beard proudly and drank deep from the goblet, reaching out and grabbing at the woman's ass as she skirted away. He screamed something indiscernible and raised his cup, eliciting an explosive chant from the crowd, and finished off the contents of the goblet with a violent belch. Applause filled the open chamber and he held up his hand to silence the people. The music ceased and the only entity that existed was the man on his throne. Every one of us waited for his next sentence as if it was to be the word of God Himself.

And then, suddenly, subtly, a thin trickle of crimson ran down from the left corner of his mouth. He coughed once, then twice, into his closed fist. His eyes bugged out of their sockets like he was choking. His face was turning a dark purple. The crowd remained silent. When he removed his fist from his mouth, it was covered with blood. The king looked down at it and raised his eyes back upon the crowd with unmistakable horror. He coughed once, twice, and vomited blood on his marten fur coat. It was black. A single audible gasp was emitted from the crowd. He attempted to stand, and stumbled onto his knees as if penitent, his eyes the only part of his face able to project the fear coursing through his veins. And finally, still with a hint of style, the dying man vomited black blood onto his throne, and collapsed. A solitary scream erupted from out of frame, and the screen faded to black.

"My guess is the redhead with the tits," said Death, filling the silence while I attempted to wrap my head around what I'd just seen. "I don't think the sniveling fella had the balls to do it."

"Are you always this unpleasant?" I croaked. "Where are the peaceful sleep apnea demises, the gentle heroin overdoses in large bathtubs?"

"The people want the greatest hits," Death said, extending its arms out to the empty theater, "I can't always be what you want me to be."

Before I could respond, Death held up its skeletal hand. "Now quiet. It's starting…"

It began with a cry and the blurred ceiling of an operating room. A lens of tears obscured the first sight of my life. Two large hands reached down around the screen and lifted up infant me, said something. His eyes were wide and blue and bright and wrinkled in the corners from the smile hidden behind his surgical mask. I then pissed on his face. This was my doctor. I had heard this story about a million times, never found it funny— but I chuckled a little seeing it as it happened. He flinched and nearly dropped me, immediately passing me off into the arms of the most beautiful woman I would ever know. In her face, I saw my own green eyes staring back through the screen. She was covered in sweat and breathing heavily through her nose. Her chest was heaving my small body up and down like undulating sea waves. But boy, was she happy to see me. She looked over to my father, still young and with an uncombed clump of black hair on his head, shaking in his scrubs, forcing a smile for my mother. I was wrapped inside a light blue blanket by one of the nurses and laid back down upon my mother's chest. Everybody seemed so happy in that room. The implication of what was to come ruined the beauty of the moment for me, but I didn't want to spoil the film for Death. Or maybe it would enjoy it; it didn't seem very engrossed in this—my original, innocent moment on Earth.

"I knew this wasn't gonna get interesting until at least twenty years in," said Death.

"Just watch the damn film," I said.

I was in an incubator. The air was orange and I was screaming. I don't know if I had blacked out or if the film was jumping around a bit. I never learned exactly when the stroke occurred, but I know it happened some time while I was still at the hospital. I thanked the empty black ceiling that I no longer possessed the memory of this experience. Knowing what had happened to this child and hearing the screams escaping from this unattended machine made me feel sick to my stomach.

"What happened?" asked Death.

"My mother had a miscarriage before she had me. I guess the kid didn't die all the way. When I showed up, what was left of him mixed all up with me while I was still a little sea monkey inside her. It did something to my brain. They said I was either gonna come out of it with cerebral palsy—never talk and never walk, just lay there drooling and shitting on myself for the rest of my life— or I was gonna die right there in the incubator. No one could explain why it didn't happen."

"Hmm," said Death, "I wonder why I didn't just take you then."

"I don't know. I figured you decided I still had more misery to endure."

Death laughed, "Ha! Ah, yeah. You wouldn't get off that easy."

I paused and looked down into the abyss of the theater's floor. "A part of me always thought I was meant to die then. Like it was this cosmic mistake. Like a glitch in the matrix. And by some fucked up fluke of nature, I ended up still here. And all these awful things that happened in my life were just part of one big sign the universe was trying to give me: 'Kill yourself.' Y'know? 'We fucked up. Our bad. You weren't meant to be here. You gotta kill yourself so we can fix the glitch.' It had to have been more than just bad luck."

Death scoffed and waved its hand dismissively. "Oh boo hoo. Don't be such a fucking narcissist. You're not the only one in the universe that floated up shit creek."

I turned and looked at the side of its hood as if there were a face behind it. "Can you tell me why you didn't take me in that incubator? Please."

"I can't remember," said Death.

There I was again. I was being shepherded through the doors of my new preschool, my tiny hand enveloped in my father's sweaty, coarse palm. He dragged me up to a desk at the entrance and began talking to a middle-aged woman in a pink dress. I looked up at her, curious as to who this stranger was that my father seemed to know. Her hair was long and straight and black, and it scared me. But she wore deep red lipstick and her perfume smelled like my mother, so I decided to trust her.

She noticed me staring, and leaned over the desk, grinning with big white teeth. "Well hello, darling!" she cooed. "Aren't you just adorable?" Her voice was soft and melodic, like the birds that would chirp outside my bedroom window when I woke up in the morning. I liked her right away.

She waited for me to answer, but I just kept on staring. I didn't know why she was being so nice to me, and didn't want to do anything that might make her stop. She cocked her head and smiled again sympathetically. "How old are you, honey?"

My father looked down at me in my silence, and back up at the woman. "He doesn't talk much. We don't know if it's because of the—"

"Oh right, right," said the woman. "Well, that's okay. You don't have to tell me."

My head swiveled between the woman and my father. He looked disappointed. She was looking away now, typing something on her computer. I wanted her to look at me again.

"I'm four and a half," I said, and held up five fingers.

The woman turned and beamed at me. I could see all her teeth now. "How wonderful! You're getting to be such a big boy! Well, its lovely to meet you, Mr. Four and a Half."

I looked up at my father. He gave me a weak smile and squeezed my hand. I smiled too.

I recognized this scene. This was my first memory.

The image of my father's smile melted away like a piece of paper lit on fire, and from behind the screen of blinking white that replaced it, an altogether new scene flooded back into focus.

I was ten. I knew where I was immediately. I wore blue slacks, dirty Converse high-tops with the left shoe untied, and a red button-up shirt sporting my grade school insignia. I stood in front of my class of snot-nosed, fellow Catholic-schoolers, reading a poem on loose-leaf paper. There was the alphabet pinned to the wall above me, fashioned out of cartoon characters with googly-eyes; the dusty chalkboard with next week's spelling homework written in delicate cursive behind me. The eyes of classmates I hadn't seen in decades were trained on my long-passed self. I remembered every one of them.

"The blonde with the gap-tooth and the eyes too close together?" mentioned Death into my ear.

"Michael Woodson," I answered. "I always hated his guts. Acted like he ran the school 'cause his daddy owned a beach house. He broke my nose in third grade for sneezing on his lunch."

"Yeah. Picked him up in 2012: autoerotic asphyxiation."

"Ha! Ha ha! Tell me Pops found him."

"Along with about half his firm—company potluck at the happy family's abode. Mikey thought he could squeeze one out before dinner. Daddy-o was never the same after that. Took himself out with thirty Xanax and a fifth of HRD two years later."

"Ha! Ha ha, ah. That's rich. How many times do you gotta tell people? Always use the buddy system."

I pointed to one of the girls waving intently at a bird outside the window. "That girl in the pigtails behind him—black hair; smiling like a retard?"

"Yeah?" said Death.

"Lost my virginity to her freshman year. She told the whole school I got her pregnant when I wouldn't do it again."

"Why not?"

"Have you ever smelled fish sauce?"

"Lovely. Four-eyes next to her—picking that gold nugget out of her nose?"

"Yep. Samantha Berns. Real bright. I heard she ended up at Harvard Law."

"She sure did," said Death. "Take a guess."

"Accident at the yacht club?"

"Nope."

"Choked on the steak at the Four Seasons?"

"Eh."

"Give me a hint."

"Think less fancy."

"Ah, just tell me."

"Craigslist orgy, truck stop motel, eight ball of coke, exploded heart."

"Beautiful."

My younger self was reading words I didn't remember, but when the camera panned to the right, everything came flooding back into me as the screen focused on the wrinkled face of my fifth grade teacher. She was crying. I was reading something that I had written all on my own, and I was moving another human being to tears. I had affected someone in a positive way from a product of my own mind. This was the first time I could ever remember doing something right.

Death moaned and slumped down in its seat. "Ugh. Why is this in here? Fucking BORING."

The words fell out of me: "This is my first happy memory."

The child that looked remarkably similar to the man watching him finished his poem and looked up at his peers. His hands were trembling and hardly able to keep the page still. All at once, the classroom broke down into laughter, pointing and hollering insults at the timid boy. As tears began rolling down his reddening cheeks, he turned again to the only friendly face he could find: Mrs. Mahoney wiped tears away from the corners of her eyes and silenced the class with a soft tone. She walked up to the trembling child at the front of the class, smiled wide with her slender hand on his shoulder, and said, "Good job, Henry. That was lovely."

The screen focused on her face for a few minutes, and then Mrs. Mahoney faded away into an altogether different scene.

I was standing in my pajamas, on the stairs leading down to the garage of my childhood house. I couldn't remember how old I was. My big sister was next to me, on her knees with a trash bag still being held up by one hand. It was torn open, and piles of vomit—red and pink and green and brown—had spilled all down the wooden steps. I could hear the puke that hadn't yet hardened dripping down onto the cement floor between the cracks. She was desperately scooping up the vomit using her free hand like a dustpan.

"Where's Mom?" she was repeating over and over: "Where's Mom? Where's Mom?"

I didn't say anything. The smell was horrible. I turned around and walked out. "Don't tell Mom," my sister said, the final word being deafened by the slam of the door behind me.

The door fell away into the open entrance of a hospital room. I stood closely behind my two parents, barely reaching my mother's shoulders. They were talking to a gray-haired doctor wearing a long white coat and a stethoscope around his neck. I couldn't make out what they were saying. Beyond the hospital room entrance, shriveled under the dimmed lights and swaddled inside layers of blankets, was the gaunt, pale face of my teenage sister. She stared blankly at the ceiling, unable to move or communicate. I had never seen someone look so detached, never seen the light in a person's eyes flickering so close to darkness. The doctor nodded to my father with a vague smile and walked away, and my mother leaned over me, speaking very softly. Her eyes were red and puffy, and she was not smiling.

"Henry, Carmen is going to have to stay in the hospital for a while. She's very sick. Dad and I are going to go talk to her now, but I want you to stay here outside, okay? It's very important that you stay outside."

I nodded. I wouldn't understand the severity of my sister's anorexia and bulimia for a few more years. At this age, I wasn't able to put any critical thought into it all, really. She just became like a skeleton one day and she would vomit into a trash bag and hide it under her bed after dinner every night. For some reason, whether by desensitization or ignorance, these were just facts that I accepted and never looked into further until her illness began to have a direct effect on my ability to function.

The final moment of this scene was the image that was vividly burned into my memory for the rest of my life: As my parents sat down next to her bed, moving their lips and holding each of her hands under the blankets, Carmen slowly lifted her neck up as if it weighed fifty pounds, and stared at me watching her from under the stale, florescent lights alone in the hallway. Her eyes looked entirely black, vacant, horrifying. She looked dead.

The whole scene was suddenly washed away as if someone had thrown water on a page of wet ink, before going dark.

A fist filled the entire screen. It was white and fleshy and covered in curly black hairs. The fist connected with my face, breaking my nose. Blood was running down my lips and chin, forcing me to spit up onto the floor as it poured into my open mouth. I was wailing and cowering in a corner, attempting to hide behind a sofa. But my father tore me from my hiding place, knocking the sofa onto its side, and beat the side of my head with the back of his ring hand. His other hand was busy gripping the collar of my ripped shirt, making sure I wasn't going anywhere this time as he laid into my belly with a firm uppercut. My mother was screaming with every inch of her breath, throwing things at my father from across the room in an attempt to stop him without getting herself in the way of his manic outburst.

"YOU LITTLE BASTARD!" he screamed. "SAY IT AGAIN. TELL ME WHAT I CAN AND CAN'T DO IN MY OWN HOUSE ONE MORE GODDAMN TIME!"

Another open hand landed against my left ear. For a moment, all I could hear was ringing and I tried my best to keep my arms up to protect my seventy-pound body before I was beaten unconscious.

"Look at you!" shouted Death, throwing its arms out, exposing its radius as its sleeve fell to the elbow, "What the fuck're you doing? Fight back!"

I was frozen in horror, watching the death of my childhood as every piece of matter between me and the boy on the screen was being torn away without mercy. I choked on the words, "I can't."

The rage was etched too deep into my father's face. His yellow teeth were bared like a rabid dog, spittle flying from the corners of his lips as he spewed pure hatred into the face of his child. He had gone mad again. Before a final strike was landed, the piercing scream of my mother came flying towards me, and before my stunned mind could register what had happened, he had changed targets; the volley of fists was being directed at his wife. I crumpled against the wall in a bloody heap, howling like Hell had opened up beneath me, watching the onslaught meant for me being unleashed upon the only person I'd ever cared about. Sliding up against the wall for support, I struggled back to my feet and hurled myself against the kitchen counter. The fight had spilled out into the dining room, and my father had thrown the weight of his body on top of my mother. Too short to see over the counter, I blindly reached across the cold granite until I got a firm grasp on the shape I was feeling for. With the last of my remaining strength, I charged into the dining room screaming. There was my father, back turned to me, laying into my mother with both fists and the weight of his 230-lbs. frame. The noise was deafening and sick. I was watching the evil of the whole world pour out onto the floor in front of me. Trying my best to hide the fear behind my voice, I held out the six-inch kitchen knife against the nape of my father's neck and roared, "DAD, STOP! I'LL KILL YOU!"

With that, every sound in the universe ceased. My father stopped, turned around. And in his eyes was the most beautiful thing I'd ever seen in him: fear.

The screen froze on his expression for a few minutes, and crumbled away into black.

I closed my eyes and wished that it wouldn't be next to me when I reopened them—but there was Death, staring into my face like a black hole. "How much longer is this?" I asked with a grimace. "I don't know how much longer I can do this."

"That is so like you," said Death. "As soon as it starts getting good, you always cash in your chips. That's what you ALWAYS do."

"I didn't think it would be like this."

"No one does," it chuckled. "Seriously, try to enjoy this. It only gets better from here."

The screen opened up to a beautiful, clear sky. I could hear the wind and smell the scent of flowers it carried. A lone bird flew across my vision, breaking the untouched scene like the wake of a ship in the ocean. For a moment, I was meditative. Then the medic appeared. Then another one. Then the phantasmal red and blue lights of an ambulance bounced off the corners of my eyes. One of the medics lifted up my head and said words in an urgent matter that faded in and out as my eyelids became heavier and my vision blurred: "What did you take... how many... you take? Henry, how many... Henry... keep your eyes... losing him... we're..." And that was it.

I was sitting in a bathrobe. I was unshaven, and wild tufts of long, brown hair stuck up out of my head in different directions. The walls were white and a woman with a pointed nose and round glasses sat on a chair across from me. Between us was a flimsy, collapsible table with a tape recorder sitting atop it. She wore a short, purple skirt, and when she crossed and re-crossed her legs it slid up just a bit more, exposing the hidden skin. She was speaking words and I was focused on her thighs.

Finally, she grasped my attention: "I said, Henry!"

My eyes shot up, wavering for a moment on her breasts hidden behind a white dress shirt, and then up to her face.

"Yes?" I mumbled.

"Are you listening to me?"

"You are the sexiest psychiatrist at this hospital, Melissa."

"I need you to focus."

"Hike up your skirt a bit."

"Henry, some of the orderlies tell me that you aren't taking your meds—that you hide them and trade them for cigarettes from the other patients. Is this true?"

"I don't know what you're talking about, Melissa."

"Please—Dr. Minerva. Well, they've shown me tapes of you doing just that. Did you know the hospital records everything in the psychiatric ward?"

"Fucking snitches."

"Henry, we need you to be taking your medication. Otherwise, you may not get out of here for a long time. You want to get out of here, don't you? You want to get better?"

I looked down at the pink hospital bracelet attached to my wrist, reached into the front pocket of my robe for a cigarette.

"No smoking in here," Dr. Minerva said. "I need you to communicate."

I remembered that only the orderlies carried matches, and tucked the cigarette behind my ear. "Okay, Doc. Communicate. How about this? I don't like 'em. They make me bloated and I can't think. I walk around with a storm cloud in my head and the static zaps behind my eyes. I get sick and I can't eat. I don't like 'em, Doc. I don't like 'em, I DON'T LIKE 'EM… and YOU can't make me take them."

The woman in the purple skirt exhaled through her nose and marked something off on the clipboard in her lap.

"Okay, Henry. I'll see you next week then."

A shrill buzzer sounded off behind me and a door opened. Two men in white clothing approached me on either side and firmly grasped each arm, ushering me up to leave the room. Before I could be forced out of her presence, I screamed my final remarks at Dr. Minerva like a bullet aimed at her chest: "YOU don't know how this feels! You'll NEVER know! KILL ME, YOU BITCH!"

The shell of my former self was dragged out of the room kicking and screaming as the good doctor crossed her legs and wrote something on her clipboard, and the screen fizzled into black.

Death slapped me on the shoulder. "This is more like it," it said. "You're pathetic, it's gorgeous. I can just feel it coming."

I stared into the gaping hole inside its hood, reached out and touched the black cloth draped over its shoulder. "Is this all you've ever been?" I asked. "Can you feel sympathy?"

"Don't ruin this for me," Death replied, "I'm finally enjoying your film. Take pride in that. You can really suffer, man. You should be proud of that."

The screen opened up to her face. I knew this would come eventually. I was studying the freckles dotting her cheeks, the strands of blonde hair messily hanging over her blue eyes that stared into the empty audience like nothing else had ever existed. Her lips parted and revealed a row of white, symmetrical teeth. She lay upon a pillow next to me, and reached out to touch the scars on my wrists. Above her face was the glow of the morning, and through the window was a swaying conifer tree, filled with green leaves and extending branches.

"Good morning, Henry," she said.

"Oh. Who's the broad?" Death chirped.

I didn't answer. This was the moment I was waiting for. The only reason why I was sitting in that theater.

"Good morning," I said, and reached under the covers to grasp her side.

"You look happy," she said.

"Why wouldn't I be?"

I slid up in bed and reached over to the nightstand, pulling a cigarette out of the carton and took a pull from the beer bottle left over from the night before.

"I'm not used to a smile, is all. I could get used to that."

"Don't do this," I said, lighting the cigarette with a match on the floor.

"How did you pull this one off?" said Death. "A damage case like you?"

Without taking my eyes off the last woman I ever loved, I mumbled, "Don't worry, I fuck it all up."

"Well, naturally."

"Are you ready, baby?" said the woman on screen.

"How could I ever be?" I said, exhaling smoke heavily through my nostrils. "Let's just stay in bed. Let's just get drunk all day and let him rot."

"You don't really wanna leave Carmen alone on this, do you? First your mother, then—"

"Stop," I barked. "She'll be as happy to see him go under as I am. The dogs can eat him, for all I care. Then at least he'll have served a purpose."

"Let's not start the day like this."

"You didn't know him like I did. You saw the end of him—the remorseful, frightened little man. You didn't really know him."

I tried my hardest to ignore the context of the scene and focus solely on the features of the woman. If I could just ignore the words, if I could just pretend this was any other day.

The phone was ringing. I shook my head and got up to piss while she answered. I could hear one side of the conversation through the open door:

"Hello? Hi, Carmen. Yes. He's in the bathroom. Yes, he's coming. Yes, I'm sure. I'll make sure. Does he wanna talk?" There was a pause as she waited for some kind of confirmation from the bathroom. I remained silent, throwing the cigarette butt into the toilet and flushed as I zipped up my pants. "I'm not sure right now. Right. Four o' clock. I'll see you there. Goodbye."

I returned to bed after grabbing another beer from the fridge, sat up and drank half it down while looking out the window. It really was a beautiful day. Life had turned out so much differently than I imagined.

"Why are you doing this?" she said.

"Doing what?"

"Making everything harder than it needs to be."

"It's easier that way."

"I just think if you talked to someone—"

"I'm not going to another goddamn shrink! You understand? I'm not fucking doing it. Stop bringing it up."

She stood up, wearing white panties and an old, oversized t-shirt I got in Tampa Bay three years before. On it was a cartoon sun with a smiley face, and the words "We Are The Sunshine State!" printed beneath it. Her hair hung down around her hips and she looked smaller than I'd ever seen her even as she stood over me.

"You're sick. You're a sick person, Henry. Why you can't admit that, I don't know. Maybe your family fucked you up worse than I realized."

"Don't."

"Don't what, Henry?"

"You bitch," I snarled, throwing the beer bottle against the wall. It shattered with a bang, and she jumped and backed away from me.

The words knocked the air out of me like a punch to the gut. I had gone over that morning over and over in my head in the days that followed, never understanding why I reacted like I did.

Tears began to run down her face and the sunlight from the window glinted in each one. "Please leave," she whimpered. "I don't care where you go, I just need you to leave. Please."

"Fine. Perfect," I snapped, and jumped out of bed, pulling a jacket over my stained undershirt. "I don't need another fucking person telling me who I am, what to do, what to think. You're no different, are you?"

"Please just leave, Henry. I'll… I'll see you at the funeral, I just don't want you to be here right now."

"I'm not going to any fucking funeral."

She had backed up into the wall. Her hands were trembling and she was doing her best to hide it, wiping away tears as they fell down her cheeks between the brown freckles I had counted a hundred times.

"Just go, please."

I put on a pair of boots and walked down the hall, opened the door into the apartment building.

"You're no different than any of the rest of them," I said, and closed the door behind me.

She slid down the wall on her back and exhaled a hard, trembling breath; wiped away the last tear before it dripped from the bridge of her crooked nose, and the screen faded away into black.

"No, no, NO!" I shouted at the screen. "Bring her back! Bring it back! How do you make it go back?" I grabbed Death by the shoulder and shook it, staring into the screen waiting for any chance that she would reappear.

"It's done, you idiot," it hissed, and threw off my hand with its phalanges. "It's almost over now, it's all almost over. Then I'll take you back home."

I focused as hard as I could on her image, tried to study every second of the scenes that displayed her face, but every time she reappeared in my memory, she burned away again like a distant dream. I was sick with myself over again, ready to do it all over again. And then there it was.

I sat with my legs dangling over the roof of my apartment building, watching the full moon glow over the lights of the city. I could count every visible star in the sky on two hands. Between heavy sips from the bottle of whiskey in my lap, I took sporadic glances down at the tiny orange lights of the cars driving back and forth far beneath me. The wind was strong and whistled in my ears every time it passed. I was drunk, very drunk. I was twenty-eight. I had been to jail, been committed to the psych ward, flunked out of college, traveled the world; lost girlfriends, my wallet, my mind and both my parents; alienated myself from friends, from my sibling; ran with the bulls in Spain, eaten puffer fish in Japan, made love for three days and three nights; worked in factories, restaurants, offices; been homeless, poor, well-off; been loved, hated, beaten, broken, afraid, depressed; been an activist, a child laborer, a king; been nothing and everything at every moment a human heart ever beat—and here I was, hanging over the roof with a bottle of cheap whiskey, under a full moon and dim stars and bright city lights, finally aware of it all.

Maybe it would all go differently next time. Maybe I'd get it right.

I closed my eyes and looked away from the screen as the man on the roof drank down the last of the bottle. Death noticed this, tapped me on the shoulder and pulled off its hood.

"C'mon, Henry—open your eyes. Don't you wanna see how it ends?"

Laurel

When I think of Laurel, the memories come in fragments: Walking outside her house after listening to Neil Young records and making love for two hours, to see the full moon licked orange from the nearby forest fires, the blue air thick with smoke; the image of her back to me, bare legs submerged up to her freckled knees in fountain water, surrounded by night-piercing floodlights and isles of bloomed roses in a park of which name I can't remember; her eyes rolling back to reveal the whites as she attempts through convulsing orgasms to breathe my name; her scent that feels like home lingering on my clothing the morning after; the metronomic beeping of the heart monitor as she lies exhausted and disheveled on a hospital bed beside me; the cold indifference rippling across her face like tremors under the earth when her patience for my erratic mania has run dry; the scalding hatred drowning it all out once the flaws we've failed to control have seeped through the cracks.

Some people are not meant to have met. The winds of the universe pull them away from each other but regardless they crawl back towards one another through the gusts as if they know better. They are so similar in their insecurities and flaws that the blood collectively flowing from their open wounds merely fills each other's gaping holes to the point that they believe they have fixed each other. The most destructive relationships can appear to be a once in a lifetime symbiosis for that reason. Of course, though, they're not. The biggest issue is that these sorts of unstable personalities almost revel in the possibility of mutual annihilation. It's what a part of them has secretly hoped for this entire time, and what better of a way to do it than in the eye of a blurry storm of sex and love and hatred. These types are ensnared by the unhealthy dichotomy of unwavering romanticism and unending self-punishment. This is why you don't date masochists. Or writers. But more often than not, you're talking about the same thing.

The first thing I noticed about Laurel was her legs. I told her that. She was expecting some romantic answer. But no, that's what I noticed first. The first thing she noticed about me was that I had a weak handshake. So I suppose we're even. We weren't flattering at first.

She was friends with my friend Scott, the overly confident semi-hipster with the bloated assumption of charisma. The first thing I heard about her was that Scott had known her for a while, and finally they'd decided to hook up after being in each other's company for however many years. I met her a week later.

We were at a bar in the north side of the city that Scott had invited me to because they had a jazz band playing every Wednesday night. Laurel and I arrived at the same time. She wore a long dress down to the ankles adorned with colorful, flowery patterns—the kind of tasteful sundress that you don't see many people our age wearing any longer. It had that slit going down one side that left the one leg bare for the purple hues of the sunset and deft admirers to gaze at. She was built thick with wide hips and full, pale thighs that were exposed just enough to be provocative when the light summer wind lifted her dress up. Dirty blonde hair fell down to her shoulders in soft waves.

We walked in nearly side-by-side, avoiding eye contact until we realized that we were meeting up with the same person.

Scott made the introductions.

"Henry, this is Laurel. Laurel, Henry."

Handshake, mandatory friendly smile.

"Nice to meet you."

There was very little recognition at first. I imagine I was more of a background set piece to whatever evening she was planning on having.

I ordered whiskey. She ordered the same lemonade she always did that I didn't realize wasn't alcoholic until a few weeks in. The three of us sat down at a booth across from the band playing in the corner.

Even through the shadowed, dim lighting of the bar her eyes burned neon green. There was a striking amount of life in her.

"Well, this is nice," Scott said. "You're my two friends that have the most sex. And you're by far the darkest. You guys will get along."

I thought that was an odd thing to say.

"Yeah?" Laurel said. "What's so dark about you?"

Scott answered for me. "We don't have enough time to explain everything wrong with Henry. He's fucked up."

"Thanks, man. That's sweet of you to say."

Her eyes flickered. "I bet I have you beat."

I laughed. "Oh, you think so?"

"I know so. Wanna go story for story?"

"Lady, you don't wanna do that."

"Oh, I do. It's *so* on."

Scott interrupted us, "Trust me, you guys don't wanna do that. This will become so depressing so fast and I'll have to rescue you from yourselves, and I don't feel like doing that today."

"I have so many mental disorders I can't keep track of them," I said.

"Me too," she said. "What else?"

"My father never should have had kids."

"Same with my mom."

"My sister is bipolar and bulimic."

"Mine is a sociopath."

"The priest at the Catholic school I went to turned out to be a child rapist."

"My dad was in a doomsday cult and made us secretly go to the services with him in the middle of the night after my mom threatened to leave him for it."

"I'm a sex addict."

"Me too, but I'm okay with it."

"I'm an alcoholic."

"Me too, but I got it under control."

"I still drink too much, so I win that one."

"Fair enough. I got married on a whim when I was eighteen and got divorced six months later. We still talk and it is most definitely not healthy."

"Oh, nice. Okay, I'll give you that one."

"Jesus Christ," Scott cut us off. "We get it, you guys are fucked up. I knew this was gonna happen."

We both started laughing.

"Yeah, I like you," I said. "We'll get along just fine."

You know, I should've taken the hint right there. I should've recognized that anyone like me was someone I should never have been around. What's the quote? I'd never join a club who'd have me as a member? But that's one of those in a long list of things that are easier said than done. Hold your judgment, though. I've already done that for you.

The first time we fucked was in public on the side of a polluted river. We were still getting to know each other and really the only thing I thought I knew was that she upheld a much healthier lifestyle than me. I was coming down off a particularly self-destructive bender that had lasted longer than I anticipated. She was coming down from a pernicious and toxic relationship, from which the scars it left on her were still slowly becoming apparent to the both of us. She had relapsed two weeks earlier but I didn't know that. We had no intention of having anything except sex.

The river was a dark green and the sun was setting. We waited until the last of the remaining voyeurs shuffled off the beach before she threw me onto my back and slid the panties off from beneath her red dress. When she slipped it in, her eyes rolled and her mouth dropped open (a tell that I'd grow to recognize). She arched her back, grinding against me, digging her fingers into the sand and against my chest until it left vicious, crimson streaks; grabbing at her neck and shaking like epileptic spasms, letting out shrieks and *oh my gods*, giggling and biting at my shoulders and neck when she bent over to feel my lips. I would look to the left and right, at the mercy of the fuck, waiting for some poor kid coming back for his beach ball to stumble upon this horrible, violent, beautiful, carnal dance; feeling the sand cake to the bottom of my legs. She was surprisingly reactive—to the point where on someone else it would look unbecoming, but maybe I was just happy to be getting laid again. I'd always wanted to fuck by the water.

I've been with enough women to know when I'm pleasing them—doing the right things, touching the right places, reaching the right angles—but with Laurel it was as if just being there was enough. I was a warm body that happened to be connected to the hard cock that was being used at her whim. She was orchestrating the event; bouncing and sliding back and forth, slowing the rhythm and speeding it up only once I let out a noise. She knew exactly what to do based on body language and guttural sounds alone. It was a symphony with Laurel at the helm of the music. It came to a final, triumphant crescendo when she slid her hand to my side, guided me on top of her and grasped at my back until I came inside her with the sand and the orange rays of the sun and the moving current and the cops on their way. I now knew something else about Laurel: she could fuck. We had woken up the world.

This was after we stood waist-deep in the water together, talking about Frank Sinatra. I was making the flubbery, middle-aged man next to us uncomfortable, taking handfuls of her ass and gripping hard while I made eye contact with him.

"Could we get in trouble for fucking here on the beach?" she asked.

"Yeah," I said. "It's a sex crime. We'd be on that list with the pedophiles and rapists and all those guys."

"Alright. I'd take a great mug shot, though."

"I think everyone says that. The only guy that ever really pulled it off was Sinatra. You ever see the mug shot of his where he's like our age? With the curl of hair coming down, looking like a sex symbol?"

"Oh, yeah."

"You know what he got arrested for? He was fucking some guy's wife."

"That's a crime?" she asked. "I should have a life sentence by now. Jesus."

"Eh, it was in the forties. Times were different then, I guess."

She paused and looked around at the people wading and lying on the beach. "I don't think we'd get caught. It takes like eight minutes for the cops to arrive at the scene of the crime. I heard that somewhere."

Purple dusk was descending over the trees once we were back in the car, kicking up dust under the wheels of her dirtied RAV 4. The cop car's lights glowed through the windshield as it burned down the road and drove past us. I think a part of her wanted to get caught.

When we hit the freeway, Laurel became quiet. I counted the freckles dotting her face lit up in the headlights of passing cars and watched the moon hanging in the sky. We didn't speak for the rest of the drive. I assumed she thought I'd soiled her. I wasn't unused to that sentiment in women who had fucked me before, and the self-loathing pulsing in my stomach allows me to reach this kind of conclusion whenever something goes right.

Once we pulled up in front of her house, Laurel remained silent in the driver's seat looking down at the sand stuck to her legs, and I waited for something painful to come out of her mouth. I cracked my window and lit a cigarette, watching a homeless woman on the street corner talk to herself. The air was abnormally humid that night.

It wasn't until the ember on my cigarette reached the little blue camel that she grew the courage to let go of the words festering at the edge of her tongue: "I think I really like you."

This was not the outcome I'd anticipated. But I could tell she was telling the truth. I could tell this was something she didn't want.

"I have a lot of shit I need to work out. I wasn't expecting this," she said. There was a moment of hesitation. "Is this the part where you run for the hills?"

"No," I said.

"I don't want you to hurt me."

"I don't think I'll do that."

"You know I'm sick, right? People can't handle that. People run away."

"I've never run away from anyone," I said. "I don't see that happening with you. I've always been the problem."

She studied my face intensely in the glow of the moon, the smoke from the end of the cigarette rising between us. "Well, we'll see."

That night we slept together for the first time, although that's really just a figure of speech; she woke me up to fuck at three in the morning, then again at five and again at eight. We never questioned any of it. The pace seemed to set itself, and we decided that it must have been healthy because, well, because it felt good. But so does heroin. Remember that next time you feel that swelling in your chest when you look at someone you think you love. Most things that feel good are bad for you.

Laurel and I began spending every day together. She kept me out of the bars and I suppose I was good company when sober. We would take long walks around her neighborhood, past the homeless on the street and her crackhead neighbors who only came out after the sun went down or early in the morning to riffle through people's trash and check to see if any parked cars were unlocked. I got used to walking on her left side, as she was born deaf in the right ear. I still instinctively walk on people's left side now out of habit.

She took me to parks I had never been to, and we sat in the grass for hours laying with each other, talking about books and writers and our past lives and transgressions. She handed me plenty of red flags, all of which I ignored and only made me think she was more interesting. At twenty-three, she had been married, been divorced, been an addict, been homeless, lived in an Earth-worshipping cult, lived on the road. Her father beat her; her mother was an alcoholic. Her friend's uncle shot her up when she was a ten-year old. She lost her virginity by being raped to "fuck the queer out of her". Her life had been shaken and stomped down more times than I could count. Yet she recounted each story with a sense of humor that seemed to indicate a wisdom that most don't

217

attain. Or it was simply a numbing disconnect that she'd learned to develop. I didn't know which one.

She was a writer, a poet—a real one. She could actually write. The first time she let me read a piece of hers—as we sat on the edge of a cliff overlooking graffiti-covered trains and the industrial area of the city—I felt a twinge of jealousy over her ability to compose words like real art. The descriptions and flow of the words detailing these painful experiences bent and twisted around each other in ways I couldn't do. She was special. Or at least she thought she was, and I was inclined to believe her. I do mean this in the most endearing way possible when I say she was the only person I'd ever met who was as—or more—damaged than I was. It was nice to finally see that familiar, distant despair in another person. But she hadn't broken. She hadn't yet given up. She was still in love with the world around her. I thought she was beautiful. It had never occurred to me that it was all an act, that she was just better at hiding the scars than I was.

For someone lugging around the weight of pain she did, Laurel carried herself with the confidence and lust for life of a much older person. She would stop by every rosemary and lavender bush on the sidewalk to pick a piece of it, smelling it like it was the first time she ever had, smile, then stuff the plant in my face and say, "Smell! Rosemary!"

"Yeah. Rosemary," I would say. "That's rosemary."

Every neighborhood cat was her friend. They would approach her and meow until she showed them affection, cooing in a soft baby voice and lowering the back of her hand for them to smell before skipping off to the next rose.

At night, we would walk the streets and fuck in parks, then come home to fall asleep together. Some nights we would meet up and jump in my car, and without another word, Laurel would say, "Go east." And I would. We would drive until the city lights burnt out and became a green and black wilderness, until we found ourselves on unpaved roads, until we were alone together staring over a cliff, and there before us was a snaking, black river and the unmasked stars. I would tell her I wanted to be great, that I had this beautiful potential inside me. That I really believed I did. And she believed me. Then we would drive back, and she would give me head as the speedometer hit eighty, and the pale yellow streetlights reappeared for us and us alone on the empty freeways to the city.

There was no fear anymore when she was next to me. There was no dread. There was now this unexplainable hope glowing within me. I was present with her. I recognized that every moment with Laurel was one I would look back on and remember as some of the greatest times of my life. I didn't need to drink. I didn't want to. I wanted to remember everything. Every morning I woke up happy, knowing that by the end of the day I'd be back next to her again. We were each other's romantic writer's wet dream that we had always wanted.

Some relationships are a slow burn, a steady incline. Some explode and rain down from the sky for everyone to see. Ours was the latter.

Something light before the inevitable collapse: There was the time I thought she gave me an STD.

We were on our way back from spending the weekend at the beach. Laurel was the first person I'd ever met whose libido rivaled that of my own, and the task of living up to and satisfying that libido was a twenty-four-hour-a-day ordeal. She was used to multiple fucks a day, going for hours until I would "fuck her into a coma" as she so tenderly put it. On days when we didn't see each other, she would admit to masturbating up to eight or nine times a day. I figured this was some byproduct of the mania brought on by her bipolar diagnosis. But there are worse symptoms than that to have. I didn't mind.

Anyway. So we were on the highway back towards the city. My hand found its way to the inside of her thigh as she drove, and slid up underneath the thin skirt too short to cover the purple and yellow bruises in the shape of my teeth. She began breathing heavily and the car was swerving a little too much outside the white lines. Her right hand grasped at my cock through my pants, and the car behind us blared the horn as Laurel jerked the car onto the side of the road. We sat parked on the outskirts of an overgrown swamp. The heat of the summer day cooked the inside of the vehicle and my skin stuck to the leather seat with sweat.

She looked around at the mounds of dirt and plants and buzzing creatures. "This'll work."

We stepped outside into the dry air and walked through a makeshift path into the swamp until we deemed it far enough out of the view of any passing cars on the highway. I could hear the sound of a small creek running somewhere beyond us. We stripped off our clothes and fucked there on our bed of bushes and flowers, the mosquitoes furiously biting at our naked bodies until they were ready to burst with blood. Laurel reveled in her ability to scream as loud as she possibly could, with no one to alarm but the insects beneath us and perhaps the passenger or two lucky enough to have the window down as they drove past. When it was finished, we redressed and walked back to the car hand in hand.

That night, I awoke in bed next to Laurel with the overpowering need to scratch my balls. I'm saying the itching was so bad it literally woke me out of my sleep. I kneaded the loose skin down there for a minute or so, thinking, *this is probably something bad*. Eventually I fell back asleep, and dreamt of exotic women in leotards scratching my balls with golden scepters.

The next morning, the itching had intensified. I got out of bed as quickly as possible and kissed Laurel while she struggled through half-opened eyes to register what I was doing.

"Gottagotoworkokaybyebaby."

I then ran out the door and drove home with a hand down my pants.

When I got there, I came crashing into the bedroom, ripped off my jeans, and sat at the edge of my bed under the bedside lamp with my cock and balls exposed for inspection. What I saw was one of the most horrifying scenes I'd ever witnessed: The entirety of the scrotum was bright red. Beet red. Blood red. Like two swollen Christmas tree ornaments hanging between my legs.

"JESUS CHRIST," I screamed. "WHAT THE FUCK HAS SHE DONE TO ME?"

The rash, chaffing and burning, extended up to the bottom of my shaft, where it mysteriously stopped in a clean line where the balls ended and the cock began. Ugly, dark blister-like shapes rose above the swollen red skin like a relief map of the inside of an active volcano. I immediately looked up the nearest and most readily available doctor and called, trying my best to mask the mounting panic behind my voice.

"Hello, this is the Montgomery Creek Medical Clinic, how can I assist you?"

"Yes, yes. Uh... yes. Is... Dr. Morris available for an appointment?"

"When would you like to see him?"

"Um, now? Yeah. Now."

"Alright, well let me see... I have an appointment with Dr. Morris available today at 4:30, does that work for you?"

"Yes, yes. Yes, that works fine."

"And what should I tell him is the reason for your visit today?"

"Look, miss, there are some things that the receptionist doesn't need to know. I don't want you to know. I don't want to ruin your day. You understand? It's in your best interest that I'm declining to tell you the nature of my visit."

There was an extended pause. I could hear the general static from the voices of the other receptionists next to the less fortunate one on the phone with me.

"Um… okay. So… 4:30."

"Right. Thank you. Have a good day."

I hung up and then called Laurel. It sounded like she was already at work.

"Hi, baby."

"Hi, Laurel. Uh. Look, I'm not mad."

"What?"

"I mean I'm not mad. But is there like… uh, something you haven't told me?"

"What the fuck are you talking about, Henry?"

"Fuck it—did you give me something?"

"Give you what, Henry?"

"Goddamnit, my balls are on fire. Did you give me an STI?"

"Your balls?"

"Yes, baby. My balls."

"No, I couldn't have! We wear condoms! What're you talking about? What happened?"

"MY BALLS, LAUREL. THEY'RE ON FIRE."

"Oh God, I don't know! You're scaring me! Don't be mad!"

"I SAID I'M NOT MAD."

After that productive conversation, I went to work.

The doctor's office was unusually warm but sterile. The woman sat down next to me and checked my pulse with a little plastic clamp around the tip of my index finger.

"So, what seems to be going on today?"

"..."

"...Just a follow-up?"

"Yeah. Let's just call this a follow-up."

"...Okay then. The doctor will be in shortly."

I stared blankly at the waste bin marked with the poisonous substances sticker where they throw the used needles and bloody surgical gloves.

Dr. Morris was a tall, bald man with small eyes that were dull and unappealing in a human sense. The backs of his hands were covered with thick hairs. If he shaved all the hair from his hands and put it on his head, he could probably have a decent toupee.

"So, what's going on, Henry?"

"Everybody wants to know that today. Look... it's bad, Doc. It's scary. It's really bad."

"Okay, just calm down. What're we talking about?"

Without further ado, I wordlessly dropped my pants and revealed the full majesty of my newfound ailment. "Look at it! Look at it, Doc! What the fuck is it?"

He cocked his head to the side like a confused animal and stared closely at the puffy mess. It took about five seconds before he answered. "Yeah, this is an allergic reaction."

I looked down at it. "A reaction? It's not anything... sexual?"

"No, no. That's just a very sensitive area of skin."

"Don't I know it."

"Have you been using a new laundry detergent, any new medications?"

"No."

I paused and thought about any new factors that had recently entered my life that could have in any way had a detrimental effect on my cock and balls.

"Well, I—hm. Okay, yeah. I had sex outside yesterday."

"Like on the grass?"

"Like in the wilderness. Like in a swamp."

The doctor squinted at me and glanced at my testicles. "Yeah. That'll do it."

So I had dodged a poorly perceived bullet. And learned a valuable lesson. The doctor prescribed me hydrocortisone and told me, for future reference, not to fuck in swamps.

"I'll give you points for safety, though," he said as I was walking out the door.

"What?" I asked.

"The irritation is virtually everywhere in that area but on your penis. I'm guessing that's because you used protection."

I made a mental note to pitch that to the marketing team for Trojan.

When I called Laurel to tell her the good news, she informed me that the same fate had befallen her lady parts. She thought it was a cute sort of twisted bonding experience for us. "We'll be laughing about this in a few days," she said. "You can write about it."

One night, Laurel woke me up at one in the morning when she bolted out of bed and left the room. I fell back asleep eventually but woke up again at five. Laurel was still gone. I got out of bed and went downstairs to check on her. She had been talking about suicide earlier that night, and about her manic attacks, and how bad her depression had gotten. She wasn't doing well.

I turned on the lights to the kitchen. The room was empty. I looked out the window to see if she had wandered off into the street in her nightgown. She had never done that before, but she had never explicitly talked to me about suicide before either.

After deciding she probably hadn't left the house, and had at least not killed herself on the kitchen floor, I noticed the bathroom door at the end of the hallway was closed. A little bar of orange light glowed underneath the bottom. I knocked. No answer. I knocked again. No fucking answer. This didn't alarm me too much, as Laurel's fifty percent deafness was really more like seventy-five percent, and she barely heard half of any of the shit I said, let alone a soft knock on a door. Nonetheless, I pictured her body laying there on the tile, razorblade in hand, the blood, eyes still open like in the movies. Fuck.

"Laurel!" I whispered in a hoarse tone, trying not to wake up her roommate sleeping across the hall. I knocked again, harder this time. "Laurel, please say something."

Then finally, there was the sound of footsteps and the door swung open. She was alive, but—

"I'm peeing blood," she said.

"What?"

"I'm having a flare-up. Like a really bad one. I'm peeing blood."

Some context: Laurel suffers from a chronic illness with a name long enough that I can't even begin to remember or look it up on the internet. I could ask her but... well no, I can't. Alright wait, I found it. Interstitial cystitis. The disease affects the bladder, causing the sufferer to have the constant, urgent feeling that he or she has to urinate, but is unable to. Along with this comes, from what I can tell, exceptional amounts of pain in the lower stomach down to the entire pelvic region. She has no way to know what exactly will trigger a flare-up, but they happen often. This night, though, was much worse than usual. She had been doubled over, alone, sitting on the toilet in pain for four hours. She had never pissed blood before.

Laurel grimaced and said, "I need to go to the ER."

She meant I needed to take her to the ER. For Laurel, this disease was incredibly embarrassing, and it was a side of her that until this point she was careful not to reveal to me. So the fact that she was willing to let me in on this showed me just how bad the situation was.

We packed up some of her things in a satchel bag that I tossed over my shoulder. Laurel threw on a dress, and with my hand against her back as she leaned against me, we walked outside and into my car. I wasn't sure what to say or do, so I stayed silent, holding her hand, and sped through red lights and the empty streets while she focused on her breathing. I watched her stare into the dashboard, exhaling, coping; her facial muscles twisted and contorted in anguish. I could see the pain she was in. It was impossible to hide. But she didn't complain. She hardly said anything at all. And when she did, it was mostly just things to calm me down. I probably looked more worried than she did. I remember tightening my grip on her hand and thinking, *this is a braver person than me.* Her hair was messy, her clothing was askew, her face was unwashed and wrinkled from stress. She looked as beautiful as she ever did.

The hospital we arrived at was where I was born. Also where I stayed for a few nights when I was first diagnosed with epilepsy. We pulled into the parking lot of the ER and stumbled together into a spacious room populated by two hospital staff members and a homeless man sitting in the corner eating a cookie. The woman in blue scrubs behind the desk asked which one of us needed help. I thought it was obvious that it was Laurel but maybe I didn't look so great either. The woman motioned to the nurse standing around next to us eating a power bar, who then finished eating and shepherded Laurel into another, smaller room with fancy equipment.

I wasn't sure what the protocol was. I had always been the person who needed the treatment, not the other way around. "Wait," I said, "can I come too?"

The nurse spoke loudly: "Well, if it's okay with her—"

Laurel grabbed my hand. "Yeah, I want you with me."

I listened to the cold ticks and whirs of the machinery and let my vision blur into the stark white walls while Laurel described her symptoms. The nurse had never heard of her condition and had to look it up on the internet before giving any advice or asking the proper questions. I wondered what this scene would have looked like before Google existed. I then realized that if this were fifty years in the past, Laurel probably just wouldn't be alive. There was a board on the wall that had written in big letters:

HOW MUCH PAIN ARE YOU IN? 1-10
CAN YOU WALK?
HOW LONG HAVE YOUR SYMPTOMS PERSISTED?

After the questioning was finished, the nurse led us into another room with a bed and a curtain for a door. She helped Laurel onto the bed and I sat down in an uncomfortable chair beside her. The lights were on. They were bright and sickening and yellow. It was finally setting in how little sleep I had gotten. Laurel hadn't slept all night. Someone new came in and put a blanket over her, drew some blood and said the doctor would be in eventually. Then they left, dimmed the lights, and we were alone.

I waited a moment before talking.

"How're you feeling?" was all I came up with.

Laurel shifted over on the bed to face me, forced a weak smile, and said, "Not so great."

"Is there anything I can do?"

"Close the curtain? I feel like all the orderlies passing by are getting a view of my ass."

I leaned over and checked. It was all hanging out down there. She had given up on trying to be ladylike. I understood that.

With the curtain closed, Laurel finally shut her eyes. She stifled a whimper and wiped away a tear with the side of her hand. "I wish so fucking badly that I didn't have to live in this body. I'd give anything for that. I'm just so tired."

"I like your body," I replied. I was trying to be funny.

"You know what I mean, Henry."

"Yeah. I know."

In that moment, there was nothing in the world that I wanted more than to take the pain out of that woman lying in front of me, shaking on a hospital bed. I wanted to take her pain and stuff it all inside me and sit there like that so she could get some goddamn rest. I wanted to tell her how beautiful she looked, and how proud of her I was, how she had been through things ten times worse, and if she could survive those then she could survive this. That if there was one person on the planet who could take all of this shit that was thrown at them, it was her. I wanted to tell her she hadn't deserved any of it, that if God wasn't sorry for any of it, then I would be for him. But she was falling asleep. I didn't want to wake her.

I must have knocked out eventually, because I woke up sliding halfway out of my chair. Laurel was up again, looking at me.

"Has the doctor come in yet?" I asked.

"No, not yet."

An alarm was sounding, and a voice came on over the hospital speakers: "CODE BLUE. DOCTOR FEENEY TO ROOM ELEVEN. CODE BLUE."

I watched the hurried feet of several hospital staff running past underneath the curtain. "What does Code Blue mean?" I asked Laurel. She had been a hospice nurse for two years. She had been everything.

"Code Blue means someone went into cardiac arrest. They're dying."

One of the first stories of Laurel's I ever read was her recounting of the time she attempted suicide with a bottle of pills.

In it, she explained how she legally died in the ambulance on the way to the hospital. She said that was called "coding." She told me nothing happened when she died. It just went black.

"You must be exhausted," she said. "Come lie on the bed with me. There's room."

"No, no, I'm alright. The chair works. I just want you to sleep."

"No it doesn't. I can sleep fine with you." She moved over and patted the open space. "Now get the fuck up here."

I got up and stretched out behind her. She took my hand and wrapped it around her chest. And we lay there together on a hospital bed in the emergency room at seven in the morning. Her scent that I had gotten so used to so quickly, overpowered the lingering stench of industrial-grade cleaning product. I buried my face into her hair and held her. Someone was breathing his or her last breaths in the room next to us. Alarms were shrieking and abrasive lights flashed in dizzying patterns up and down the hallway outside. I was exhausted and confused and worried. Laurel was twitching in pain, sleep-deprived and aching from six hours of muscle contractions. I had never felt so lucky in my life. I was in love.

How do I start this?

I think the beginning of the end was the night I showed up drunk. That was Laurel's one rule: *Don't drink around me, don't show up drunk*. Well, I did that.

The particulars of what led to me stumbling into her room at midnight no longer matter. None of it really does. I remember sitting across from her, unable to detect the disgust, the recognition of the ugliness welling up from inside me that I knew would inevitably emerge. The self-saboteur. I rambled through double vision—something about suicide, something about how I would never be good enough, something about how I always knew I would fuck it up. Ugly words. Pathetic words. The diseased raven within me coughing up blood in a last-ditch effort to ruin this ephemeral happiness I could never get used to. My own repeating, self-fulfilling prophecy.

Laurel had no patience for it. Her eyes turned cold. Her mind threw her back into a broken past I no doubt reminded her of.

I remember the tirade. It's really all I can recall.

"Stop. I know what you're doing. You need to give this shit up. This self-hating bullshit. You're not fucking Bukowski. This fucking character you play—this drunken, depressed, romantic writer. Give it up. You can't hide behind your flaws forever. You can't just fetishize your sadness and pretend what you do is admirable. You romanticize these awful things about you and make them a shield as if it's attractive. I'm looking at you, and do you know what you look like, Henry? You look fucking pathetic. Drop the fucking act. Get the fuck out of my house."

I left.

It had always been easier to lean on my shortcomings and call them my strengths. You would never have to change—or answer the question of whether it was even possible to change. You could maintain the poisonous behavioral patterns hardwired into you, making the same mistakes over and over. That you've simply been on a predestined path since birth hurtling you towards failure becomes a fathomable reality, and you can give up comfortably. The record can keep skipping, and the music will always sound the same. And once you listen to the same song for long enough, you forget there was ever anything else to hear.

But there were some shortcomings I hadn't counted on returning.

Laurel took me back after a few days, on the condition that I would NEVER DO THAT AGAIN, and that I would stay sober. For the most part. And things smoothed out for a while. But I was growing uncomfortable with my happiness. Over twenty-three years of life, I'd become so used to a chronic state of depression that once the feeling left me for as long as it did while I was with Laurel, it literally felt like an integral part of me had withered away. I didn't know how to function in life without that sinking feeling in my chest, without the disassociation, without the lingering thoughts of suicide when my mind grew quiet. I couldn't keep this up. There was this part of me that had to destroy anything beautiful once it came too close, lest I find myself in an unknown state of being where I wouldn't know how to react. It was an entirely subconscious defense mechanism that served no purpose but to return me to a familiar and reliable level of functional mental illness. So it's for this reason that I think the episodes began to happen again. These relics of my unstable childhood.

I would begin to shake, and my mind would fall out through the bottom of my stomach. This undecipherable terror would leak out of me until I was drowning in it. I would start talking erratically, making no sense, babbling incoherently to try to stay on top of the swirling thoughts smashing against the insides of my head: KILL YOURSELF KILL YOURSELF KILL YOURSELF. RUN. FUCKING RUN.

Every irrational fear and painful memory I had ever kept locked away inside a bottle of whiskey would spring forth out of me in the same earth-shattering moment, as if the gates of Hell had opened up beneath my feet and I was the only one who could see the flames and death reaching up at me. My eyes would glaze over, and tears would pour out of me, and my chest would tighten until the knot was so powerful that if I were to take a single moment to breath or attempt to break out of the tunnel of paranoia I had been shoved into, my ribcage would shatter and my fucking heart would explode.

Laurel told me what I was experiencing were manic attacks. And they began to happen more and more. And each time they did, her patience deteriorated to the point where her apathy was akin to that of a sociopath. It was a side of her that until then she'd been very careful to hide. But after so many of my exhausting episodes chipping away at her, she no longer had the energy nor saw the purpose for sympathy.

The night before she ended it I had gone insane again. We were in her room. It had just washed over me. There was never a reason for it.

She was lying on the bed. I was standing over her trembling, horrified by an indiscernible entity, as if possessed by a demon but acutely aware of it. I choked on the words in a harsh whisper: "Please help me. I don't know how to stop this. Please, I can't calm down."

"You fucking figure it out," she spat back at me, no longer any sign of warmth in her eyes. I'd by now drained it all from her. "I won't deal with this. You always have to make everything about you. You never think about *me*. What about *my* problems? Figure it the fuck out yourself."

A jolt of pain and frustration ran down my spine, crumpling me under its weight. I twitched erratically to balance it but fell to my knees, attempting as well as I could through the chaos inside my head to explain to her: "You don't fucking understand. Just be nice to me for a second. You're making it worse. Please just be nice to me, Laurel. I just need to calm down. I can't breathe. I can't breathe. I can't breathe."

I devolved right there in front of her into a frightened child, a cornered animal; no longer capable of logical thought, only able to regurgitate the words screaming the loudest over the rest poisoning my mind. She turned over in her nightgown and occupied herself with something else, anything, just to illustrate how little my unflattering outbursts mattered to her.

"JUST BE FUCKING NICE TO ME," I screamed, now solely focused on bringing back the humanity in this woman that I was beginning to worry had only ever been a meticulous fabrication.

She then turned back around just long enough to show me it wasn't going to return, and said very calmly: "I'm never changing. You will never make me change. I don't have to do a goddamn thing for you."

Those were the last words I ever heard her say. I walked out the door and left, bought a bottle of whiskey on the way home, and drank it in bed until the voices quieted. Laurel had reached her breaking point.

The next morning I awoke doused in guilt and apologized like I always did. Laurel responded swiftly and bluntly via text: *It's over.* That was it. She meant it this time. This had happened before, more times than I'd like to admit, but she really meant it this time. I knew it right away. It wouldn't have felt so abrupt if I'd been able to recognize how quickly my thin veil of sanity had been dissolving before her eyes in the last few weeks. But the man talking to the lamppost is always the last to find out it's a lamppost.

I texted her back begging to drag me out of this prison I'd accidentally locked myself in, regressed into a state of panic after receiving no response, called her twenty times to no answer, vomited, packed a bag, threw it in my car, and drove south for an hour. I didn't know where I was going. I didn't know where I was. I didn't know who I was. My mind could provide no appropriate reaction but to run, as if somehow I could physically escape the consequence of my actions. I swerved in and out of traffic, narrowly avoiding enough accidents that I still have no idea how I wasn't arrested, until I eventually pulled over in the parking lot of a church in a small town I'd never been, gave up and turned back, defeated.

When she finally answered my call after a long string of particularly vitriolic texts, I was confused when the voice on the other end of the line was not Laurel's, but a stern, nasally female voice that I didn't recognize.

"You need to stop," I heard the woman say from the depths of my insanity. "Don't call this number again."

I didn't. And that was it.

After that, I got drunk for six days and six nights. I was diagnosed with bipolar type two; the family curse I had hoped for years that I'd somehow avoided. I hadn't. Big fucking surprise. But it didn't change a thing. It was too late. I had undone any progress made during those brief, dreamlike summer months. I had fulfilled the one promise I knew I could keep—the promise echoing in my head the night Laurel and I talked in the car that now felt like a lifetime ago: That whether by choice or through some vengeful, omniscient force operating beyond my control, it was going to be me who would bring it all toppling down around us. I wasn't sure if there was even a difference. What they tell you about history is not true; sometimes no matter how aware of it you are, you may still be doomed to repeat it.

By the time I dragged myself out of a perpetual drunk, the rain began to fall. The summer was over.

It wasn't until many nights later that I realized what Laurel had been to me. I had simply traded in one vice for another: Liquor for Love. Two drugs no different from each other in that they both provided the same desired effect: A respite from the crushing loneliness that came with a mind prepackaged with the inability to feel less than too much. A numbing agent. I was never better. I was never healthier. I had never been anything more than an addict. And now, bleeding through every nerve ending in my body was the inevitable withdrawal from what always only could have been a temporary fix to a deeper problem. The final, soul-wrenching question I was faced with was: *Was I ever in love with her, or was I simply in love with the desperate, euphoric relief of a briefly quieted mind?* The answer to this question was something I didn't care to know. It hardly mattered any longer.

In a clouded haze, I remember walking into the bookstore we had gone to together when times were better. I walked through the isles of books, lurking like a specter through the places we had been, reading the novels that she had picked up and handed to me. I sat down in the corner that she had said was her favorite—where they kept the independently published and local writers; writers whom I found awful, but whose books I nevertheless quietly wished to one day see amongst my own—and I waited there. I waited for a small, freckled hand to touch my shoulder. To turn around and meet the gaze of familiar green eyes. To see the smile bright with compassion that at one time existed. For her to sedate the crying child inside me. No one came.

I walked back out of the bookstore under the rain, and drove alone to my old bar.

The Guilty Sparrow was exactly how I'd left it. I sat down in the same seat next to the same regulars who would sit next to me every night, and ordered the same drink from the same bartender who was in the same place as where I'd left her.

"Where you been, Henry? It's been a while," she said, and slid over the drink in the same filthy glass it had always been in.

"I've been around," I answered. "How've you been, Anna?"

"Ah, you know. Nothing changes around here. You didn't miss much."

I stared into the mirror and watched the same expressionless face drink from the glass until it was finished.

"Another one?"

I nodded.

The floor was still dirty. The lights were still dim.

I looked around and there in the middle of the room was an elderly couple I didn't recognize dancing slowly and methodically to a song I'd never heard. It was a lone, solemn piano, played delicately and soft. I watched them like that, swaying and spinning to the notes, their white hair thinning and their wrinkles hidden behind the darkness of the bar. They seemed happy.

I watched them dance until the song was finished, and I drained the rest of my drink. Then the old man unclasped from the old woman and staggered over to the jukebox in the corner. He slipped in a dollar bill and selected a song. And from the speakers came the same tune that had just played. The haunting chords filled the room, and they returned to each other's arms, and they began dancing again. The same dance: slow and methodical and melancholy. They didn't miss a step, as if they were trying to perfect it and couldn't get it right.

The bartender saw my empty glass and returned next to me, poured the cheap whiskey to the top. We watched the old couple together for a moment. "They've been dancing to this song since they came in," she said. "I don't think anyone's noticed."